Chapter 1

"Give me one word to describe you," the voice in Hailie's head demanded.

"Agoraphobe," she said.

"Not your condition, but you," the voice shot back.

"Agoraphobe," Hailie replied loudly.

"Okay, who are you today?" The questions were forcing her to look more deeply into her motives.

"Mrs. Prescott," she answered.

"That is not you anymore. You got divorced ten years ago," the voice reminds her conscious brain.

"Today, I say I am Hailie Prescott and I am amazing. What do you have to say about that?" She taunted her inner voice to conceive a better answer.

She waited for a reply. There was silence. The voice was finally outwitted. She contemplated the sanity of feeling happy about out-reasoning herself while noticing that the wood floors weren't even daring to creak like they had all morning. The whining sounds the pine floors allowed to escape when her feet crossed them were like a doubting echo all morning. Now the echoes had shushed in awe of Hailie's determination while she slipped her blouse over her head. Hailie spun around from the mirror to face her doubting thoughts.

"Are you saying that I can't do this?" She lifted her eyebrow and squished them together in an effort to intimidate the inner speaker. Breath escaped her lips and furled the nostril hairs of her momentary tormenter.

"You are a little close." She said in an even tone, staring directly into the inner demon's pupils without changing her expression.

"So are you."

"I am doing my job. You want me to keep you in check when you are reaching beyond your capabilities. Well,. . ." the imaginary speaker paused for effect. "This is beyond your capabilities." There was a rushed but earnest tone to its voice.

It put Hailie on edge. Involuntarily her teeth chattered, tingling ran up her spine like a sprinter on speed moving through her nerve endings. "I created you, so disappear!" she commanded.

Hailie stood alone in her bedroom. The floor-to-ceiling blue damask draperies were tied back, allowing sunlight to penetrate the room for the first time in a decade. She was wearing a sharp suit as dated as the calendar from 1999 that hung on her wall.

She stepped out of her cubby-like living room to cross the threshold that had defined her for the last decade. She wanted to be armored to face the world, so she went shopping, but no matter what she bought at Tiffany's or YSL, she couldn't build the confidence to step out into the world.

Today, she had decided, things would change. They may not change for the better but she was finally willing to face what she had run from for the last decade.

The sky seemed to hang low with threatening tears of her impending failures. She looked up at the sky and said in an off-handed manner, "I feel the same way. Just don't cry right now. It will kill my hair."

She chuckled to herself. What did it matter if the sky cried? Nothing would change. She would still be herself and her life would still be on pause. Her ride pulled up to the curb.

RoseRosa reached over, unlocked the door, and swung it open. "You are really going to do this?" RoseRosa was a good friend and had been with her through it all.

Tentatively, Hailie whimpered, "Yes." Her voice trembled as she began to second guess herself.

She tried again. "Yes, ummm, no." That was the truth. She questioned herself before speaking again. "I think so."

This was definitely her final answer. It was a confidence plateau she could live with.

While cookie cutter McMansions, struggling to find their unique identity, whizzed by the window, Hailie thought over her situation. She, too, was a grand exterior but the weather of life had strained the structural integrity of her mind and body. The beauty of her abode was ageless, the staircases of opportunity within her were opulent, the floors were polished within an inch of its shiny life due to constant mental clearing of the cobwebs. Wide hallways stretched the expanse of this home, but only echoes of half-developed thoughts and the shadows of former knowledge filled them.

The walls were empty where tawdry galleries of family historical busts and good times were displayed. When the sunlight of memory hit the bay window in that room just right, the refracted beams would paint glimpses of artwork or fleeting shadows of the petite statues that stood proud in that spot. If only she could remember and return the possessions of her mind, but no matter how she strained her mental facilities, she couldn't recapture this or other dormant rooms from the past in the vast blank corridors of her mind.

Fortunately for her, one of the select few rooms that were in tip-top shape was the kitchen. She could fire that gas oven or range to prepare an idea from start to finish. She didn't want to admit it, but evidence of age and overuse were starting to creep in. This frightened her and her thoughts would often settle on the what if's during the preparation. What if this part of her reasoning became like the perishables stored in the mental icebox? What then? What do the dates labeled on those containers of inspired notions say?

After a meal she would stand in the doorway of the formal living room of her mind with anticipation, but she never summoned the willpower to enter. That room had too many implications and expectations of proper actions. Instead, she would opt for the den with a more casual feel and a lowered bar of concentration. A variety of movies spanning all genres were neatly arranged along the shelves below the high definition television of events she could recall . She knew from experience and hard knocks that only the comedy films were available to watch. The other movie containers held nothing in the cases.

While Hailie mentally scanned the covers of movies within her own mind, she instinctively went through the motions of exiting the car and entering the four level building where her first presentation to a client would be.

She sat in the chair of the main lobby where her entire life's happiness would be determined and yet in her mind's eye, she sat on a loveseat holding the case to a comedy, balling her eyes out. All she could project to the world was the comedic aspects of her personality.

"Ms. Wilmington-Prescott?" the perky, stereotypical secretary called out as she stood glancing over the unoccupied smooth black leather chairs with a discerning eye.

It was time. "Now or never," she mused to herself as she snapped back to reality.

Hailie rose to meet the speedy sweeping gazes of the assistant. They both knew she was the two o'clock. Hailie and the protector of the boardroom were well past the age of imaginary play fellows, and as there was no one else present, there were no other options.

That is exactly how Hailie felt, as if there were no other options left to her. She looked to the left and the right like she was crossing the street. Deciding to commit to her course of action, she rose. "I think that's me."

"Oh , good! I was about to cancel your appointment."

Hailie desperately wanted to ask her why. Obviously, she was sitting there waiting to see her boss.

"You made it in the nick of time. You know, if you're not fifteen minutes early, you are late," the secretary chirped.

Hailie wondered how many times the micro-mini skirted secretary had been reprimanded for the same offense. A chuckle escaped the back of her throat into the audible realm. Her escort for the seven steps it took to get from the edge of the reception desk to the doorknob looked back over her shoulder. "You Okay? What's so funny?"

There was a long answer to that, and an even longer list of mistakes. The statuesque Helen of Troy that stood before her didn't want to hear any of her tales, nor would she care.

"Life," Hailie exhaled. Her shoulders dropped and the growing knot of stress between her deltoids released. "Just life." She breathed again and pulled the door open.

Hailie went about setting up for her presentation. It didn't take long. She welcomed all to the meeting and thanked them for the chance to be considered. Her audience and she knew that no matter her experience or abilities, she would have this opportunity. Unbeknownst to them, what was more concerning to her was not the presentation, her ability to perform, or the fact that she was a shoo in for the job. She worried about how much work it would be to prove her own competency in an arena such as this.

Hailie dropped the remote down her blouse and was going on a fishing expedition worthy of a deep sea rod and a proper charter fishing boat. She pushed aside her right breast and blindly searched, patting, pushing the b sized mounds protruding from her chest until she retrieved the blinking laser pen and black remote.

She vaguely overheard the comment, "I hope there is gold in there."

Her head snapped up and she scanned the room. Unfortunately in her hurry to place blame, feel embarrassed, and reel in her lost piece of technology, she had not looked down. In her hand, cozily sitting like a scoop of ice-cream atop a cone was her left bosom. It was as free and happy as those pictured in 80's style National Geographic.

This was not going as she planned. Not at all. Now she understood the skies ominous threat to cry when she left her home this morning. It was crying for her.

* * * * *

 Rose arrived five minutes late to the meeting
she had arranged so Ms. Wilmington-Prescott
could sell herself for all she was worth instead of
the discarded fashions she had cocooned herself
in for the last decade. She hoped against the
odds that maybe, just maybe, Hailie could have
the life she imagined daily.

To this day she swears she saw the electrical
charges rapid firing between her synapses.
"Surprise!" she exclaimed.
She took a quick memo for herself. She would
need to sign up for some type of shock therapy
so the current in her mind could upgrade.
 "It is like that right?" she questioned no one in
particular. " You add RAM to a computer for
better memory so you add electricity to
humans?"

Chapter 2

 "Hit the lights," she whispered in a voice suitable for any civilized royal court.

Darkness spread across the conference room. With the press of a button, her perfectly timed slide show began.

Air conditioning flowed in abundance in the room. That was the first thing she noticed. No maybe about it. That was why she was shivering. She only hoped it wasn't noticeable to her audience.

"For your spring gala," she started the presentation with a montage of pictures showing their failures and accomplishments, "you had numerous accomplishments as you learned the ropes of the business. It is important you continue to take away valuable lessons from these well-earned triumphs and failures."

The weary members of the board were all products of the charity, Experienced People, and a reflection of its past and present. The worn clothes, threadbare socks, and jeans they lived in were a reflection of the battles they'd fought on their way to the top.

A twice-divorced single mom sat in the corner, fatigue painting a broken capillary dark brown in a half-moon shape under each eye. Her best efforts to prop her eyelids up into an open position were failing.

The polo clad middle-aged man to her right was impeccably dressed. Knowing the story of the polo that clung to his brown, mountain-like biceps and understanding why he chose this shirt instead of one that displayed his millions was part of knowing this man.

Every thread bore a tale, just like the temporary residents of the table, but while each tale was different, they had the same ending: this table and Ms. Wilmington –Prescott's long, boring presentation.

Oddly enough, the tapestry of life events that wove their lives together could not have made a more exquisite cross-section of contrasts than the men at opposite ends of the table.

"Wendy." She pointed to the slides of the "Silent Party" charity ball they ran the previous year at a twenty –two thousand dollar loss.

"Granted," she continued, "with the personnel assets gathered around this table, it is inevitable that the event was excellent in its execution, but what we must all ask ourselves is 'Where is there room for improvement?' What I have listed is one area my company can answer for you."

Polo shirt had read ahead and was the first one to compose a question "Mysterious is not what we have in mind. How do you explain wanting 'mysterious'?"

He chuckled as he looked around the room. "The last time my company wanted to be mysterious, we had three lawsuits filed."

Trying to turn attention away from the joke the snotty Polo made, she directed their attention to Page 8. "You want a venue that people yearn to see inside. They want to say they experienced the venue. Once you have curiosity piqued, then all you need to add is anticipation of a spectacular, sophisticated evening."

Polo respectfully declined by not bothering to lift the report off the table. She ignored him and continued with her presentation. "There are a few suggestions on how we could take advantage of venue excitement."

"Why do we need you?" The distinguished head of the charity spoke.

She focused her gaze on her challenger. "As I said before, you all have some remarkable triumphs, but your ROI is off. Way off. It is hard to help others if you are not bringing in the sponsors you need. As you see on page 18, the charts and numbers don't lie. Your average expenditures compared to your received donations for these events are quite lopsided."

The members of the board poured over the last two papers that listed her fees and the options she offered for payment. In the total silence that descended as they read, her mind drifted to images of cardboard boxes and her days pushing the infamous homeless cart.

The images were too real. She shuddered and clenched her teeth as she thought about the reason those images existed. Somewhere in the infinite alternate universes, there was a version of Haillie enjoying the life she was drooling over right now.

"A snore fest" was the affectionate name many of the single mom's coworkers labeled her post-event accounts summaries. For some, this was the first time the numbers were in front of them and not just projected on a screen. Like the magazine companies, she knew the importance of involving the other senses in making a sale. The screen was removed from them and so aloof that it made the ramifications of these figures unreal. For them to see a side-by-side comparison of the fundraisers income versus the event expenses was crucial. People usually tackled an event with the same tactics they employed to dissolve their own life problems: as long as it worked out in the end, learn from the mishaps and be happy they landed on their feet. In truth, many event planners accepted the same motto when they were in a bind. It was practically a trade secret of how inexperienced planners dealt with their first years. Standing in front of them was one of the planners.

It took hard knocks that Mike Tyson would have struggled to bounce back from to make the beast of the planner that stood in front of them. The wear and tear of ten years of isolation had taken its toll on her, but in this presentation, she would be the beast of the past. If she counted the years that she consulted for her own business, the sum total of years spent in the war of budgets, floral arrangements, venues, and deadlines came to twelve.

While she waited for the twelve members of the board to finish reviewing the notes, her thoughts blindly bumped along the corridors of the forgotten times. The doorbell of reality rang, sending her racing down the hallway of awareness to answer the person on the other side for a moment before she uncovering a memory. Meeting her at the entrance to the present was the scrunched face of the charity's president.

His lips turned up at the right hand corner, subsequently making his cheeks look fatter, like he had jawbreakers stuffed in his jaws. An idle thought passed through her mind. He had gotten fat, maybe by about forty pounds.

The weight had not done anything for his baby face features. His bottom lip folded into his mouth, the top row of teeth caught it, and he began to literally bite back his words. As his eye darted down the page, his cheeks went rose garden pink to a smoldering mad bull red.

* * * * *

Rose arrived five minutes late to the meeting to give Ms. Wilmington-Prescott the opportunity to sell herself for all she was worth, instead of the discarded fashions she had cocooned herself in for the last decade. She hoped against the odds that maybe, just maybe, Hailie could have the life she imagined daily.

Nine other members read ahead as Hailie spoke. Rose shut her report within the first fifteen minutes. Her decision was made.

While she watched the screen and listened to her speak, Rose was beaming inside. She looked over the table at the expressions of the other board members. Hailie had managed to make them chuckle repeatedly. It was clear Hailie was able to get them to understand what Rose had been saying for the two years she'd been their treasurer.

"Donations," Hailie explained to the housewife, "are covering your overall expenses, but if you'll notice, your three large galas are draining the budget by $10,000 three times a year,"

 "I understand that." Polo raised his voice an octave. "So why should we pay your fees and hemorrhage more money?"

Rose wanted to rush to Hailie's defense, and explain to this idiot that a professional would do nothing but help because it could not get worse, but she held her tongue. Everyone on the board knew the two of them were friends. Speaking up for her would only hurt Hailie's case, not help it. Virginia, the fiancée of Mr. Prescott, spoke like a child dipping her toes into a cold pool, "I think..." The ten other heads gathered around the conference table snapped in her direction, as if they were all daring her to add her two cents. Virginia continued as if unaware of them, "What she is asking for is fair if she can reduce her cost like page twenty-six said. I know what she said about venue selection sounds odd to you. I sat through enough of these meetings to know how you select your venue and I want to say that it is wrong. None of my friends want to go to a gala in the first place. If you want to attract the clientele you seek, you will need to listen to her. We don't even think about attending an event in a youth center with nothing there to interest us. We are not even known in the trendy circles. I have to hide the fact that I am on this board. It is so not cool. We make an exception if the charity is known for throwing the hottest events in town or we need to network. Maybe you will notice that all our donations are from baby boomers. Soon the old folks will die and then where will you get your money? What this lady is offering is a middle-of-the-road gala. Besides, the baby boomers are retiring. You know what happens after retirement? Death. And that is really boring."

Ms. Williamson-Prescott concluded on those words. There was nothing else to be said. Virginia's word was as legitimate as law considering that she had every social and party girl badge attainable, and she'd validated every point Hailie's presentation made.

Halfway through sliding the glass door to the conference room, though, she heard a boisterous, "I don't think this job is a fit. . ." The president was poised to start the overqualified speech.

The rest of the board cut him off before he could press the accelerator on his speech. "We like you."

Rose watched as Hailie twirled around, looking at the people who had given her a second chance at life despite the fact that her professional reference sheet was lacking in experience. Visible to all was the disgust the president felt over their decision, but he had no real power to overturn their decision. He was stuck with their future professional arrangement.

* * * * *

Virginia was the first one out of her chair welcoming her to the thirty-employee office. "It will be a pleasure working with you!" She squealed as she snatched her Prada glasses and purse, extended her hand as an afterthought.

Hailie readily accepted it for fear of a hug followed by excited jumping if she didn't follow suit. Hailie relied on all her knowledge of etiquette and social expectation as she calmly reached her hand out to shake Mr. Williamson-Prescott's hand. With the coolness of the Sinatra rat pack, she presented her hand to him. She made sure to only extend it halfway. He took note and with a slow deliberate motion, withheld his hand until a few seconds past proper decorum.

"Thank you for this opportunity." The phrase sounded icy to her ears. She was surprised she could summon that much chilliness.

"Welcome to Experienced People." Devoid of inflection, he held their hand shake and they both smiled at the occupants of the room. Polo, the single mother, the blue collar worker who still would lay floor and build a wall with the guys filed out of the office along with the others. Each of them stopped to congratulate her. The single mother wished her luck. She warned that she would need it. Haile smiled and replied "I know I am going to need it."

"You are a professional. You will be fine." The mother continued.

Haillie said nothing. She could tell by how her face glowed and her shoulders had dropped a fourth of an inch she was happy the stress was gone. Her voice told another story altogether. Hallie wanted to ask why the single mother would want to hold on to a position that caused her so much stress. Walking toward the door the mom rolled her eyes. She left the room leaving Rose and Hailie as its only occupants.

* * * * *

Rose sat three chairs down from where the new employee stood, steadily filling in the missing information in the independent contractor agreement. Scouring through the pages, she searched for any oversight that could be exploited to sever the connection between the two companies. That was the last thing she needed. She had strong flags of allegiance planted in each party's camp.

Rose's hands shot up far above her head when she felt a tap her on the shoulder, breaking her intense concentration.

"Umm...I just wanted to say thank you," Hailie explained.

"Sorry, Hailie, I'm just really focused right now." Rose's heart rate steadied. "I want you to sign this before you leave. I don't want them to get buyer's remorse and give you the boot."

Hailie frowned, "Can they do that?"

Rose shook her head. "No, that was a joke. At least, I can't think of an instance where they did, but then again, this is a...unique....situation," Rose slid the folder to Hailie, "to say the least."

"Sign here," she pointed to a tab "and here." She flipped a page while Hailie waited patiently for the pen to sign. Seven signatures later, AEP was no longer surviving on a hope and a dream.

Rose stood with Haille and embraced her. "Sis, this is the first step. I'm so proud of you."

"No, this morning was the first step. This is the first leap, but thanks. It is a long way from here. I fear the battle is all uphill." As they exited together, Rose gave her some advice. "You may want to think about shopping your resume around again before you accept this position." The elevator doors opened as people filed out one-by-one. "Oh, I want this. I want my own. I have dreamed about it, and I'm going to have it."

Rose frowned. "You never dreamed he would be part of its fulfillment"

She watched as Hailie got on the elevator, "I don't care who is in the reality. Just as long as it's happening."

The doors closed and Hailie descended down to the lobby.

Chapter 3

In the parking garage, Hailie searched for the top of Rose's car. She stood on her tippy toes because her five foot one inch stature would not extend any further no matter how hard she tried to stretch it out. She made a note to herself that she needed new stilettos if she was going to work here.

The blue convertible beckoned to her from the fifth row in section C. "Finally." She exhaled .

Quickly she snapped up the keys from the bottom of her purse and opened the doors before igniting the combustion engine. An incessant buzzing alerted her to the need to answer her smart phone.

Rose blurted "Where are you?"

"Parking garage," she replied, surprised by the question.

Rose's voice was hesitant. "I turned in the contract to Human Resources. He, Micheal, has personally decided to handle your employment process. Debbie from Human Resources . . ."

Hailie felt like a fire ignited in her belly. "I know what he is up to." She shut off the air-conditioning, killed the motor, and slipped on her shoes. "Rose, I am on my way up."

She could hear the frown in Rose's voice. "I don't think you should come up."

Hailie was determined. "I am coming up and that is that."

* * * * *

Rose covered her phone ducked into the nearest cubicle. She wasn't going to pass his corner office and chance the possibility of being pulled into a web of woes so complex even Charlotte couldn't find her way out.

"Sweetie, I'm telling you . . . " she started before realizing that Hailie had hung up. "Don't do it, Hailie," she muttered in frustration. She punched Hailie's number into the phone and prayed she would pick up.

"Rose."

The sound of Mr. Prescott's voice behind her startled her. She froze, dropped the phone, and shot upright in the chair in the cubicle. "Yes, Mr. Prescott?"

"Are you on the phone?" To lie or not to lie. That was the question.

She decided to stick to the truth. "Yes, sir."

"Is it a company call?" His voice sounded skeptical.

"Yes, sir." That was the truth. It was a half truth, but a truth. Hailie was now working for the company, which made a call to her technically a company call. "That counts right?" she rationalized.

"Hello?" Hailie's voice came over Rose's speaker phone.

Mr. Prescott's brows furrowed.

Hailie sounded puzzled. "Do you have me on speaker?"

Rose's thumb had brushed against the speaker phone emblem in her rush to try and terminate the call.

"Do you mind?" Mr. Prescott asked, his flat palm extended expectantly.

Rose handed over her smartphone sheepishly. If this had been a workplace only situation, she would have kept her property and accepted a reprimand, but only after quoting the company manual as a precedence.

This debacle she had caused was a steaming pile of poo. She didn't want to swim in the deep end. "Hailie. What was it you were trying to pull?"

"Pull? What do you mean pull?" Haillie stepped off the elevator, waving to the lot attendant over her shoulder.

She mouthed "Thank You!" as a gesture to both commend and mock his behavior.

* * * * *

Hallie was in the elevator smashing the button repeatedly. The doors wouldn't be hurried, so she started punching the button. She was getting angrier with each unanswered blow. Tears of desperate frustration bubbled up from her inward fiery fury.

"This is my time! The first thing that goes right and you try to take it from me?" She pulled her arm back and, using all the strength she could muster, gave the button a knockout blow.

"You know the gym is on the second floor?" The parking lot attendant's words flowed like syrup.

She was startled by the smooth tenor voice. Most girls flipped over a baritone voice, but not her. She wanted something light and soothing, like the waves in the early morning. The owner of this voice, she hoped, was looking for a tenant. She looked up.

His eyes were filled with amusement. "You okay, Ms?"

She filled in the blank. "Ms Willamson-Prescott."

His eyebrows raised slightly. "Oh, I didn't . . ." He stuttered, as if grabbing for words. " Mr. Prescott has a daughter your age."

He stepped on the elevator. "Tell you what, I will ref your fight with the lift."

Referring to an elevator as a lift was distinctly British, but the accent didn't match. "You British?"

"No. I just thought saying 'fight with an elevator' would be ridiculous."

She opened her mouth to respond with feigned indignity, but had to agree that a fight with an elevator was sophomoric even if her job was on the line. He waved his hand over the panel "Where would you like to throw the first blow?" She smiled and laughed. "Second floor."
He reached out to push the button.
She stopped him. "On second thought, fourth floor."
He nodded. "Off to see Daddy?" She wanted to will the words to come out of her mouth, but they insisted on taking their own slower-than-a-tortoise pace.
"Yeah, I had a rough day." She finally pulled from the depths of empty, readily-available socially-acceptable responses.
His fingertips skimmed over the selections of floors, stopping at the close door choice. The two of them rode in silence. She positioned herself in a corner that was in his blind spot. Ten years as a depressed shut in, mourning the loss of a marriage, made her susceptible to any

stimuli, especially young and hot. She noticed he didn't have a ring. With her swelling confused emotional state right now, all she wanted was to let it out on someone or something.

Actually, she had tried the something, and her knuckles were throbbing from the losing battle with the elevator. Guess she needed a ref after all. She was glad he came along. Maybe it was time to try someone.

But what does one say she asked herself. *How old was he anyway? If she invited him to the back seat of her car after dealing with Micheal, would that be too forward, slutty, or just considered hooking up?*

Realizing her age and how much dating had changed according to reality television, she was frightened to realize she had no answers to her questions. She decided to let the whole idea go instead of embarrassing herself and betraying her inept old ways of striking up a date.

Since she couldn't enjoy herself, her mind drifted from the real problems only two floors away. As a distraction, she decided to just look over his derriere as many time as could be discreetly fitted into the ride.

She glanced once while he spewed some positivity chatter. She wondered how it would turn out if she acted on her thoughts about his derriere. Perhaps if she allowed her arm to take control of itself and press button three or four, then slyly graze the red stop button, what would happen? Her mind built the following scenario: "I have three questions. Do you mind answering them?" she would ask.

"Sure," he would tell her.

She would smile and look him in the eyes. "First, I am thirty seven. Am I too old for a guy like you?"

She imagined him smiling in return. "No." She would take a step closer as she asked the next question. "Second, am I attractive?"

He would look her up and down and maybe swallow a little. "Yes."

She would close the gap between them as she asked the final question. "Third, can you go on break now?"

He would tell her, "Yes," and she would press one. The elevator would plummet safely to the first floor and then she would have some long overdue fun.

The attendant spoke, breaking into her fantasy, his words shaking her back to the then and now.

"I hope your day improves. Ms. Prescott. I'm sure your father will know what to do."

"I'm sure he will. Thank you," she said to him as her phone rang.

She was thrilled the victor was her frontal lobe and she hadn't reached out to grab his booty or asked any of the crass questions in her head. She reasoned herself out of speaking another utterance as the doors parted, he put his arm over the black midsection of the elevator door, and gestured for her to have the right of way.

Right then, the metal cage tried to close. He put his hand out and the doors snapped back to their open position. He waved a regal goodbye before going back to his domain.

Letting his flat palm come to his waist, just above his hip bone and he bowed from the waist with a wink and a smirk on his face. A giggle–followed by a gasp escaped her lips at his actions against the auditory background of her new boss's verbal rants encroaching ever closer from the background. The doors closed, whisking the young attendant back down to the underworld of this Olympus and depositing her directly in front of Mr. Michael Williamson-Prescott.

* * * * *

Micheal Willamson-Prescott shut the doors to the office suite that consumed an entire fifth floor as he unofficially awaited the arrival of his ex-wife. He was ready to pounce on her as soon as she entered.

The leggy blonde and her two sisters that guarded the conference room, the front desk at the entrance, and the charity president's desk respectively also had a perch on that floor. Normally they would be sitting at their posts, but they were short-staffed this week.

Veronica and Samantha were away in New York. The three strikingly gorgeous triplet secretaries considered themselves to be starlets last year and started taking turns auditioning. Rooms went silent when they entered. While the other two –thirds of her posse were away, she was working three times harder than usual. Hailie's first comment as she stepped off the elevator told him she hadn't failed to notice. "The sister's are missing."

She looked around at the mahogany, brass, and gold dipped everything. "This office would make Scarface proud."

"What are you trying to pull? You know what I mean." He kept his back to her, not trusting himself to maintain composure.

The sarcasm dripped thickly from her voice as she replied, "Yes, Sweetheart. I always know what you are thinking. I am your personal oracle."

"We both know that's not true." He wanted to end this now. There was no need to drag their musty ten year old laundry out of the hamper and attempt to rewash the same stains. They had set in for life at this point.

"You would have foreseen me leaving you," he jabbed. "This is my point. You are always trying to evade the only question I ask. What are you doing here? What do you want? Is it to prove you are still valid?" He turned to look at her. "What is your angle, you conniving wench?"

"I don't have some 'angle.' That is your job. I'm trying to work." She straightened up, sucked in her tummy and bellowed out, "Is employment some criminal angle?"

"What do you need a job for? I pay alimony!" He looked her in the eyes, knowing she was like a deer that could hear the bullet hurtling toward her at top speeds to open her skull and spill the emotional gelatin holding her thoughts together. "Employment may not be some criminal angle, but trying to put a crazy notion in Virginia's head will be grounds for termination. I want you to know that.."

He wanted to push her until she was no more, until she returned to a corner in a dark room mumbling incoherently yammering in between sobs. She did not belong here standing in front of him. She was interfering in his happiness and quickly becoming an apex in the geometry of his harmony.

"Grounds for termination." She started reciting them from memory, listing all twenty-three grounds listed in her contract as she inched toward his desk, placing her hands on it and looking at him face-to-face. Inches separated them. She could feel his breath on her top lip. Their stares became intense and his was traveling. She continued enunciating the rest of the list.

"Number twenty three If the probationary ninety days . . . " She continued. Their eyes bored into each other's, mining for memories, battle scars, elation, accomplishments, and failures. What they found was not pretty. Empty pits had developed where wheels turning their love in to fuel powering their success used to be.

"It doesn't matter what you signed. You mess up, you are out on you're a**, and back to your corner of the town house sobbing." He verbalized his uppercut to stop the pull of his attraction to her. The black tar pit of emotions surrounding her had the power to suck him right back into his past with her, and he wanted nothing to do with that.

* * * * *

Hailie found herself amused as she stepped into Michael's office. She suspected that this was Michael's version of quality. His place looked like the Trump Plaza casino. Any second, she expected to see a rotary phone and a cell phone the size of someone's head.

The brown leather chair faced her instead of the man. She half expected him to be clad in John Travolta's dancing suit from Saturday night fever and the Bee Gee's to come blaring out the speakers.

She ended their inevitable argument with words she knew would deliver a death blow to that oversized ego of his. "I got the divorce," she pushed off from the desk, turned and walked toward the door, "and the vacation home, too," she added as the door automatically slid open and closed behind her.

She ended the mental scenario and finished up her niceties with the scentar standing guard over her ex-husband's domain and readied herself to start the verbal fisticufs for real this time.

If only the situation would actually play out as it did in her head, where she was the victor.

His bulging eyes and the jumping vein on the side of his neck grounded her fantasy faster than gravity. It was inevitable she would have to come down from her imaginary win. What goes up . . .

Unlike the strong lady that lived in her head, who found the power to push off the desk and walk away with stinging last words a mere twenty minutes after she boinked the parking lot attendant, in reality Haillie took the verbal blows like an amateur sparring with Tyson.

Somehow, feeling the spittle on her face as Micheal tore away the flesh surrounding a necrotic sore of her mental fragility, listening to him rip her to shreds and mowing down any new personal growth, she felt at home.

To onlookers it was insanity, but for her it could be compared to pulling the boat into dock on a cloudy, dreary, drizzling day knowing warm soup and a hot fire were inside. A few inches and nothing stood between her and a warm potbelly stove.

Worn boots soaked through to the socks dragged up those last few steps, turned the knob to the right, and she felt the warmth welcoming her home in return for the effort. Inwardly she smiled from ear to ear. Her food wasn't too hot or too cold. Her comfortable ottoman chair was perfect. The bed wasn't perfect, but she remembered it well and appreciated it for its flow. That is what made it hers.

"What did you do that for?" He whispered. They were so close, although his imposing desk provided a buffer between them. His body seemed frozen in position as he leaned over the desk. His knees were bent, his finger was in the air. His back was still stretched out.

She had spent a decade in their formerly shared posh home, shuffling from room-to-room, asking herself what - just what - could have gone wrong? When had things changed? Everything had a starting point, a middle, and then an end. She knew the beginning and the middle. She just didn't understand the end.

By the expression on her EX- she reminded herself - husband's face she knew where he was. He was inside that same vault with her, one where the boxes of their shared life were stored, and soon those boxes would be opened. Memories of happy times, sweet kisses, dinners of his favorite foods shared on a blanket by the blazing fire in the dead of winter. Neither party wanted that.

He asked her again "What did you do this for?" She couldn't help but taunt him. "You know why. You are my oracle. Remember when you said that before you left? You told me you knew my every move. There was nothing exciting about me."

She sashayed away "You know everything about me, even why I evade your direct questions. So you tell me."

* * * * *

Micheal was taken aback. Where had she found the back bone to talk back to him and defy answering his question? Sure, Hailie had been like this when at work with her coworkers. That fire was what had initially attracted him to her. But for her to bring that into their marriage? It was so unlike her.

He caught himself mid-thought. Not marriage. This was a work relationship. That is when he recognized his miscalculation. He wasn't speaking to the Hailie he'd known during their marriage. He was in debate with her professional side.

A desire he hadn't felt in more than a decade blossomed inside of him and a need - a hunger - he couldn't explain overtook him. He reached out, grabbed her face, and roughly but passionately kissed her.

She didn't pull back from him. She was his for the taking. He would possess her like he always did and then exorcise his desire for her from his soul for good. She would have no more power over him.

To his surprise, Hailie ended the kiss with a violent shove to his chest. He remained standing over his desk in his fighting stance.

She glanced down and noticed the three top buttons undone on her blouse. He smiled at the sight of those firm, tight breasts and looked back up at her, daring her to finish what they'd started.

The expression on her face told him he'd badly miscalculated. The kiss had not resurrected the ghost of Hailie the doormat wife he'd come to loathe. He tried to dismiss his behavior with a shrug. "Old habits, you know."

Without a word she turned and walked out of his office. His eyes followed her.

* * * * *

The kiss was as sudden and unexpected as it was passionate. Hailie's mind twisted in a whirlwind of 'what if's' for the future and 'oh my, this is right' of the past. Somewhere in the back of her mind, the professional inside her was yelling sexual harassment and face rape. She did not want to listen to that voice, but she knew she ought to.

The unwanted kiss was becoming a mutually enjoyed fervor, but Hailie forced it to end with a hard shove to Michael's chest. The cool breeze on her breasts made her look down. She noticed three buttons were undone, and while Michael was still standing in his fighting posture, his gaze was firmly affixed on her chest.

A devilish smile spread across his face, but she didn't smile in return. Satisfying their mutual desire would only end like their marriage - in a joint culmination of hate expressed as mutual destruction. The outcome was familiar and comfortable, but not where she wanted to be.

He made no apologies to her except to smirk and toss out a lame explanation. "Old habits, you know."

Disgusted with his behavior and her response to it, she walked out of the office without a word. She found herself anticipating the return to the lot. The encounter with Michael had inflamed passions that she'd allowed to lie dormant for the better part of a decade, and she was eager to pioneer new trails in her fantasy land.

The elevator doors opened, but the attendant was nowhere in sight. Thinking quickly while trying to retrieve information covered with more cobwebs than an attic corner, she flipped through the dusty archives of her dating moves memories folder by folder. She settled on an oldie but goodie, and began putting it into action.

First, she scanned the parking lot. She cautiously took hesitant steps forward, her face clearly displaying a mental fog. As she strolled the aisles, combing through the cars, she ran scenarios for what to say, and how she would respond and still be witty. Nothing came to mind but bad opening lines from men in a bar. Deciding on the most recent one she'd heard, the direct approach, she started mumbling it to herself. First impressions were the lasting kind. Pushing aside all the articles on how to recover from awkward first encounters to one side, she stepped toward him.

Half-winking, sporting a crooked wince with a scrunched face and a dazed expression, was the wardrobe she unconsciously wore when she happened upon the parking lot attendant. The professional he was chatting with had him by an inch in height. The attendant's mannerisms and word choices said he had an east coast education. Upon spotting Hailie, she handed him a card and the patron went on his way.

Still bouncing around in her cranium were many conversation openers, some of them clever, many of them just grossly wrong. Before uttering "I share a fire because you are smoking" as her introduction, he attempted to assist her. "Ms. Prescott, your car is in E3." Hitting his stride as she followed behind him, she pondered her next statement.

"What's your name?" she mumbled.

He broke his stride, paused, and asked "What?" Shaking like leaves on a tree on the inside, her fingers tapping on her thighs like a piano keyboard, her freshly kissed lips shivered like she was stuck outside ice fishing. Her confidence turned tail and started running in the wrong direction, driving down a one way street of self-esteem. Seconds before the electric impulse to speak and act fully formed, stupidity came galavanting through her voice box. "Are you single?"

He answered, "Yes."

Ask another question, she thought, something reasonable. Her confidence left skid marks as she hit the U-turn trying to escape this perilous situation. When she started to speak, it grabbed her confidence by the back of the collar and dragged it back to its appointed destination.

"Would you like to have coffee?"

He didn't say anything. It felt like hours passed before he answered.

She gave him an out and started walking away. "Or not." Her hips that sashayed away from her ex now awkwardly swang like a monkey swinging from vines for the first time. First, her backside cheeks whipped right then vibrated from the extreme weight until both cheeks arrived left. The green straight pencil skirt was tight, thereby holding her gelatinous fat. If it didn't, the fat would break free and attack any onlooker's eyes.

* * * * *

"Coffee is fine." He said before he looked up and saw her walking away.

"Where are you going?" The woman was a genuine puzzle.

She turned to look at him. "I didn't think you were interested."

He could not understand her. "Of course. Why wouldn't I be?"

She wrote down her name, time, and phone number. "Hope you don't mind." An attractive blush crept over her face. "Me being so direct." He grinned. "Nope." It made the whole thing a lot easier when a woman was clear about what she wanted. He took the card, flipped it over, and read it. "I'll definitely be there."

* * * * *

It wasn't until after she gave him the card that he took his hat off. Smack dab in the center of his head was a shiny bald spot and half a cowlick. He looked like an aging Alfafa from Lil' Rascals

Oh sh**t her inner mind yelled. Every myofascial muscle froze in place from years of debutante training so she wouldn't offend him or betray her true feelings.

"I'll call you later." He said. As he walked away, he scratched his bald spot.

She quickly found Rose's car in the dimly lit garage. She relished the warmth of the late afternoon sun on her face. Her thoughts made her feel as toasty on the inside as she felt on the outside.

Her first day out of her home since her ex had left her and the nineteen year old perky blond slut doll he was dating had turned against him to help her land a job. She'd landed a date and, in reality, had beaten her ex-husband two times in one day. Well, three, if she counted not fully giving in to her carnal needs and fulfilling a manic cheaters desire for a quick snack.

She deserved chocolate. That was another treat she'd missed in the last decade. She knew right where a Coldstone used to be. She hoped it was still standing.

Chapter 4

Rose dragged herself up the stairs and slammed her shoulder against the door while balancing two full handleless paper grocery bags. She twisted the key in the lock while corralling a runaway onion with her left foot. All her charges, including the onion, made it in the apartment safely.

She dropped some of the bags on the nearest couch. The onion escaped again. She watched it careen across the rug and attempt to hide under a T.V. stand at breakneck pace. She dropped the keys and hoped wherever they landed wouldn't be too much of a bother to retrieve them in the future.

She was worn out mentally, emotionally, and physically but the physical part was from the trek up the stairs. The rest of her bagged food supplies she haphazardly tossed on the counter, taking a moment to find a clear spot, because the eggs were on top. Hoping they landed upright, she went straight to the wine. Swinging her bag strap precariously over the back of the high bar stool, her purse began vibrating off the chair. The first goblet of wine was in hand before she attempted to answer. The smell of the Merlot filled her nostrils, rolled off her tongue, and jump started the salivary glands, preparing them for the incoming liquid.

Behind her, the the cellphone had escaped the confines of the purse to slink across the three by three tile. When it started to follow the path of the delinquent onion, she noticed the vibrating phone, but ignored it.

The first sip of the evening had to be consumed before she could even consider sliding her bum off the stool that was missing the purse strap. Merlot coated her palate and she slid away from the counter. Reluctantly, she snatched up the phone.

Sliding her thumb up the screen she put in her birthdate on the keypad. Her sister had called. She was unsure how she felt about that. Her sister's favorite saying,

"A good deed never goes unpunished," came true today.

Two more glasses filled to the brim with wine and at least one episode of any mindless reality show and then she would be ready to call her sister and enter the mind twist of her life.

It was ridiculous. Her sister had only been out of her house for twenty-four hours and was already entwined in an incomprehensible mess.

Next came the pouring of the wine as a source for a happily-ever-after for her hard day. On second or maybe third thought, she realized what she needed was another bottle. Fortunately, the wine cooler wasn't far from the couch. It was within arms' length. The third ring from the speakerphone livenrf up the room.

Rose sipped. Gulped was closer to the truth. Downing the wine in her glass helped to blur out the day of being constantly chewed out by Micheal. She finally understood what her sister saw in the man.

He was a handsome, six feet tall, broad shouldered man with pecs that could belong to a thirty-year old. Even when the man was pummeling an employee verbally, his swagger had a classy essence to it. It was like a perfume. The phone rang again. This time she answered it.

* * * * *

"Hello," Hailie repeated herself "Hello. Is anyone there?"

With a little worry in her voice, she yelled out again "Rose? Rose! Sis, you there!?"

Her sister's voice came back finally. "Yeah, just drowning."

"What? Should I call 911?" Hailie took a moment to catch up. "You wouldn't be able to tell me about it if you were drowning."

Rose sighed. "No, just drowning in the events of the day and some merlot."

Merlot sounded incredible right now. "You can't tell me you are drowning in Merlot and don't intend to share."

Rose chuckled. "How was your first day as a working American?"

"I got a date!" Hailie squealed.

* * * * *

Rose silenced a giggle. She did not mean to doubt her sister's words, but her last steady boyfriend stood six feet three inches of well - built man. Hailie often detailed the wonderland he called a body. His abs were so flat they could be used for beer pong. The sex was steamy enough for a *Hustler* anthology.

Years of drooling, late night fantasies, and hot dreams were spent in envy of her shut-in sister's love life. Heck, she put him or his twin on her wish list and dropped the letter into Santa's mailbox at the local Macy's.

A chick who had not scored a serious date in a year is willing to expend any amount of energy on finding a man like hers. When Rose finally got the guts to come over to spy on her sister and her date, she found out first-hand that men like him don't exist.

Almost a decade had passed. The boyfriend who proposed twice was all a figment of her imagination. Hailie had invented him so she wouldn't get bored or lonely. "I don't mean to be rude, but is this a tangible person?"

* * * * *

Hailie didn't know why on earth Rose was acting like this. Jealousy could have taken over, she thought to herself. After all, her sister was the voluptuous one in the family.

By voluptuous, Haillie wasn't referring to the internet fake picture dating site appearance description. Rose had curves like Selma Hayek. Everything was there and nicely packed into her vertically challenged stature.

"Put simply, can I meet him?" Rose inquired again.

Ohhh now Haillie understood. She was referring to Mr. Too Good To Be True. Honestly, she had assumed that everyone knew a man with a sense of humor, great looks, who always had a complement, enjoyed creating gourmet dinners for two, with physical skills to match his culinary talents, and showered his woman with gifts for ten years had to be fake.

No man on earth was that perfect. There was one group of men excluded from that generalization and they were found in romance novels. Even those men could only keep it up for a few hundred pages.

Hailie brushed off Rose's skepticism. "In my defense, I never said you could meet Matt."

Rose sounded amused. "Okay. Does this date have a name, a job, a car? Any of those normal manly things that will help me believe he is real."

Hailie rolled her eyes but answered her sister's questions. "Yes. His name is Jake. Yes, to the job. No, to the car. He has a moped. He's very eco-friendly."

Rose made a noise that suggested she wasn't convinced. "And you are still sticking to your story that he is real?"

Now she was offended that Rose wouldn't believe her "What part of my story doesn't sound real to you?"

* * * * *

Rose thought it over, but her vehicle of logic could barely see through the Merlot fog. She gave up concentrating. If she had wanted to spend her evening thinking, she could have worked late.

Rose shrugged. "Where did you meet him?"

Hailie was struggling to contain her enthusiasm. "Today at work."

Rose sat up. "There is no way. Then I should know him. What department does he work in?" Rose frowned at Hailie's reply. "Cars." Rose scratched her head. "We don't have a department dedicated to cars."

Hailie sounded impatient. "The parking garage." Rose nearly spit out the sip of wine she'd just taken. "I'm going to fess up now. I am near the end of my second bottle of wine, so I must not have heard you right. You, of all people, are going out for coffee with a poor man? This I have to see."
Hailie seemed intent on ignoring what Rose had just said. "You mean café?"
Rose could not believe what she was hearing. "Whatever. This man is broke? You know you have never dated anyone below a six-figure salary?"
Hailie's response was a little on the defensive side. "So? I thought he was cute. It's been a ten year dry spell. He was nice."
Rose couldn't help but point out the irony of her admission. "Has it been ten years since Matt?"
Hailie sounded hurt. "You have jokes. I was emotionally paralyzed, not insane. I know Mateo is not real."

Rose's brain was starting to catch up with what Hailie was telling her. You're awful! You mean those fine, tall younguns that watch the parking lot?"

Hailie sounded smug. "Yup."

Rose almost lept off the couch to do a joyful dance, but restrained herself. "Which one is it again?"

Hailie repeated her answer from earlier. "Jake."

Rose could picture them both in her mind. "He's the youngest one, right?"

Hailie sounded confused. "I don't know."

Rose chuckled. "You sure you don't mean James?"

Hailie's sounded doubtful. "No, I'm pretty sure his name is Jake."

Rose rolled her eyes. "You didn't ask him, did you?"

Hailie seemed reluctant to admit the truth. "Not exactly. How did you know?"

Rose explained things. "James and Jake have a running joke between them. James always loses his badge. Jake is a worry wart, so he literally keeps a bin of tags at work in case he loses one. Rules say if you don't have a complete uniform, you can lose your job. Jake never has that problem because he has those extra nametags, but James wouldn't remember to put his head on if it wasn't attached. They get three warnings before termination. James is on his second, so he often borrows one from Jake."

Hailie gasped. "How does he get away with that stunt?"

Rose shook her head and grinned. "You saw James, right?"

Hailie's response was an emphatic, "Yes!"

Rose figured it should be self-explanatory.

"Okay, well, that should answer your question. Also, wearing someone else's name tag is not against the rules, but the nametag missing is grounds for termination. You just looked at what the tag said, didn't you?"

Hailie's response was uncertain. "He pointed it out, I think."

Rose grinned. "First time he pulled that stunt, the boss wrote him up for it. He thinks it is absolutely hilarious. I should tell you this funny story about James and Micheal's betrothed." She sipped more, "Virginia came to the office consistently after she was appointed to the board. James struck her fancy and she put some time and energy into trying to get him to do some underground parking."

She took another sip before continuing.

"Micheal caught on about the second month she was working there. Now, he makes her call him when she is 5 minutes out so he can park her car and she never has to talk to James.

The really funny part is Micheal hired someone to review the footage to make sure James didn't do extra "parking duties" for Virginia. James didn't give in. Him and Micheal are good friends now. Virginia has taken to telling everyone the story about how Micheal got jealous over a parking lot attendant."

Hailie made a noncommittal noise. "Virginia makes him sound petty. She must be more of a woman than me to get him to react like that."

Rose snorted. "No, she's more girl, and a whole lot less woman."

Hailie gasped. "Are you saying that she is skinnier than me? I should take offense."

Rose didn't answer that. She didn't need to. "

Hailie sounded doubtful. "That does not sound like him."

Rose snorted. "And you know him so well? You haven't even had coffee yet. Oh, and Virginia mentioned he was handsome." Rose stopped herself from giving Hailie too hard a time. She was glad her sister was finally showing some life. "Wow! I still can't believe it! This is great news after the day I had."

Hailie's voice sounded concerned. "What happened to you?"

Rose let out an audible sigh loud enough to blow down a straw house. "I got you a job."

Hailie's confusion was clear. "Yeah, that is a good thing and I am forever grateful..."

Rose grunted in frustration. "Micheal, my dear brother-in-law, had a few colorful and some drab words to say to me today."

Hailie gave a full-throated laugh."Are you starting a coup?"

Rose snorted. "Yes! Yes, I was. Apparently, I wanted to undermine his authority. He asked me to resign."

Hailie sucked in a breath. "Are you going to?"

Rose shook her head. "No, something like that would be up to a board vote. When they drafted the papers, the votes were weighted so he couldn't dominate the charity without regard for the other board members. They made sure Michael had no power besides Public Relations. He is a figurehead."

The smile in Hailie's voice was clear. "It's about time someone out-smarted him."

Rose raised an imaginary toast to the board. "These people grew up with him. They are from the same neighborhood so, yeah, they get him."

Hailie's curiosity was aroused. "What else did Micheal say?"

Rose chuckled. "He had some interesting names for you. None of them were creative."

She didn't sound surprised. "Explicit. I'm sure."

Rose took a sip of her wine and thought about how to put it. "Let's just say that if he was a rap album, no kid could buy him." She opened a new bottle of wine, poured, and swirled it around the glass. A few drops sloshed over the sides. She drank, letting her fingertips catch the droplets. She sucked the sulfate-free liquid . "He does *not* like you." She put extra emphasis on the not.

Hailie sighed. "You know, he looks manlier when he is enraged."

The wine was working its way through Rose's brain, unloosening the normal tight grip she had on her thoughts and feelings. The words were out of her mouth before she could stop them. "It is the extra color in his cheeks when he is angered. Between the pink cheek and how he swells his shoulders, he looks rugged."

She paused for a moment as she pictured it. "It's an . . ."

Rose's words startled her. "Aphrodisiac. Are you crushing on my ex?"

If Rose allowed her mind to wander into a land of circus mirror rationale, then the answer would probably be yes. She could like him. He did have the raw sexual prowess that spoke to a woman's hormones. His problem was his mouth . Every time it opened, he would say something so repulsive it could make upchuck sour.

"No! No!" She answered quickly and adamantly "Even if I were, I wouldn't tell you."

Hailie sounded amused. "You could if you wanted to. I would help you."

Rose rolled her eyes. "I don't think you would be my ally of choice. He detests you now."

There was a hint of feminine satisfaction in Hailie's voice as she replied to that. "Yeah, but my cleavage doesn't turn his stomach, as he attested to this afternoon with an unwanted kiss." She paused for a moment. "Unless that was part of his interrogation technique."

Rose was appalled. "Talk about sexual harassment. You should report him."

Hailie sounded surprised. "For what? Kissing his wife."

Rose found herself angry for her sister. "Ex-wife, and if I were you I would chalk it up to not having a goodbye evening of love . For both your sakes, view it as a goodbye."

Hailie snorted. "He has Virginia."

Rose cautioned her sister. "He has a body and a trophy. You are going to reconstruct yourself.

He knows that. Then, what will he have? It won't be you."

There was the slightest hint of something in Hailie's voice that Rose hoped was NOT hope lingering in the question she asked. "You think he wants me."

Rose tried to cut this off at the pass. "Nope! No matter what you do, he will want something new and better." She could feel Hailie's heart free falling, destined to smash on the cement of Michael's heart. Hailie was inclined to believe that love springs eternal despite the arid terrain of the ruins of their relationship.

Rose changed the subject, hoping to distract Hailie from further thoughts of Michael. "Apparently, Micheal is history anyway. You're dating James or Jake now, right?"

Hailie took the hint. "Well, it's just coffee."

Rose smiled. "You know they say coffee is an audition, not a real date."

Hailie sounded puzzled. "That's a rule now? I didn't know. I would have asked for dinner, but I wasn't sure he could afford it."

They sat in silence, both reviewing the day and the decade before Michael.

Hailie broke the silence. "Thanks for the support."

Rose smiled. "What are sisters for if not to support you?"

Hailie sounded serious. "I didn't mean just today."
"I know." Silence fell again.
Trying to lighten the mood before they hung up, she joked. "Remember to support me when Micheal tosses me out on my bum for swaying the board to hire you."
Hailie corrected her. "Remember, you didn't hire me. The board did."
Rose nodded. "True that . I was just one vote."
"Recall that, and bring up his lack of sway over his own board if he tries to blame this on you. He hates to feel his ruling dictatorship is not fully under control."
Rose ended things on that note, "I need my beauty rest, so I have got to go. I'm glad you had an amazing day."
"Except for the Michael part," they said in unison before hanging up.
 Rose sat in the middle of the wine rubble. Wine bottles were scattered by the wind of her buzzed extremities. Tossed here and there, she dropped

the wine glass in with the litter and went to bed. Tomorrow would be stressful, also.

* * * * *

"You know why I'm confessing all this to a parking lot attendant?" Michael had asked one night as James poured him another drink. "Because stopping at the bar for a drink might get me another D.U.I., and that's the last thing I need right now."

"My ex-wife, that cow, took those little D.U.I's and spun them into exaggerated tales that her divorce attorney ate up like cotton candy. You cost less," he'd said as he sipped his drink. James didn't mind. He was being paid either way, and although it wasn't the most prestigious of jobs, as long as it covered his bills, it was fine.

"Our divorce was just like our marriage - her making a bunch of endless demands and holding a bunch of impossible expectations. I couldn't stand being around her. The bar was the only place I wanted to be after the office closed. I'd stay there until the place shut down in the wee hours of the morning just to stay away from her."

Michael took another swallow. James didn't bother to point out that although the ex was no longer present, Michael was still drinking. Some people just needed someone else to blame for things.

"Virginia is different. She may be young enough to be my oldest grandchild, if I'd had any, but she cleaned me up. When she's around, I can't help but love life. My lifestyle is better, my business is better, hell, everything is brighter," the smile that came over Michael's face as he thought about Virginia lit up his face for a moment before the clouds descended again and he frowned. "Of course, that's not how the press sees it. They hate me. Calling me a cradle robber, like Virginia's not plenty old enough to make her own decisions. It's not like she's underage or something."

He took another sip of the drink. James worked up the courage to ask Mr. Prescott for permission to date his daughter.

"I met your daughter today. Lovely woman. She dropped her wallet in front of me."

Michael's head had snapped up and he looked at James. "My daughter?"

James steadied his hand as he mixed another drink to refill Mr. Prescott's glass. "Yes," he said and then proceeded to describe the woman he'd met in the parking garage. "I was wondering if you would have any objections to me dating her?"

To his surprise, a huge smile spread across Mr. Prescott's face. "Why, James, I think that would be great. She doesn't get out nearly enough. I've been telling her that for years. I'm sure the two of you would get along just great."

* * * * *

Michael Prescott couldn't believe his luck. The only woman that had visited him today was his ex-wife, not his daughter, and if there was anyone who deserved a money-sucking leech like James to be attached to her, it was Hailie. She had embarrassed him in front of everyone today and taken a job that she shouldn't have. If this parking attendant wanted her, that was fine by him.

He knew Hailie's weaknesses. If the man's physical prowess was as good as his features, she would be hooked. Her emotions and his alimony nectar would make a vacuum in Haillie's pockets so large black holes would be envious.

He'd never let this parking attendant anywhere near his actual daughter. She was a successful blogger. But Hailie was another matter. That was a match he could easily approve.

He spent some time giving James a few tips on how to win Hailie over. It was the least he could do to repay her.

* * * * *

Haillie heated the bread and cheese in the broiler to avoid the extra calories. She preferred to butter both sides of white bread and put extra sharp Vermont cheddar in between it before putting it in the frying pan. It was a simple dish but it was her favorite. With dinner, she drank a glass of water and for fun she grabbed a tablet and paper.

Looking over her schedule the single mom dropped off on her way out, she grabbed her cell. A minute crease on her face gradually grew into a scrunched up face of stress. Twelve mesaley days bridging the spring fling party and her present situation.

Minutes ticked off into oblivion while Hailie worked her way around the problems created by accepting this job. Why hadn't she really investigated the only place that accepted her resume? It had been a decade since she had worked properly.

AEP events took care of themselves and took care of her. Alimony also helped, she added as footnote to the main statement, although it was more than a footnote in her bank account.

She set aside that set of problems and filled another bracket of the dangers at work. She had to figure out how she was going to deliver what she promised. Her contacts were ancient. Were they still valid at this time?

Her phone rang, and she picked it up. "Hi, it's James."

Startled, she hung up without a word. "Oh, my god ! He called. How did he get my number?" she asked the empty dark house. The answer was obvious. She had written it down,

Hailie had been better for a year. April the 22nd three hundred and sixty five days ago, she bought her first dress on the laptop in her bedroom. She'd called Rose and told her, "I'm coming back to life today." Rose had shown up at the front door holding a club dress, matching shoes, and a purse full with a night out essentials.

"Let's do this." She had exclaimed over-zealously on her front step

Hailie had explained her plan for re-entering the world. Step one was to go outside and get the mail herself. Every week, she would buy budget clothing for the day she would walk out that door for a job interview. Next came business. She started that in January. Each morning, she would dress according to the activities she imagined herself doing that day.

On the weekdays, they were long workdays. Normally, she watched television and pretended she was in the office. On the weekend, a morning run was on the top of her list. Saturday nights were date nights with the perfect man.

By April, the classifieds were a paint-by-number masterpiece, but no one needed a ten year recluse with a decade-plus-old technology consulting firm. Between the regrets around selling her original firm and her relationship failures, she would find herself sitting at the dining room table with steaming hot smothered fried pork chops, Michael's favorite dish, decorating the dinner plate and her wedding album for company. The lit candles made it resemble a Victorian ballroom.

"Good times." She echoed as she turned the pages. Many people would think this would depress her and send her spiraling back into the abyss.

The simple fact was that this was her safety line. She needed to beat the man that stole her life in the arena of corporate success. As she turned the pages, tears dropped, and were replaced with hardening steel. If she shed tears in his presence, they would be bullets of verbal venom. Bullets welled up in their tear ducts when then hand vibrated and slipped through her finger tips.

Seconds tucked by as she recalled the routines of the past year before the sound of the phone ringing and the possibilities she was missing in that moment registered. She dropped to her knees and snatched the phone up.

"Hello, James, right?"

"Yes," the male voice on the other end of the line confirmed.

"Sorry, I guess the phone dropped the call," she told him.

That was the best excuse she could come up with for hanging up on him. Now, she was scraping up what courage she could find not to hang up again while also scanning her archives for possible conversation pieces that didn't include explicit conjugal details. Added to the awkwardness of the greeting was the ever-present fermented slur.

"Don't worry about it." He said, filling the silence her fermented fruit energized brain was attempting to fill.

"Hi, Ms. Willams-Prescott." James said again.

She wanted him to use her first name, but she had a sneaking suspicion he thought she was the daughter of Ms. Willams-Prescott. If he thought she was the younger Ms. Prescott, she wouldn't give away the secret. After all, the secret was only one sided for now.

"Yes. It's me." She smiled into the phone.

He sounded relieved. "I'm sorry. I thought I lost you again."

"No. I'm still here." She was smiling again. Her cheeks were stiff and her eyes were not used to the gesture. They had produced tears and complemented fleeting moments of half joys throughout the solitude. Mirrors in her home remained covered since the day Michael left. She did not want to see the body that had failed her. No reflection was needed for her to know she wasn't happy.

"Not a problem." His voice was soothing to her. "I was calling because I couldn't read the name of the coffee bar."

"The Café?" That place had become her favorite over the last year.

"Yeah." He sounded anxious, and that made her smile. It felt good to have a man nervous about talking to her instead of the other way around.

"It's around the corner from where you work. It's a small café, but it's nice." She could picture the two of them sharing a small table in the back.

"Thanks. I'll see you then." James hesitated for a moment and Hailie wondered if there was something else he wanted to say, but then he just finished with a quick, "Bye," and hung up.

She was a little disappointed at the brevity of the conversation but supposed it was to be expected. They were just getting to know one another.

She was mid-way through texting Rose that he'd called when the phone rang again. It was him. She thought maybe he'd butt-dialed but decided to pick it up anyway.

"Ms. Prescott, it's me, James. I'm sorry. I know we just got off the phone, but there was something I meant to ask you. I just didn't get it out."

While she waited for him to ask his question, she quietly tied Rose into the call, snickering to herself. This would prove to her sister Jake or James or whatever his moniker happened to be was a real person. She sent a text explaining things to Rose: "He is on the phone now."

* * * * *

Rose heard the chime and bell ringtone from across the darkened, spinning room. Guided by the annoying, disturbing sound, she found the phone. "Hello?" formed on her lips, but before she spoke, she registered that another conversation was going on. She was on a conference call.

Listening to the terribly corny banter, she put names to the voices. It was her sister trying to firm up the date with the parking lot attendant. This left her with one question. Why was he calling her Ms. Presscott and not by her first name?

She wondered if she should tell him, but if Haillie was okay being Crystal, Mr. Presscott's daughter from his first marriage, who was she to spoil the best real thing that had happened to Hailie in the last seven years?

"Will you meet me for breakfast instead of coffee?" James asked

"Why?" Hailie sounded confused.

"No," Rose thought. "Don't you dare. If this doesn't work out, you will be back in Micheal's arms or worse - dating your next pretend boyfriend."

She decided to intervene in a way that only a sister could. She lightened her voice and peeled back a few years from her larynx to match Hailie's and usurped the conversation for it's embetterment. "WHY, sure. When?"

The smile in James's voice was evident. "Seven tomorrow. Thank you. I was worried that you would be scared off by breakfast instead of coffee. See you tomorrow." He hung up.

Hailie's panicked voice broke in. "Hello! Hello? Are you there?"

Rose grinned. "Yes. I'm here." Hailie deserved this for waking her up.

Hailie sounded exasperated. "Not you. I meant James."

Rose chuckled. "No, he hung up."

She could hear the doubt in her sister's voice as she asked, "Was that my fault?"

The truthful answer, "Yeah, probably," would only mean a slow calculated regression to shut in status, so Rose chose to be supportive. "No. Truthfully, you were both quite awkward, but you did well considering the circumstances."

She sounded relieved. "Thank you."

Rose sighed. "Congratulations on your first post-divorce date. Now, if that is all, good night. I have to work tomorrow and so do you. And you have an early breakfast to attend, I might add."

Hailie sounded confused. "What work? I don't have any work to do tomorrow. There's nothing on the books."

Rose swore. Wow, could her sister make a grown woman shed tears of frustration over ineptness.

"Voice mail." She deliberately said each word with painstaking slow pronunciation. "Dear sister of mine. We have gone over this before. Your voicemail is the answering machine of the twenty-first century. Check it. Daily."

Hailie's response was overly dramatic. "But, Rose, what does it do in the twenty-first century?"

"Geez!" Rose's brain was slow to catch on. "Nothing! It is the same. Since you have time to agitate your tech tutor, tell me how do you retrieve your messages again?"

Hailie's answer was less than confidence building. "Something about a pin number, like an ATM pin. One, seven or two. Right?"

Rose groaned. "It is two in the morning. I can not explain it again. You are on your own."

Hailie apologized. "Good night. I promise I will let you get a good night's sleep. No more calls from me."

Rose grunted. "Good night." She'd almost hit the button to end the call when Hailie's voice interrupted.

"Just one more thing." Hailie quickly spoke into the phone.

Chapter 5

"Admit it. Tonight was a failure," Michael told himself as he chewed another chalky antacid which he followed with a warm milk chaser. The clock in the library read 2 am in the morning. He'd still be asleep, but Virgnia's restlessness woke him. She told him it was stress, but he wasn't sure.

Fleeting thoughts of good old days with Hailie had interrupted his attempts at making love to Virginia for yet another night. Virginia made him feel alive, young, and virile again, but Hailie was undeniably amazing in bed.

"Yum," he startled himself with the sound of his own voice as the memories of that body rose to the surface and his manhood with it. He began pacing. Temptation tugged. He could…he looked at the cell phone on the edge of the desk and shook his head.

"Nope." He refused to revisit those memories. He mentally tucked those safely away into a shoe box and decided he wouldn't think about her, or the wrongs she'd inflicted on him by showing up in his life again so abruptly.

But some memories refused to go down. The lifeguards and barricades he'd erected surrounding his past with Hailie came crashing down when that fenced member stood up.

A brief spark of guilt crossed his conscience for the mental infidelity to Virginia, but he knew the truth. His charm, for her, was in the bank account and not in the bedroom. He knew why she wanted him. He knew why most women wanted him.

Most of his peers told him that at his age, he should be with someone who loved him. He had been, but his second wife, Erica was dead now. He'd found consolation in Hailie, but it hadn't lasted. Virginia was the latest, and he knew already that wouldn't last either.

His answer to his friends was always the same, "I should love what I have, even if it is only for a short time." Nothing he loved ever lasted.

He gazed at the empty glass of milk, trying to gauge whether or not he'd given his bedmate time to fall back asleep, but his mind wasn't up to the task. Instead, he poured himself a glass of amber liquid, the cognac that he used to drown out the memories of the past and silence their persistent voices, and then found himself thinking about how much like Hailie and he this liquor.

They were so well-matched, and yet complete opposites. One was strong and one grew to appreciate the taste as well as the effects. The other was soothing to the body and the palette. Both were soothing, just with different properties.

He walked across the teak floors to the granite wet bar with the towering oak book cases, drinking in the smell of the room and the distinguishing scent of stale Cuban cigars and single barrel reserve bourbon combined with imported French cognac and old American books dating back to the eighteen hundreds. His books were appreciated, but the liquid behind the counter was needed.

She had to go. He couldn't go another night at half-mass, leaving Virginia wondering as to his heart's state of affairs and him questioning his mind's obsession with Hailie. A flash of her hips bucking upward beneath him shot through his hippocampus to remind him of all that he'd left behind.

"To the way things were," he said as he toasted the empty air with his high ball. He swapped the eight-ounce glass for the bottle. He was going to have a dreamless sleep one way or another.

"To Hailie and all of our unmentionable memories." He lifted the bottle and, foregoing the formalities of a toast, raised the bottom of the bottle until its contents were gone. But there wasn't enough liquor in all his cabinets to chase away the memories of her.

~ ~ ~ ~

Virginia was wide awake, filled with anxiety, heart throbs, and butterflies. She'd pretended to go back to sleep after Michael awoke, tired of the failed attempts to please her. They seemed to drag on forever, as if he thought he could make things work by sheer willpower alone.

She knew what had changed and when. Ever since the AEP had shown up on Michael's desk as an approved independent contractor, he'd begun experiencing these complications. She couldn't remember the last time she'd actually enjoyed sex.

These days it felt like they were on the same yacht but in different wings, sharing a bed but nothing else. She longed for the days like when they first met. She'd been so eager for their special breakfast in Paris.She hadn't meant to oversleep. She wanted to be wide awake, but she was done for by the time they entered the last time zone during their red eye flight.

He'd awakened her with fresh squeezed orange juice made from the Spanish Valencia blood oranges growing in the backyard of his Parisian home, with egg white omelet spinach feta and nine grain toast made in the kitchen by his personal chef. The gleaming expression of self-satisfaction spreading from cheek to cheek was enchanting, and he'd walked through the door frame, taking up the majority of space. She'd liked the sheer mass of him.

His pecs were solid mounds of muscle, swollen biceps that held the antique 1930's breakfast tray he presented with one, bulky manly hand. He'd placed the food down with flair while the other hand swooped around her waist and he pecked her forehead with soft pink lips.

Butterflies, balloons, and bubbles seemed to tickle her insides. She was definitely being swept up in the magic of the moment although her two feet were rooted on the ground. These days, it felt more like she was six feet under and life was searching for new ways to bring her even further down.

She was nodding off by the time they connected with their 6:35 am flight to Paris. She watched as cognac from France splashed around the two ice cubes in his high ball glass. Tilting his head back, he knocked back the drink. She watched him hypnotize himself while turning circles with the glass as the ice cubes danced with simplistic grace, each one colliding into the other occasionally and then skidding away to their respective corners.

He tilted the glass, sending the ice cubes smashing into one another as he sipped the diluted liquid. Virginia pondered what he found so beguiling about ice and crystal.

"Ha!" The triumphant sound startled her, and she watched as he poured more amber liquor over the cubes before sending them down another white rapids ride down his esophagus.

Her last conscious thoughts before dozing off were about those past moments. How much pensive ice cube gazing was about her predecessor? He'd been doing an inordinate amount of bottom glass gazing since she was selected as a finalist for the contract. She felt asleep, dreaming of the surprises that tomorrow was sure to bring.

Hailie found herself clinging desperately to a small, seaworthy vessel of sanity bobbing along in an ocean of fear that had flooded her mind in the week preceding the presentation. Giving into tidal waves of panic, she reached desperately for the comfort of sleep, but compounding stresses competed to keep her awake.

There was one act she was confident would knock her out, but she lacked the key ingredient required: a gentleman. Despite the absent material, she determined to put herself to sleep by any means necessary.

She reached into her nightstand, with a sleep mask firmly affixed so she wouldn't disturb the beginning stages of rest, and fumbled about until her fingertips found the elongated shape they were seeking. She turned until she found the appropriate setting and turned the object upside down to enjoy its promised pleasures before searching once more to find the liquid that would ensure a smooth entry into her temporary paradise as she popped the first two sleeping pills into her mouth. She fell into a fitful sleep filled with dread of any surprises ahead.

Chapter 6

Hailie woke to the blare of sirens. Her feet hit the floor, missing the quick access slippers she kept beneath the bed for just such occasions, but she heeded the call of urgency to leave her house and moved forward in her bare feet. Visions of plumes of smoke climbing the stairs in search of a resident to char triggered a fear that she was going to be roasted alive in her own dwelling. The thought of being trapped inside, burning up alongside everything she owned, was one that had haunted her since she was seven years old. She considered slipping on her robe while scurrying to leave, her eyelids still pasted shut beneath the sleep mask, as she sprinted down the stairs to the door. The click of the Jazz-era, Harlem-style repurposed door helped a few fragmented thoughts settle into place as she stepped out into the safety of the open air and the breezy late summer coolness began to slip around areas best not shown in public.

A new fear displaced the fear of burning alive, dulling the ordinarily pleasant sensation of air drying her more private crevices, and she found herself mentally reviewing her nightly routine with a silent prayer that she had not actually forgotten to put on clothing in her haste to exit the building.

She began by patting her face. Her dermis was moisturized. That was the step that always came before unfolding the pajamas which were neatly stored at the end of her bed each morning. There were two bottles for her nocturnal skin routine, used at the apex of the routine pyramid, followed by her underpants, a roller for her bangs, and her pajamas.

Denying the evidence to the contrary, she reassured herself that she simply must be wearing the pajamas. Putting them on was the last step she took before climbing into bed each night. She must be overreacting. The fresh air caressing her curves was not proof of a reality she would rather not face.

Starting at the crown of her head, Haillie began patting the naturally curly mane, now brushed into a bun, down her neck and to her shoulders, and then onto – her breast and nipple. Naked. She was bloody naked!

All other thoughts attempting to whimper forth were drowned by these deafening words exploding forth.

The horrifying reality confronted her. She left the building hoping to preserve her life, but now found herself silently wishing that the ground would open beneath her and swallow her whole. The irony was not lost on her.

Her hands flew to cover areas only a doctor or husband should see and her eyes darted back and forth, checking for any entrepreneurial types with a phone and access to YouTube. The day was off to a bad start. Reliving it in a public forum and seeing the comments below would put be the nail in the casket of her recovery. She jotted down a quick mental memo to develop a lack of reliance on technology after this incident of embarrassment. A footnote to the body text she added to always put on a robe before leaving the house.
A quick double-check for morning joggers, people

e strolling about, or the random peeping Tom relieved her mind. A small sliver of hope that no one would come by before she could make

her way back inside began to make its way to
her brain. It was the crack of dawn. Surely
nobody else was awake yet.

The road clear, she bent down and blindly patted
the stoop for the spare key under the fake rock in
the giant planter on the left of her front step. The
key was hidden between bushes in the flower
box. She turned over the rock and the key fell
down in the dirt next to the cement encased steps
leading to the front door.

A sense of urgency filled her mind. There were
already plenty of tidbits available for a morning
matinee viewing and she had no desire to
uncover the few pieces she could hide with her
hand and forearms.

Sorting through the dirt, expletives began
streaming softly out of her mouth, when she
heard a man's voice coming from the sidewalk.

"Are you okay?"

She froze before sneaking a peek at the owner of
the voice from between her knees.

A light sheen on his forehead from his morning
jog gave him an effervescent glow. The six-foot-
three-inch guide was talking to her two airborne
cheeks. Her hands were temporarily painted dirt
brown black. Her face had smears of topsoil on
her front and back cheeks. Her hands were still
resting on the pot she was searching.

What could he see? How much of her body bits were open to his view? Did she do enough exercise to be standing with her back end spread eagle? Was her full moon firm and her cellulite appropriately hidden? For the first time in her life, she considered the merits of bleaching her excrement orifice.

If she had to let her little moon shine, it might as well be in its full glory. She stood up, covering her breasts and lower area as she turned around to face him. "I'm fine. Why do you ask?"

"You looked like you might need help." His eyes took in the whole of her.

Having already began, she doubled down. "No, just air drying."

A slight smile touched the corners of his lips. "I hope no policemen or young children come by." She hoped he would hurry on his way so she could get back to looking for that key. "Me, too. Have a nice run."

"Have a nice day." He extended his hand. "I hope you get back in your house, Ms…"

"Prescott." She extended her own hand, revealing a c-cup bosom.

He looked down at her hand, one eyebrow cocked up and melting into his hairline. Haillie noted his widow's peak, speckled with salt and pepper, but full unlike James. She blushed as cool air continued caressing her exposed areas. They stood shaking hands while she gaped at him, taking in the full impact of his masculinity. "I never said I was locked out."

Realizing how dirty her hands, not to mention her thoughts, happened to be, she snatched her hand back and wiped the dirt on her thigh. "Sorry."

He stared her directly in the eyes. "It's been a pleasure meeting you." A grin stretched across his face. "Enjoy your morning."

Salt and pepper man put his earbuds in and sprinted down the sidewalk. He became a bobbing dot in the distance and she stood, motionless, with her hands by her side.

Cling. Clang. The key hit the cement on her second try to get into the front door. Picking it up, she entered the house hoping for a non-eventful rest of the morning, except for breakfast with James.

Safely back in the confines of the opaque solid walls of her town home, she skipped the preliminaries on her to-do list and jumped straight to putting on her robe. Although it was too little, too late to benefit her during her outdoor adventure, she did enjoy the belated comforts of the satin that slid against her skin.

She glanced at the mirror before heading to the shower.

"It's nice to be clothed again," she thought as she stepped into the porcelain tiled tub. Pellets of water rained down in drizzles that slide across her back making her feel as sedated as an overcast morning. She needed every drop of water from the rain shower head to calm down.

*****

Anxiety woke James long before the alarm rang. The idea of dating his boss's daughter filled his mind. He contemplated what to wear for a full fifteen minutes, staring at the seventeen pairs of plain white shorts and pressed jeans that hung in groups of two beside the dress khakis.

He decided that if he was going to be seen with a woman like her, he should make an attempt at looking classy. He picked out the khakis and paired them with a blue checkered buttoned-down dress shirt along with white dress shoes.

*****

Haillie wrestled with the pullover knit sweater, the wet fabric twisting inside out beneath her arms, as she wrapped her fintertips around the upside down polyblend cloth to begin a tug-of-war that would eat away at yet more of her precious time. She refused to admit defeat rather than disrobe and select a less skin-hugging garment from her collection.

Any piece of clothing that showed her curves in a way that benefitted her was worth the battle. There was an impressive age gap between herself and James. This piece of attire stood between her and a twenty-two year old six pack belong to what she assumed must be a pot head. He did have a tendency to lose his name tag, after all.

A familiar siren sounded and she glanced over at her iPhone, which was reminding her that she was cutting the dressing part of her day dangerously close to what she hoped would be snuggling time. She momentarily retreated from her battle with the sweater to retrieve the phone and silence the cling clanging of the same alarm that had sent her bolting from the house that morning.

She padded back to the bathroom feeling two shades stupider than when she left, but the phone was quiet at least. Declaring herself the victor, she stuffed the knit shell into the waistband of her dark pants suit. Accessories and a spritz of vanilla from her kitchen pantry, a scent she'd been assured in a career women's magazine appealed to men, were her final touches. He would never notice the difference between the cheap scent and a luxury perfume. He was a man.

Suitably attired, the search for her car keys began with vigor. Twenty minutes were trashed with her mental attempt to place the misplaced keys in her house before attempting to look for them. This hold up was an annoyance. She was being mugged of her remaining seconds to take a deep breath before leaving her home on her second shot at finding happiness again in life. Her keys were not on the key holder near the door or on the change table next to the couch. Frustration bubbled over into frantic action as Hallie tossed her couch cushions on the floor even though she was sure she had not been in the vicinity of the living room. She fell to the floor, repeating the act of patting and running her hand over the surface of the tiles, hoping this time she would come up victorious.

She was hopeful they had fallen out of the purse she'd last carried to sign divorce papers, but it had been so long since she'd last seen them that she knew the hopelessness of the situation. Desperation mounted as the second hand began its fourth sweep around the clock face. It was now 8:04 am. If Lady Luck decided to stroll into the café of her life and throw a little good way into this situation, she would not be upset.

Luck stood her up. Again. She was keyless. Fortunately, Haillie had ideas for creating her own luck. She had a mental deck of cards which she shuffled, dealt it out, and stacked that deck in her favor with one phone call.

"Hello, this is Ms. Prescott. I need a car immediately." She spoke from rote memory, not having used the car service in ten years. There would be a price to pay if Michael found out, but until then she would enjoy moving onward and upward to James.

Having dealt herself a club flush, it seemed she'd earned Lady Luck's respect and good favor. The missing keys were found in the umbrella holder to the side of her front door. Smoothing out her blouse, she immediately put her hands on the perfect pair of shoes, which were also next to the door. A club flush was now a straight flush. She swung open the door.

The driver pulled up to the curb. "Good morning." He held open the car door for her. "Where will I be taking you today?"

She stepped into the car. "Café Around the Corner."

*****

The coffee shop named Around the Corner was a few blocks away, but around the corner from Haillie was another coffee shop. Her thoughts were preoccupied with sliding into the car backside first, pressing her legs together at the knees, and scooting back she turned and pressed her feet firmly against the floor. He shut the door and got into the driver's seat.

"Which one did you choose?" The driver turned toward her, the confusion written across his face. Haillie realized her need to clarify. "Not the one around the corner. The one named Around the Corner."

He nodded his head and faced forward. "Thank You."

The black Lincoln cautiously pulled away from the curb. Like yesterday, she watched the surroundings pass through the tinted window. Unlike the day before, she was going to work. There were new developments in her life. She knew the road she chose was as full of potholes as the Baltimore highways. James would be a complication more than relief, but it was one she was prepared to add to her life.

The immense mansion of a past she couldn't remember and the reflections of those she could were closed to visitors today, including herself. Instead, she closed her eyelids, shut out the world, and let her mind paint a water color masterpiece of how breakfast would go in step-by-step detail. Unfortunately, the art on display in her mind wasn't a watercolor, but a perfectly preserved photograph of her past.

Dabs of mental paint brushed across the canvas to create a sketchy figure similar to Michael. There were blades of grass. He held her hand. His large, strong grip enclosed hers, making her feel protected. They approached a blanket on the ground with a picnic basket spilling over with food.

Her favorite fruit was plucked from the basket and hand fed to her. She laid on her back and stared at the sky. He gently slide his forearm under her head to provide a little comfort.

"What do you see?" he'd asked her.

"A triceratops," she had told him.

"Where?" He strained his neck to see the same thing she'd seen. She'd traced the outline of it in the clouds that paraded across the impossibly blue skies.

"How?" He looked again. " All I see is a potential downpour."

She lifted her head until she was about two inches above his face. "You are looking at the clouds from the wrong viewpoint."

"Really?" He smiled devilishly. "How should I look at them? Glass half-full?"

She'd shaken her head and returned his gaze. "Forget the glass. Rules don't apply. Just open

your eyes and imagination. You can see water
without glass or any other container, if that is
what you want." He closed his eyes tight.
She was about to object to him doing the
opposite of her instructions when he opened his
eyes. Cool air poured into his eyes She opened
her ocular orbs and now they looked like a bug.
She roared in laughter.

Chapter 7

Around the corner was a delicatessen that ran like a Nascar pit stop for the entry level corporate ladder climbers. Accounting clerks stood next to eager beaver college grads with more energy than sense. All them were jam packed in like commuters in a subway car.

Behind the counter, a combination of baby faced workers and nearly dead retirees jumped to attention at each jingle of the bell located above the door. Hustling and bustling like bees around a hive, they efficiently churned through coffee requests made by the respectful co-workers we all know and love to hate.

James found a chair on the outskirts of the craziness in the suburbia of it all. He stared at the sun absently, watching the people scurrying about on the sidewalks, as aimless thoughts bounced around his head like a pinball.

****

Haillie's car drove two blocks in the morning's traffic jam costing her fifteen minutes. Now twenty-two minutes late, she was certain she was going to be tardy on her first day. The car eased its way over to the middle lane toward the curb. Horns honked when it finally stopped to let its passenger disembark.

Pushing and shoving past the line of pre-caffeinated souls she tried her best to see over the six foot tall human traffic jam. Her five foot one inch stature was having no luck. Out of the corner of her eye, she caught a glimpse of a group sitting at the tables in suburbia.

Those occupying the seated section were relaxed, lingering over sips of organic coffee and herbal chai tea while chit-chatting about the puzzle of world problems. Amongst them was James. If her eyes weren't deceiving her, she might have thought his baggy jeans were neatly pressed. Before approaching, she spent a split second imagining their first words to each other.

She saw herself walking over to the semi-circle of the socially-conscious and fiscally unresponsive before sitting down on James's lap, leaning in and kissing him. Not some peck, but a full on French, while whispering in his ear that she would offer him a backseat ride to work. Hopefully he would understand. She did worry.

Just three steps away from her date, she contemplated the day dream again, weighing its pros and cons, then scrapped the notion of being that forward. Instead, she placed her hand on his shoulder and waited. He looked up.

James pinched the stirrer between his forefinger and thumb. The stirrer did a round de jam, making the creamer streak the brown coffee like a jet's path across a pure blue sky. Haillie patiently waited for him to speak coherently about the conundrum he was in by leaving what looked to be good friends to her to begin their first date. A slip of a thought shot discomfort through her body. Was she supposed to join them as a group date of sorts?

James stood. "Ladies and Gents. I leave you to your wonderful association."

"Good luck." the group answered back.

Arm in arm James whisked her to an empty table in the corner of the restaurant.
"They know about us."

Screeches came from the chair legs scraping the tile floor as he pulled it out for her. They both gritted their teeth "A woman like you I would tell everyone about."

He leaned down to whisper "You look amazing"

She smiled. "These old things?"

"Classics never go out of style." He sat across from her. "What do you drink?"

"Whiskey." She laughed at her own joke. "I'll take a caramel flavored macchiato, upside down, heavy on the whipped cream."

"I'll get it for you." He stood quickly and darted toward the long line like he could magically make it shorter and hurry back to Haillie's side. She had meant to watch him walk away. Those broad shoulders screamed to her inner thirst. Arid lands had reigned for so long that just a spark of a drop was like a deluge.

Instead, she caught his glance back at her. If she remembered those gleaming eye signals correctly, his eyes were communicating adoration. What was she to do with admiration?

She could understand lust. She was looking for lust. It was half the reason she had agreed to coffee. Lust is a satiable urge, but admiration leads to emotions that she'd left confined to a dark corner whimpering in the mental living room with a pint of Nelson's chocolate dutch ice cream.

She knew the feelings that had moved into the mcmansion of her heart while the body she once fully inhabited with a full range of her emotional state was languishing in the haunted memory walls of her winnings from the divorce.

What she needed to fight off his admiration was at her fingertips. Still a tiny wayward feeling poked a needlepoint hole in something, of what she couldn't be sure. A whisper made it through the punctured membrane, instructing her not to reach for that heartbreaking lie she wanted to use to send him running from her.

She couldn't handle admiration. She still had to unpack how she felt about yesterday with Micheal. An involuntary reaction caused her to shiver.

****

He glimpsed at her quickly showing his pearly whites in a reaffirming manner. James couldn't believe how fortunate he was to be with the daughter of his employer. She was perky, and had an old soul.

He was surprisingly happy to see that in her. He was aware he was jumping ahead of himself. They hadn't talked, but he had a feeling. How did this happen he thought? He pinched his arm to make sure this was real. He gave himself a self-assured, knowing nod. His dating prowess gave him a barometer for the socially vapid sorts.

"What would you like?" Behind the counter the barista spoke.

James stood there, speechless, before composing himself. "Sorry," He sputtered. "I want a pumpkin latte, upside down, no sugar added with extra whip."

"Pumpkin's not in season." The pimple faced, buck-toothed girl behind the counter told him, her expression flat as she waited for his revised order.

He flushed. "Oh. Right. I mean caramel." He plunked down his money. The change sounded like wind chimes as it hit the countertop. James never noticed the whimsical, almost melodic rhythm the change made hitting the counter. He reigned in his emotions with a quick reminder to himself. *Get it together, man. This is not a Disney movie.*

The barista scooped up the money. "You can pick up your coffee over there."
She pointed to the left.

James shuffled to the side as instructed. While waiting, his mind drifted to topics Haillie may consider charming, and suitable to their vastly different stations in life. What would a parking lot attendant talk to the boss's daughter about during their first date?

"James. Macchiato." The words drifted into his train of thought from outside his cerebral borders. "James."

Caught up in a winding web of lies not yet told and expectations he wanted to unfurl around her like a cocoon of infatuation, the syllables making up his name started to come through. A distracting thought from inside his mind led him away from the outside world again.

Interacting with her father could be a registered act of infuriating frustration. He should know. The man chatted with him every evening, his entitled attitude making James both furious and frustrated.

He weighed whether the web of lies or the truth about him and her family was in her best interest to share. He was familiar with Micheal's first wife and the jarring shock it had been to those outside their family bond when Micheal and she broke up. He tried not to stare at the demure young lady that came from that union.

A rollercoaster of affection was an understatement as to what she must have gone through with her father and the many partners he chose to share his life with, especially after the last and very public divorce from Haillie. *What happened to her?*

The male baristas words suddenly became comprehensible to him. "James. Macchiato."

"That's me!" He raised his hand. "Right here."

"Cool, dude." The barista said as he handed him the drink.

James returned to the table where Haillie sat waiting. He placed the drink in front of her and all the conversation stakes he had plotted out dissipated. The silence that hung in the air was heavy with anticipation. James opened his mouth to speak syllables that didn't materialize.

Haillie sipped the coffee. "Thanks. This is different, but I like it."

Gazing into each others' eyes with no words coming to mind, the half-truths each kept weighed down the atmosphere. The absence of words made it more difficult to navigate towards the safe and smooth passage of a good first date conversation.

James lifted his cup to take a sip and changed his mind. The cup landed with a thud. They both looked down at it.

"Thanks for inviting me to coffee." Haillie's voice was timid. "I don't date often."

"That's understandable." He gave her what he hoped was a reassuring smile. "It must be hard to meet new people. I mean, you are who you are?"

With a sigh and inward cringe, she kept her gaze on the coffee. "Yeah, it's just hard. You know?"

He didn't, but he could imagine. "Yeah."

Silence overtook the conversation again. James tried again. "How bout this weather..."

Haillie's voice overlapped his. "This place is quaint. How did you find..?"

They looked at each other. She smiled. "You go ahead."

He chuckled. "I was just going to talk about the weather. When in doubt, weather it out. At least, that's what my mom taught me."

Hallie's laugh was light. "Well, the weather has been nice."

James smiled at her from underneath thick black lashes that caught Haillie's attention and held it. "My mom's wisdom hasn't failed me yet."

She returned the smile with a coy glance of her own. "Now, we are getting somewhere. So, you are a momma's boy?"

James held up his hands, eyes widening in alarm. "Wait. No. I just listen to her advice."

Hallie laughed at how easily he'd been thrown off his game. "Just kiddin'. I think the ice is officially broken."

A grin crept across his face. "No kidding. So,"

She winked and took a dainty sip of the coffee. "Buttons."

His face was blank. He clearly didn't understand her meaning. She explained. "That's one of my mom's sayings. Now we are even."

He gave her that quick grin. "Even footing. I can dig it." He smiled. "Tell me something about growing up?"

****

"One thing I learned early is to not care about being a Prescott." Mentally she told herself she wasn't lying, although she was impersonating her step-daughter. She grew up a lot during the divorce from Micheal.

James scrunched his nose. "Huh,I never heard that before" He stirred his coffee, apparently trying to figure out where to go next with the conversation. He glanced at the clock and winced. "I'm going to be late." He looked up at her. "But…"

The way he looked at her made Haillie's voice catch in her throat as a feeling of warm anticipation flooded her body. "Yes?"

"Oh!" There was a slight frown on his face. Haillie's hopes wilted. His actions betrayed what his head was thinking. He clearly wanted to run and find shelter in a younger, more energetic version of her.

She looked down into her cup. This morning coffee was a misfire. Prescott had ruined yet another thing for her. She knew that ninety percent of the blame lay at her feet. The last gulp of her beverage sloshed around at the bottom of the recyclable biodegradable cup.

She took the shot of reality to the head, not losing the irony in a comparison of the beverage container to herself. The scraping of the chair across the floor announced her leaving.

James looked up from the cup, surprise written on his face. "You don't have to go."

Haillie's voice was crisp, an effort to cling to the shreds of her dignity. "I will be late for work like you, and it is my first day."

"He's your husband." Her heart lept into her throat as she heard his words.

Neither of their expressions changed, but the micro climate spoke for them.

"I mean, he was your husband." His voice was soft. She could barely hear it as she pushed the chair under the table.

She felt her face flush in embarrassment. He looked into her eyes and gave her a small smile. "I just wanted you to know I figured it out while we were chatting. I'm not mad. Honestly, I don't care. You are fun and funny…"

She stood still, listening even though she felt like rushing back out into traffic, climbing into her car and heading back home. It was early for whiskey, but who would know if she were all by herself?

He looked out the window. "I'm nervous, so my words just won't come out right." He looked back up at her with those puppy dog eyes that seemed to just beg her to scoop him up and take him back home with her. "I know better words. I swear."

She relaxed and laughed. "I still have to go." She gathered her purse and other belongings, along with the used coffee cup. She turned to leave.

"I want to do this again." He blurted the words out. "You fascinate me in words I can't explain."

Haillie froze. Her purse strap was above her elbow when it started to descend toward the floor.

James stood up and reached for her, turning her back around to face him. "You are like the eye of a hurricane. You are calm and clear while everything around you is swirling and tossing. You leave hope and reconstruction in your wake."

His voice lowered and she felt like she would melt into a puddle of goo on the floor right there.

"Then there is this essence of a quality I can't put my finger on. I want to know what that is, so no, I don't care about that your name is Prescott, be you born or married into the name, it doesn't matter to me. On another note, I don't care about him. I am a parking attendant for crying out loud!"

"I guess I am going to be late." She said to herself

 She texted her driver to pull up to the curb outside the restaurant. She extended an invitation to him to join her. He accepted. She knew this was not the way for them to discover why she was like the eye of a hurricane, but it had been such a long time since . . .

Chapter 8

Haillie's town car pulled over to the curb outside the office building. She gathered her nerve as she readied herself to enter the lion's den. She could practically hear Micheal licking his lips at the idea of her fragile self-worth entering the building.

She reprimanded herself for spending money she didn't have on her luxury ride to work this morning as a stroke to her confidence. She was not sure how the tinted windows and privacy partition of the mid-sized town car connected to her self- esteem, but she was filled with hubris from James.

An inconsolable one-third of Michael's triplet three-pack glanced up at her as she passed by the receptionist desk. The misery written on her face, undoubtedly from separation anxiety, couldn't make her joy stretch to a genuinely fake smile. This behooved Haillie to pause and briefly check in on her first hire from the decade prior.

She layered her voice with a measure of sympathy. "What is wrong?"

The girl was barely holding back the tears. "I think my sister got a modeling gig in New York for the next two weeks. It was supposed to be a day or two, but now I'm stuck here without her."

Haillie smothered the urge to laugh. Michael wouldn't be happy about losing one of his trophies. "Is that something we should be sad about?"

The girl shook her head. "No. It's just that she is going to be gone for so long. It's going to be quiet around the house."

Haillie was confused. "There are three of you?"

The girl shrugged. "Yes, but they needed twins, so both of them are gone for the duration."

She saw an opportunity to kindle a new friendship, and perhaps recruit a spy for her team, all at the same time. "I tell you what? When our day is over we should go out and grab a drink." Haillie had no idea where someone like her would grab a drink these days. *Was there a posh place around here? Was she even that cool? The answer to both those questions was no. What was she going to do?*

To her surprise, the girl swallowed the bait as if she were a starving salmon and the offer of drinks was a tender, juicy worm. "Yeah, Where are we going? Do you think the papers will cover us going out? Yee!" she shrieked.

Hailliee flashed the girl a smile. " I'll search and find a place you may like. You won't like my usual haunts. "

Her first day and she didn't want to be uncool to the supporting staff. She had so much to worry about today. Making friends with Michael's receptionist was hardly the largest of her concerns. She couldn't afford to allow worries over the poshest cocktails, cutest servers, and hottest party spots to occupy space in her mind.

Right now, she needed every square inch of grey matter to be at optimal running speed with thoughts of decor, caterers, and venues. One misstep here could cost her the whole recovery journey and the money to keep the brownstone.

"Great!" The girl half-mumbled as Haillie started to stroll away from the reception area.

She was scoring nada antes It was 10 o'clock and time to enter the lion's den.

In a mood change so quick the Guiness Book of World Records should have been there to record it, the triplet spoke. "Ms. Uptight Single Mom is waiting for you."

Haillie froze. She could only imagine what the extra emphasis the receptionist had put on the word *you* meant when she arrived at her assigned space. What did she mean by yoooou? I'm not that old. How can she justify using you like that? I can still party like I'm 22, Haillie thought.

She opened the conference room door only to be met by a barrage of concerns over Haillie's employment contract coming from the single mom. Haillie could care less about the covert attacks hidden in the words the woman fired like arrowheads at her.

The woman opened a portfolio and began spreading papers from the tattered folder. "I picked out what I think are the best options for us." Haillie noted that folder had seen more good old days than the greatest generation. The woman's finds were strewn across the table for easy viewing.

She paused for a brief moment to look up at Haillie. "See? I do a good job at this. I can handle the heavy lifting on this. Why don't you take care of the...finer details. Everything is well in hand. Just follow my lead and I'll get you through this."

If she wasn't mistaken, she was being pushed off her own project by one of her ardent supporters from yesterday before she even did an ounce of work. She wanted to yell, "Heifer, you don't have a charity gala in the recreation building on the less than impoverished side of town unless it is for the neighborhood," but this was her only job for now. She had a full year contract contingent on this meeting. Fortunately for her, she couldn't fully focus on this insult to her profession because she was a YOU.

"What did that mean? I am not old." Haillie realized she'd spoken that out loud when Lisa, the single mother, turned and gave her a strange look. She wished she could take it back.

Lisa straightened up with a frown on her face and crossed her arms over her chest. "What are you talking about?"

Haillie gave her a rueful smile. "Lisa, I am sorry. I was a little side tracked."

Surprisingly, Lisa let that truthful statement pass. "It is hard the first time someone calls you old. I get used to it. The kids always say I am old."

"But I am sure I could party with the best of them." Haillie debated her, although there was nothing to debate.

Lisa shrugged. "You probably could. Depends on who is partying with you."

Haillie sighed. "The receptionist wants to do something with me."

Lisa glanced over at her. "To welcome you back?"

It was more of a question than a statement. A very open-ended question that she wanted closed as soon as possible . Lisa did not need to attach herself to her invitation.

* * * *

Lisa could sense Haillie's hesitation to invite her along with the triplet. She decided to add an incentive she knew Haillie wouldn't be able to refuse. "I can tell you why the board unanimously voted for you instead of the other candidates we'd seen earlier that day over drinks."

As she'd known it would be, the proverbial carrot was too tempting for Haillie to resist chasing, even though Lisa was certain she didn't really want to add someone new to the after work outing.

Haillie flashed a smile at her. "Sure, you can come." She laughed politely.. "You don't have to bribe me." Lisa could tell she'd added that last part out of civility. She was definitely interested in the bribe.

"Where are we going? " Lisa's question added no hint about the promised carrot. Haillie wasn't going to learn the answer to the biggest why question of her day so far that easily. Lisa wanted to wallop her with the proverbial carrot.

* * * *

Haillie decided Lisa was nothing more than a proverbial carrot tease. "I don't know. Some place that fits her."

She threw up some air quotes "the YOU!"

Lisa chuckled. "Yeah, you don't deserve the 'YOU.' At least, not quite yet. That only matches us when we get our medicare and a retirement check."

"And then maybe not then." Haillie and Lisa both had a good mellow and resentment clearing laugh.

Lisa sat back in the chair and smiled at her. It was not a menacing type that displays the teeth as weapons. Haillie had been on the wrong side of that deadly chomping smile and razor sword-like tongue for years. This was an affable smile of peace mingled with trepidation.

Haillie wasn't about to bite the hand that had just tried to snatch her job. Haillie smiled back in an effort to turn the peace bow into an advantageous friendship for their mutual survival.

Oh, who was she kidding? Her survival. Lisa had navigated her way around this place for years. They shared common ground.

Haillie gave Lisa a rueful grin. "I'm actually happy you are coming with me. It is nice to go into a new situation with someone that has shared part of my past."

Lisa raised an eyebrow and chuckled. "You mean the bad part of your past."

"No." Haillie watched Lisa's shoulder relax in the chair. She took it as a good sign.
"I met you when I met Micheal. Therefore you aren't the bad part."

Lisa raised a hand. "Now, now. Micheal isn't all bad." She paused for a moment. Of course, it's thinking like that makes me answer the phone when I ought not to for him."

Haillie looked away, suddenly feeling a sharp pain in her heart. "I've never had that problem. He hates me."

Lisa shook her head. "Oh, I'm not sure about that. I feel the gentleman doth protest too much when you were hired."

Haillie swatted the words away with a playful hand gesture. "He called me back to his office after I signed the contract for the job and tried to intimidate me into leaving the company. I think hatred is the right word for what is between me and him."

Lisa rolled her eyes. "Let me guess. He tried to kiss you. You know he believes make up sex is the best sex."

"Well." Haillie started. Her eyes darted from Lisa's back to the papers. "You have some...interesting ideas. You have a handle on the budget. My hat's off to you on that front."

Lisa gave a mock curtsey. "Why thank you, milady." She jested.

Haillie was catious as she formed the next sentence in her head and let it roll of her lips like an inflatable tube down a lazy river in the afternoon. This had to be that smooth a transition. "We should stick it to Micheal like he does to us."

Lisa raised an eyebrow. "Color me interested. Do tell?"

Haillie allowed a slow grin to spread over her face. "The gala is the one night we can get away with not watching the budget and busting his. Let's go for broke. His broke."

Lisa snickered as she crossed her arms. "What do you have in mind?"

"I'll show you." Haillie opened her laptop, "I'll print my ideas out for you."

* * * *

Haillie picked up one of her hot-off-the-printer papers in the midst of the cubicle pit. Scanning over the printed words, Lisa pondered what would make her pick this place.

It was smack dab in the middle of an area that still had pre-civil war hatred for anything not Lily white. One-third of her donors definitely didn't fit that description. "You like that one? It is a little expensive."

Haillie shook her head. "It is two thousand for the night. That is not expensive. You do recognize this night will get you the majority of your operating funds for the year, right?"

Lisa stiffened. "I do recognize it, but you don't seem to recognize that I have done this for the last six years and we seem to do well."

* * * *

Lisa's more colorful past personality and vernacular were starting to surface. Haillie was aware of who she was and what connection they had to her ex-husband. She was not trying to challenge her standing either earned or by birth.

Haillie kept a smile on her face but inwardly groaned. Less than a minute ago, Lisa seemed to be all in on this idea. Haillie couldn't help but wonder what had changed.

A whiff of Rumors, the Britney Spears' perfume, entered the room.

Lisa made a face. "Phew." Her dark brown curly bob flung around as she exhaled, turning to follow the scent. "Who is that?"

The squeal from the little future Mrs answered their rhetorical questions. The response to their mental query was met with an eye roll.

"I asked Michael" the girl started. Just what she needed. Nothing for her benefit ever started with those words ever since his fianceé came along. The girl continued, oblivious to Haillie's feelings. "if I could make sure Ms. Downs" she turned to face Lisa, "was playing fair."

Lisa's eyes cut to evaluate where the former Mrs Prescott Jr stood on this issue. The former Mrs Prescott Sr. was Micheal's first wife. Was she an ally or enemy? Did she understand the struggle of the underdog? Or was she an elitist like Ms. Perky tits?

"Lisa is doing just fine. She was showing me some of her ideas." Virginia's bouncy curls were as jovial as she was. They were such a close facsimile to the innocence of Shirley temple locks, but the roots and highlights in no uncertain terms stated she was not twelve.

As Haillie thoughts landed on the curly mane, a passerby stopped to admire those same tresses. The girl was a knockout from follicle to phalange. Haillie sometimes consoled herself with the unarguable fact her replacement was as beautiful as she was smart, savvy, and gracious.

What she didn't want to do now was alienate her. "Why don't you sit in? You seem to have a knack for this and we could always use another board member's input." Haillie's mouth said while watching herself lose ground with Lisa.

"I would love to." Virginia beamed and pulled out a leather rolling chair from the conference table. Somehow Haillie felt she had just gotten played. Lisa turned her chair, knocking her pen off the table. It rolled half the distance between her and Haillie.

Lisa bent down to scoop it up while mouthing "Really? She doesn't need to be here."

Haillie said nothing. She just slid the floor plan for the venue they were just arguing over toward Virginia. Lisa slammed her pen down in silent protest to them ganging up on her. Haillie acted as if she hadn't noticed.

Lisa pushed her venue forward. "This is the first place we were considering."

Virginia scoffed and looked at Lisa in amazement. "Why? No one would come here? It's such a backwards backwoods establishment."

Lisa crossed her arms defensively and Haillie recognized the signs of a cat fight in the making.

"It is easy on the budget. If you recall our goal is to raise money for our cause not to entertain your privilege . . . "

She decided to intervene. Lisa trailed off as she handed out a binder to each of them. This gesture was premature, but she could see she needed an olive limb with as many branches she could get for the three of them to come to any sort of peace without face slapping. Immediately Virginia started flipping through.

Haillie took the opportunity to explain what was in the binders. "These are a couple of banquet halls, restaurants, and hotels that have your dates open. Some of them are, as Lisa put it, easy on the budget. Others are worth the investment for name recognition, decor, and food. An all-in-one deal."

"If it is all-in-one, what did we hire you for?" Lisa shot at Haillie, glaring at her for the perceived betrayal.

* * * *

Virginia laid a hand on Haillie's arm. "Please excuse Lisa, Haillie. She has no imagination."

Haillie said nothing. It seemed she was trying not to take sides in the ongoing war between the two. Virginia continued. "It's always about the bottom line with her. "

She turned and sat, silent for a beat, to give her next sage words a bit more emphasis. "Not every answer can be found in a budget. Sometimes you need to open yourself up to the more luxurious things in life. I mean, you can get life experience outside yourself, if you just stop worrying about cost."

Virginia folded her arms and sat back in the chair. She obviously felt her point had been emphasized. The silence in the room she felt extra content. Her two seniors were definitely considering her words of wisdom.

* * * *

Haillie sat straight up with hand equidistant form the life guru in a teeny bopper's body and the single mother. Virginia's smug smile had nothing to do with an oral battle carefully strategized and well-fought. Haillie knew this for certain because she had taught the adolescent Virginia to survive through middle school and beyond after her first three moms picked out colors for their nurseries while dwindling Virginia's inheritance down to the pittance she would now receive through this engagement to Micahel. There was no doubt in her mind that Virginia's words of advice were spoken without malice.

A tsunami sized swell of anger began raising Lisa's blood pressure. She was actually seeing red, bloody red, sheets of red flapping in the breeze like they were hanging in the fresh air on an outdoor laundry line. An o shape formed on her lips.

Haillie spoke before voice could be given to whatever words Lisa thought about putting after the shape. "We each have added something valuable to this process."

"Wha, wha, what" Lisa stuttered stumbling over the flood of enraged words"did she add?"

Haillie avoided answering that. A description of what Virginia thought she said would serve no purpose except to tick off Lisa more. Seeing that Lisa was near stroke level, Haillie decided against being a translator.

On the other hand, she did see some benefit to all the heightened emotion in Lisa. Now, Lisa would accept and respect what she brought to the table.

With more than an overture of sarcasm Lisa demanded "I'm waiting?"

Excitedly, like a puppy wanting to be petted, Virginia also waited. Fortunately for Haillie, they all received a text as the lone receptionist walked into the conference room with Rose by her side. Rose was texting and had not looked up to see who was sitting with her sister.

"Liam-Gavin Prescott is ill at school. Can you bring him home?" Rose and the receptionist read it aloud for the benefit of the room.

Lisa's open hostility was clear in her voice. "We can read,"

Rose smiled in Lisa's direction. "I will pick him up okay?"

They all wanted to say no and give a reason so they could be the best mom to Liam. Michael popped his head in the room. "You do know that Liam is sick and between the four of you, you couldn't find someone to pick him up?"

They stared.

Micheal pointed at the women and named off their responsibility to little Liam "His mom, his step-mom, aunt-in-law, future stepmom and his pretend auntie?" he chuckled exiting the room mumblining "Women."

They looked at each other. No olives were needed. Rose took a binder out of her sisters' bag , then joined them in their unified boycott of his orders. The nice thing about working for Mr.Prescott was the eventuality that the line of personal and business would interfere with office operations.

When those two territories crossed borders all that was meant to be kept secret became public knowledge to those sitting in that conference room. With all of Rose's five foot stature, she wished her sister had not been in this conference room to witness how Michael balanced his charity with his life and new female accessory.

Knowing who her sister was before her voluntary incarceration, she knew her analytical problem solving side. It would be no time indeed before Haillie would become more than a challenger to his authority. She would become a real adversary the board could get behind. This was her first hurdle.

"I know what you mean?" Cried Virginia; jarring Rose back to the meeting. "Lisa is such a spendthrift, but at least we can all agree to satin tablecloths, right?"

Virginia took a breath. The other ladies did not engage in conversation with her. "It has to be extravagant. Oh, I know! We should do a 1920 speakeasy."

Cautioning against the jejune shrills of the husband stealer, Haillie pointed out "We don't have a place to put these lovely satin tablecloths, unless we are going to postpone this event for a picnic day."

Lisa was leaking patience like a hole riddled gas tank. "Where are we having this shindig?" she spoke sternly, her eyes the only clue to the furnace expelling the warm vapors of anger.

Not so oblivious as to miss's blatant ocular clues, Lisa forged ahead with her stubborn adherence to her impossible budget. When she spoke this time, it lacked all respect. "We will have it here in the office. The theme will be working for the less fortunate."

Her lips sternly flattened their plumpness into a thin line of determination. They dared Haillie to cross this statement and take the leadership she was granted by the board yesterday.

In response, Haillie backed down. She knew this was about far more than a venue. As the baby mother, for lack of a better term, Lisa was entitled to her say and her insane stance.

Finding a solution to the mess she had trotted her way into, Haillie declared, "The board will hear your proposal first, Lisa."

With no other move availed to her, Lisa gathered her stuff from the oak tabletop with a sweeping wipe of her forearm, and left. Rose and Virginia sat staring at her back as she went toward the elevators.

"She wasn't even supposed to be here." Virginia said. "She called Michael this morning and said her son was sick. Micheal was going to call for a nanny so she could go into work."

"But..." Rose egged her on out of morbid curiosity.

Taking the bait Virginia continued. "He mentioned how she must be relieved to have more free time since you." she pointed to Haillie, although they all knew who she was talking about. "are handling the events calendar.."

In an effort to clarify Virginia's understanding of the job description, Haillie spoke up. "I don't..."

Virginia kept right on with her story. Haillie hung a mental post-it from her frontal lobe next to the one saying "Secure a venue" that said, "Handle this miscommunication about her responsibilities at a later time." The last thing she needed was Miss Preschool over there asking for sold-out tickets to assist with her social life.

A full mental debacle played out to the tune of humiliation. Virginia using her as a concierge service. What a joyful thought. The sarcasm in her tone would have melted paint if not for the fact it was all in her head.

The three shared a half smile and an eye roll, before Virginia began to ready herself to follow behind Lisa's footsteps, leaving Rose and Haillie in the room to dish.

Rose's slim, petite white manicured hand skimmed the lines of her sister's event packet. "That is not a good idea."

Anxious, Haillie rushed to her side to look over her shoulder. "What part?"

Ignoring her sister's inquiry, Rose continued. "But I have a feeling you know that." She turned the page. "Just like, you know, somebody in cardboard boxes out there will report her behavior to..."

"Michael" she cut her sister off in mid-sentence. Rose had not missed the endearing tone related to her ex's name.

"She is his mother, you know. An ally, and not one to cross." Rose lifted her irises from the pages, and peered at her sister's expression.

Haillie crossed her arms over her chest and looked away. "You look crazy when you stare at me like that."

Rose snorted. "I am aware of what I'M doing."

Haillie felt a flush on her face. "I am not foolish."

Rose put an arm around the back of her neck, gently patting her shoulder. "I am not saying you are. It has just been ten years since you had to deal with anyone slightly close to the word sneaky."

Brushing Rose's hand off the shoulder, Haillie rebutted " Ten years meditating gives me an upper hand."

The two of them rounded the corner to another set of twelve cubicles. These were vacant from a fresh round of pink slips. A twinge of guilt stuck her side. She had a job and whoever sat there didn't have one anymore. Ignoring any other feelings she responded to Rose's earlier words. "Sneaky is being locked in your own head with your own treacherous thoughts."

Rose sighed. "That is a little dark."

Haillie shrugged. "Dark or not I can handle this, I promise. And it won't send me backwards."

Rose passed a new hire named Janice. She plucked a pencil off her desk. "Hope she doesn't mind."

Haillie rolled her eyes. "I'm sure she won't."

Haillie walked toward the door Lisa had exited. Rolling her chair away from the desk and reacquainting herself with the stack of account receivables, she watched Virginia bounce toward the elevator. Her shiny ring lighted the way to the exit.

There goes Michael's corporate harem. She chuckled.

Chapter 9

Haillie had nothing to do with the rest of her day. That thought dawned upon her as she went hurtling downward in the elevator to the front lobby. The next scatter brained idea sputtered to life, then gathered traction in the race to become fully formed.

It had been nagging at her ever since she pushed the button upstairs calling the elevator to the floor where she was working. Light lit the circle above her head illuminating the number two, then she came to the realization she had taken a car to work.

Haillie's original thought was to stay at work all day until the four o' clock meeting, but now that she was leaving early the time she told the service was invalid. It was the lack of pull on her left side that gave it away. There were no keys.

As she descended, the elevator car jerked to a stop two floors from her selected stop. A gentlemen with a tailored Hugo boss suit joined her. Her libido started to surge again. She had just fed it all she was willing to give into its demands.

Calming her mind and her thoughts, she shushed her inner voice. Yesterday it had gotten her a date with a young man that thought she was her former step daughter. No matter how strange she felt about lying to him at the beginning of it, he had proved he was worth the eventual ulcer.

Her psyche had something different in mind and started its speedy debate about this male meat in the elevator with her. *You spent ten years growing cobwebs on the southern hemisphere. The quick dusting from earlier did not get to every crevice.* That was her first justification.

She was sure others would follow and they did. *You had a hard day,* followed immediately with, *You deserve a little flirting. What harm could it do?* And, finally...*If you don't try, you'll never know.* Convincing herself she could call not doing any of those options a victory over her carnal lust, she patted herself on the side of her abdomen between her rib cage and her pelvis.

Not escaping her notice as she gave herself the gratuitous pat down from the shoulders to the waist, she was stealthily drawing his attention to the fact that she still had the waist of a twenty-year-old. That wasn't bad, she thought, as she began a new appraisal of the man. Her hand lingered in that smooth nook and caressed the curve, remembering James' hand from earlier.

She was in love with herself at that moment, and the knowledge that she could make a man many years her junior crumble. An interjection of self-confidence shot through that was as intoxicating as the high preceding work day's start. It was heady.

Her victory was short-lived, because the red light flickered beneath the circular plastic encased number three hanging overhead. She was heading back up.

Her resolve began to flounder as she steadily climbed up the floors. She thought of those broad shoulders in the fine, precise stitching of the quality fabric. Her forefinger began tapping his shoulder.

He turned his head just as a pen was released from her non-dominant hand, tucked safely out of his field of vision. His face looked vaguely familiar, but she couldn't place exactly where she'd seen him before. She was pretty sure she'd remember a pair of abs that fine tucked into a suit of quality to match. Her hopes for the old-fashioned trick paid off.

Picking up the cool steel writing instrument he said. "You dropped this."
He handed her the sleek ink container and she coyly accepted. At least, she hoped it was coy and flirtatious.

She was supposed to say something, but instead she released the pen again to tumble back to the floor. "Did you drop your pen, this time? Slippery little devil aren't they?" She gave him a meaningful look while trying to keep her voice sounding innocent.

He looked at the collection of doodle buddies in his pocket. Audibly he counted "1,2,3,4,5,6."

"No, mine are accounted for. It must be yours." His lips tilted up in a smirk.

Did he have a sneaking suspicion it wasn't his pen before she asked about the writing utensil that looked exactly like the one he had picked up before? He had seen the ink smearer roll from her direction, hadn't he?

****

Checking his pocket thoroughly, he assured himself it wasn't his. He was certain the pen had rolled from her side of the car, but slipped his hand into his inner pockets to double check that the item wasn't really his.

He decided to go along with it. Clearly, the lady was playing this charade to talk to him and he was more than willing to play with her. There was no reason to mess up a good thing.

He hadn't been the object of someone so obviously hitting on him, nor had he seen this tactic used since junior high. Whomever he was sharing the elevator with was definitely a go-getter and she was hot.

Her being hot made up for her shortfalls. He would have used a better word, but adolescent stunts beget adolescent words. He gave her a michevious smile, but it came off as a smirk.

****

The reasonable, disinterested side of her mind kicked in. She felt aggravated. Where were you ten seconds ago, before he gave me the 'I'm not into you' smirk? She bade herself to answer.

Why, oh why, did I bother? She spoke to the irrational side of her mind, which had no answer. Even her loins were cooling off. She reprimanded both her mind and her box into submission.

First, you berate me with your haunting echoes of 'you're an agoraphobe' and 'wasn't this morning oh-so-fun'. Now you want me to act like some desperate cougar. She looked at the man, his powerful stance taking up the entire area in front of the button panel, his physique practically beckoning her to touch it.

The visual input began butting into the middle of her disciplining soap box speech. Her rational side added, "He's more like your peer." This started an entire conversation between the two.

"He can't be my age." She sneaked a peek past her rationale guards as she tried to scroll through her list of previous verbal scoldings to find her place so she could begin again.

"That depends on how old you are." Shoot. She recognized just a second too late that she had said that out loud. What should she say next?

"Act like you're better than him," her rational side strongly suggested. *"That way, it's not him rejecting you. You're rejecting him."*

"What?" she responded to such a sophomoric idea inwardly, or so she thought. "That is so junior high"

"I know I shouldn't ask a lady her age, because it is impolite, but middle school is a bit of a stretch, even for someone as young as you." His joke and attempted half- smile caused a light bulb to go off in her head, a light so blinding it halted all other nerve impulse traffic. He was the jogger from this morning.

Could this day get worse? She silently prayed that God would send her an angel and get her out of this mess. As the elevator paused once more, a proverb came to mind. "Knock, and it shall be answered."

The doors opened to the elevator and there was Michael, shoving Liam on to the elevator with them.

Liam was clearly upset. "I didn't want you to pick me up."

Michael was fuming. "Shut up. Be grateful someone came. Your try out mother wasn't coming to get you, nor were any of the other women. Be happy I paused my day to pick you up. You aren't even sick."

Haillie tapped the one guy on the elevator she knew would be happy to see her.

Liam's face immediately brightened. "Auntie Haillie!"

He turned, scowling, back to Michael. "I am going with her." He threw his backpack at her feet and took her hand.

Haillie was grateful for the diversion. She didn't think she could face up to Mr. Perfect Suit and Body now that she knew where they'd first met.

****

Michael was happy to concede. Liam had complained and whined the entire drive there. I want chants, and I need cries were still echoing in Micheal's ears. That boy was more like his mother than he remembered. He wanted nothing to do with his upbringing for the next twenty four hours.

Before the stainless steel doors to their box transport closed at his offices, he exhaled and gave Haillie a command. "Take Liam to your house and watch him today. Don't come back in tomorrow. I can't handle the drama you bring with you. We'll reschedule your meeting for next Wednesday night. I should be ready for you by then. I'll tell the receptionist that you are taking two personal days." The doors started to shut.

"I don't have vacation days. I'm a contractor." Haillie shot back.

Michael shrugged. "That isn't a problem." Micheal started to turn away from the trio. "You do have a check I can dock for the missed days if you choose not to do what I say."

****

Haillie couldn't see his face for the last part. Unfortunately, his words about her check made it to her ears just fine.

A few short blinks of the light above their heads later and the gentlemen' was preparing for his exit. "What do you do?" asked the jogger as the elevator slowed.

Haillie blushed as his attention turned to her. Thoughts of what had transpired that morning crossed her mind. "I am an event planner."

"Oh!" he stepped through the gap in the opening doors and swiftly executed a three point turn. A pen flew in and landed on the floor at her feet with a note attached.

She picked it up, read it, and smiled back at the man, who was grinning ear to ear at her. It was the first time he had seen her fully since he got on the elevator. He went against his character, and blurted out "Do I know you? You seem familiar?"

"Aaaaa sh. . .!" She shivered from the vocal explosion of shrills from embarrassment.

Liam's eyes went wide as he watched the tableau play out before him. "Auntie Haillie, you've got game!"

His voice oozed respect. She smothered a groan. "Sssh" she put her finger to his lip. "He may still be able to hear us."

Liam rolled his algae-covered pond green eyes. "Paranoia" he hissed.

There were ten floors in this building. She descended six and ascended eight. Fourteen floors is all it took to become a streaker, prove she was childish to the best looking man she had ever seen, gain the responsibility of motherhood, and put her job in jeopardy. Compared to what could have gone wrong, she considered this to be a good day.

That is, if she went home right now. Resurfacing from the not-so-far recesses of her mind, reason bobbed its head above to reclaim her conscious mind. She had no car but had acquired a kid.

"How did you get here?" She asked Liam, hoping for some ingenious answer to head off the embarrassment awaiting her in the parking garage. She was going to a parking garage to look for a car that was not in the lot in front of the guy she dated this morning with a teenage boy at her heels. There was going to be a lot of explaining to do.

As she waited for Liam to answer, all these thoughts whizzed by her. She prayed the universe would even the score for the last forty-eight hours with whatever words tumbled past his lips.

Liam grinned. "Dad let me drive."

She mouthed a thank you to the universe for divine intervention. "Do you have keys?"

Liam pulled them from his pockets with a smile. They left the elevator and started wandering around the parking garage. "Where did you park?"

Cartops gleamed like ripened wheat in a field compared to the greyish darkness of the parking garage. Unfortunately, they needed to find just one stalk of wheat among the many.

Liam passed a Ford Focus from two thousand and one, and whimpered. "I can't believe my mother drives that car."

Haillie raised an eyebrow. "That is your mother's car?"

Liam grimaced. "Yes."

Ooh, that is sad, she thought. She was shackled with a child and this was Lisa's first gift from the family. Didn't Micheal have the decency to get at least a Range rover for his baby mother?

Parked next to his mother's car was his gift. Unlike the four door antique rust bucket with it's nearly bald tires, the vehicle they were about to use for transportation was only half of a car. She slid her bum atop the two wheeled ride. Liam handed her a helmet and she secured it under the chin.

"Shouldn't I be driving? You're sick." Haillie shoved him into the back. "What is wrong with you anyway?"

Liam shrugged. "I think they said it's the flu."

She huffed. "Great. There goes another three days of pay down the drain once I catch the flu."

He rolled his eyes. His voice was impatient. "Are we going?"

Haillie nodded. "Yeah sure." She fired up the scooter "But where are we going?"

Liam was firm. "Home."

Pointing the front tire in the direction of the exit, she went squealing and burning rubber toward sunshine. Wafting smells of gasoline, mingled with oil and transmission fluid from the cars nearby, they approached the gate to the parking lot. Her new beau stepped out to collect their ticket.

James smiled at her before turning his attention to Liam. "Liam! You got your ticket?"

Liam shook his head. "No."

Haillie said nothing. She didn't want to have to explain how Liam, a boy old enough to drive, was her responsibility for the day. James knew she was ex-Ms. Prescott, but she worried that seeing Liam would firmly put her into the old hag area.

She revved up the scooter. She wanted to blow right past him. No need to linger like he did this morning. She glowed at the thought of that.

"Let's hurry up and find it." What she hoped would be a stealth departure was working out nicely. Just finding their vehicle without his assistance meant success.

Liam asked to drive seven aisles closer to the exit to pass his dad's Bentley. He demanded they stop. He hopped off two slots to the left. Under the sign was a key fob.

"Found it!" echoed through the cavernous lot. "I hid it there so I could get in and take his bribing stash."

The car chirped. The lights blinked and he pulled the door handle open. Haillie stayed with the scooter.

Anxiously, she listened for James' footsteps. "Hurry up." She whispered.

Liam rifled about in the car a bit more. "One more minute."

She wanted to scream. *I don't have a minute. One more minute, and I have to face the ghost of mornings past. Okay, just this morning, but she had no desire to meet the consequences of the first 48 hours of leaving her house for the first time.*

James appeared, as if those words had summoned him. "Hey, Liam. It's been a while." Liam gave James a grin. "Yeah it has. Wuz up with you?"

James extended his hand to meet Liam's. "Still here." He front bumped his fist, popped it up in the air from beneath his fist, and swatted it down from the top.

Liam shook his head. "You still doing the same handshake? That's old, dude."

James got down to business. "Why are you here? Your dad put you on the don't admit list ever since he put in the new policy about bringing kids to work."

****

Liam shrugged his shoulders as he inhaled the oil stained air of the garage. He understood why his father felt the policy was necessary. His mother was always challenging his father on all the bull he pulled because he could.

He knew his mother didn't want to pull punches because life didn't offer her such courtesies. She wanted her former lover to take responsibility for their eighteen-year old mistake, the son he'd walked away from without a second glance.

His mother had demanded the best for him. She told his father that Liam needed good schools, the latest gadgets, and tutors that would drill the importance of a Harvard education into his head by thirteen so he could pass an entrance exam for a prep school that could open the world to him.

His father had stopped listening to her pleas three years after he took his first breath. At her wits end, she did a lunatic mother's approach and brought Liam to work every day for a month. It saved her a ton on child care, and it annoyed his father. He had to face the child he wanted to ignore each day.

Co-workers showered Liam with candies, gave him toys, read to him on their lunch breaks. His father had just walked hurriedly walked past them as if it were normal. Day thirty-one, he broke his silence and opened his checkbook, along with everyone elses's eardrums, from the screaming match that came before his generosity.

Doing the right thing is doing the right thing, even if you do it begrudgingly or half-heartedly. That started the no child policy at his father's business, a policy his father had ruthlessly enforced.

This was a story his mother had told him so often he could knew it by heart, and being reminded of it was like salt in an old wound. The knowledge that his father's generosity wasn't out of love but simply due to not wanting to be harrassed by his mother still stung. "I don't have a ticket to get out of here, so I thought I would drop by dad's car and grab parking garage money. How much is it now? $75 for a full day?"

****

James's blue eyes sparkled like sunbeams off the ripples in the ocean. His plump rose petal lips curled up into a smile. He laughed. "Weren't you the one who told me to have some ambition?"

Before Haillie could protest James's words, she remembered she had became a motivational speaker to Liam once or twice, and she blushed under the helmet with the face guard.

Haillie nodded beneath the helmet. "Yes. Listen to your elders."

Liam rolled his eyes. "Oh, my god, you're old!"

Why was she agreeing with James? Why was she caring for him? He was a lust release and, obviously, younger than she was. She wanted to echo through the garage. She gripped the handles on the scooter to get a hold of herself. The wild horses behind the material of her pants suit bucked against their corral.

She exhaled to cool herself. Relaxation washed over her and she released the stress of the day, closing her eyes and letting the buildup escape. So did the scooter. When she opened her eyes, Liam was staring at her. James had taken off after the scooter. He was gaining on it.

Liam was doubled over, his hands on his knees. Haillie's first thought was "How am I going to explain this to Lisa?" How would she explain to his mother that her son was hurt under her supervision? After this morning's disagreements with both his mother and his father, who would believe she had no malice in her heart toward either Liam or Lisa?

****

James patted Liam on the back of his leather jacket. "You okay?"

A loud snort and a cough followed the trio of pats as Liam waved away James's assistance. "Yeah. I'm fine."

James stepped back to give the boy some space.

Wiping tears, Liam pulled himself up to his full five-foot nine inch stature. He shook his head and looked at the petite woman beside him. "Aunt Haillie, you are hilarious. Dad said if I put one scratch on that scooter there wouldn't be a new car in my future." He laughed. "He's going to be so mad when he finds out you broke it."

Attempting to take the pressure off Ms. Prescott, James stepped into the conversation, calling out, "It's not broken."

He stood the scooter up from the pavement. James could see anxiety mounting in Haillie's eyes over the two wheeler. He gave it a proverbial dusting off, and started looking it over. The whole time he was flashing Haillie a knight-in-shining-armor worthy smile. Digging up tape from his back pocket, he wound it around the mirror's base until it stood in its proper place.

Liam hopped onto the back while Haillie

situated the bike. "I'll see you later, right?" Liam slid the helmet over his head.

James gave him a thumbs up and signaled he would see them around three. Haillie burned rubber getting out of there as if she couldn't wait another minute to get out of there.

James yelled "Get home safely," into the puff of exhaust it spit out.

Chapter 10

Rose ventured to the water cooler filled with electrolyte enhanced, melting mountain snow sourced water nine times that day. She was getting antsy. Haillie went toward the elevator in a huff an hour and a half ago and had not returned. Certain of her sister's resolve to keep this job and make a real go at a life outside the house, she hovered around the window, waiting for her sister's return to work once she cooled off.

The white disposable paper cone cup touched her lips as she parted them to let the liquid soothe her anxiety. Partially covering her left eye, the cup tilted toward her head and the water flowed into her mouth. Out of the corner of her right eye, she saw Haillie's 90's decade leather jacket disappearing into the distance. Her cup dropped into the trash. She slid a hand into her pocket and pulled out her phone with one liquid motion. She listened to it ring.

"Am I looking at you out the window or not?" she left on the voicemail as she walked back through the maze of cubicles. What was Haillie doing leaving when she had a presentation at three o' clock and still had to get approval from three board members before she could even think about showing her work to the major donors and full board?

She tapped number three on her speed dial. If she used voice activated dialing, she risked alerting people to Haillie's absence. She got the voicemail again.

"Shoot." she muttered under her breath, pulled out her roller chair and rubbing her temples as she sat down. She clicked through her emails aimlessly.

There were three expense reports coming in from two board members, one call from a donor, and a memo from Michael. The memo was a brilliant yellow post-it with red scribbling across it. The chicken scratch handwriting spelled out 'Liam is with Haillie'.

Rose crushed the cup in her hand. She wanted to go to his office suite in her wrath and deliver her opinions about his overbearing manner. There were benefits to being part of the family around here. She could march right up to the secretary's desk and demand an appointment. The girl would clear room in his schedule this afternoon.

This was something a board member couldn't manage to do for their biggest donor, but for the show of putting family ahead of all business concerns he would allow the appointment to be added to the schedule. Of course, there was no guarantee he would actually show up for said appointment.

Rose rolled up to her desk, arranging and rearranging pens and pencils and other items on her desk just to give her mind a place to focus on anything but what she was imaging. Scenes of Haillie being tossed out with two armed guards escorting her off the premises, Micheal physically removing her from their ex-home, or. . . Before she even started to consider another option, she recalled the picture of her sister leaving. Rose was huffing. Haillie had someone on the back of the bike.

"She was with another guy?!"

As luck would have it, Micheal left his office with Virgina behind him, riled up. She was expressing her extreme dislike about something he had done. The couple walked through the cubicles, pulling random staffers into their discussion. Anyone standing there with their jaw opened was immediately drafted into the fight on either side.

This was fortunate. She was due for some luck, and his exit from his office was the luck she needed..

" You can be such a . . " he drowned her first words in a paragraph of legal mumbo jumbo at the top of the next page and he missed the select curse words his fiancée had started to lob in his direction. "Hole." She concluded the cursing rant and started again, this time more sensible and even toned. "She is not a distraction or a bad luck charm."

Michael glowered at Virginia. "It has been a half-hour since she left and already I have my contract and got the e-mails I've been waiting all day for from three people." He shrugged. "She leaves and my good luck returns."

Virginia's tone was scathing. "It is only eleven.Hardly all day."

Michael was scanning the third paragraph, and making it very obvious he did not wish to continue this conversation.

Rose knew she'd found her opportunity. "Mention Haillie or Liam, and he'll do anything to clear out that room."

Tidbits of conversation from surrounding cubicles floated to her ears. " I don't think that is good for his. . ." and "If you want the new knot dress from Dianne Von. . . " followed by "I didn't say anything."

She watched as Michael and Virginia walked toward the elevator in silence. Three full minutes passed. He must have read paragraph four through six five times. Frustration clear in his voice, he started reading aloud "The..the...the,. ." Something was clearly distracting him.

* * * *

Michael frowned. it was no use. He wouldn't be able to cite the rest. His mind was in limbo between the candy shop that just left his office and the Morton's steak dinner that worked two offices down. He wondered, after yesterday's dalliance, if there was hope of eating a full course dinner at Morton's again.

Granted, Haillie would not be the type of proprietor to let him slip in on a bribe. He would have to spend some time on the waitlist. He could do that. A romp with her was worth it.

To shake the two females from his brain, he needed to stretch his legs. There was a treadmill on the next floor down. He needed more than a jog, though, to clear his mind. He needed a cold shower.

He decided that some light conversation and a quick reprimand of some slacking employee would help divert his interest, or at the least, divert the use of his brain power.

Micheal walked by and heard Rose's declaration. He knew Rose was no office gossip, so her exclamation could only be about Haillie. Since her sister's arrival, her four-foot eleven inch voluptuous mama lion stature had been in constant striking position, ready to protect her cub from any danger.

Rose was worse, he mused, because of her vertical challenge. A lion you could see coming, but she always got unexpected blows in.

He snuck up on her in the cubicle. Rose returned to her job, giving it her full attention. He lowered his head and his voice to her ear "Who has another man?"

* * * *

The voice in her ear made Rose jump. Her mind scurried around, hoping to bump into an explanation that was two clicks away from the truth, but still believable. She wasn't a liar, though, so the truth tumbled out instead.

Micheal didn't add to this conversation. He didn't seem to have anything to say. Quickly remembering why she was angry with him, she decided now was as good a time as any to soothe her fiery anger. She jabbed a finger in his direction. "You made her leave."

* * * *

Michael stood, dazed by the news about his emotionally inhibited ex and the other man Rose had mentioned. Jealousy flared to life. What man? Was he a gentleman? A young man? A sleazy man?

A picture formed in his mind. He decided it had to be sleazy. Who else would hit on a thirty two year old shut in? After all she was...he wanted to say hideous, but that wasn't true. He'd just been thinking about the delectable entrees she offered.

He settled on awkward. She was awkward, like a lanky teenager just after a growth spurt. At least, emotionally and maybe even mentally. But the rest of her was 100 percent fully grown woman.

His mind was so engaged in thoughts of Haillie, her many delights, and the idea of a new man that he didn't even hear the three sentence curse of damnation on his black hearted soul that Rose delivered before returning to the personnel files of two new hires.
"Who was the man?" Michael heard himself saying before he could stop the words flying out of his mouth. He wanted to know who the interloper was that threatened to snatch his prey away from him.

Rose didn't look up from her keyboard. He thought she hadn't heard him. Rose's reply was quick and casual, as if it should be self-explanatory. "James, the hot garage guy."

The exchange was a quick answer and response, with a tempest effect. Fifteeen keystrokes went by before he saw Rose's hand slap over her mouth.

Michael turned on his heel, stomping his way back toward his office. The images in his head haunted him. He needed a glass of scotch. Maybe a round of golf and…

Feverishly patting his pockets, he searched for his phone. If he called a buddy or two, they could meet him. Running his finger up the screen, his list of contacts rolled by. He stopped on M and tapped the Google phone screen. Matt Patterson had a helicopter.

By the third ring, he was about to give up on Matt. His waning disappointment in his fellow retiree flatlined at the sight of a tailored Hugo suit waiting for him. Under his breath he muttered a curse word then plastered a hasty smile on his face and extended his hand to the suit clad gentleman standing in front of him. "Brandon, what brings you down three floors?"

The man smiled. "Our two o'clock appointment."

The appointment had slipped Michael's mind. He chuckled, as if he'd made a joke, trying to smooth over his mistake as he unlocked the door to his office. "Welcome."

* * * *

Rose put her head in her hands, groaning at her mistake. She'd slapped her hand over her mouth, trying to gather up the crumbs of her words and stuff them back into her mouth, but there was no way to undo the betrayal.

Later, when she explained this to Haillie, she would say it was just a mistake. She watched Michael's body stiffen and his face set into a deep frown. He turned about abruptly and stopped in front of his office, staring at his phone.

An impeccably dressed man in a tailored suit stopped in front of Michael. They spoke briefly and Michael opened the door to his office. The two made an odd pair.

The stranger's broad, manly shoulders and the comely smile which were embedded with endearing dimples along with a halo-like aura gave him an innocent, school boy charm. Yet there was a spark of bad boy as rebellious and freeing as a motorcycle on a wide country rode that shone in his blue eyes.

Rose was grateful her sister was not here. She'd have been practically defenseless against the pure sexual energy of the devil-angel battle waging between the innocence of his looks and the promises made in those black fringed, gorgeous eyes.

Michael was the polar opposite, his form a mature fineness with an aura of worldly knowledge. He was the classic man, offering stability and a ripple or two of excitement. The controlled sophistication Michael exhibited was like a gauntlet, practically challenging women to do their best to be the one to unleash whatever it was he kept under such tight lock and key.

Rose knew better than to take that bait. She'd seen the devastating impact of Michael at his worst. She was still helping Haillie to pick up those pieces.

* * * *

The Senior offered the junior a seat and sat behind his desk."What can I do for you?"

Brandon gave Michael his lady charmer smile. Micheal knew in an instant that he had given away his secret. Brandon knew that Michael had forgotten.

"I came down to give you the check." Brandon's smile grew impossibly brighter. "Or don't you remember?"

Honestly, Michael did not remember. He'd been too distracted with the women in his life to focus on mundane matters like money, but instead of asking what check, he extended his hand to accept. Brandon obliged.

* * * *

Brandon peered around the office as he waited for Michael to open the door. He'd come down here to see the girl that in the elevator, or at least her work space. He was curious about her. He didn't want to leave without finding something out about her from the old man.

In an effort to stall this perfunctory, biannual money suckling ritual, he asked the old man about their only mutual friend. "How is Virginia?"

Michael's face froze. He looked stern. Even his wrinkle seemed to settle deeper into his face. It was clear that the older man didn't care to answer his question. He could tell that, as far as Michael was concerned, he was just a piece of gravel in his shoe. He finally answered the question. "She is fine. She has her hands full planning the wedding."

Michael gave him a smile. "That is good. I hope she isn't stressing to much."

Mentally, he groaned. He had used up all the cordial talking points. He could revert back to the old English technique of engaging in polite chatter in the hopes of finding a way to steer the conversation in the direction he wanted it to go.

Seven seconds went by. Ticking could be heard from Prescott the former's clock. The two men stared at each other. Then their eyes darted off to the view outside of the window. A seagull flew by.

Michael clearly wanted the meeting to end, but Brandon was not ready to adjourn it, not until he got the information he wanted.

Michael cleared his throat. ""How are you and . . .? Ummm..."

Brandon realized that Michael was trying to remember the name of his current girlfriend. He decided to let the man off the hook and supplied the name. "Danielle."

The relief on Michael's face was practically palpable. Brandon knew that Danielle was not the kind of woman that would draw Micahel's attention. She sported a more girl-next-door kind of beauty than Virginia did.

Brandon had selected Danielle in part for that exact reason. She might be what others considered an ugly duckling, but ever since Virginia left him for Michael, he'd decided that he would only let himself fall in love with women whose inner beauty exceeded their outer beauty. It was a safer strategy for finding a faithful partner.

Most men, especially men like Michael, never bothered to look past the outer layer. In their opinion, it was preposterous to be young, virile, wealthy, and handsome without enjoying the fruits of God's gifts. He'd lost count of the number of times older men had shaken their heads when he explained his reasoning, saying, "You'll learn in time."

"Doing well, thank you for asking. While I'm here, I'm looking for.." he began to rattle off a list of things he wanted. Michael looked like an executive bobble head moving with the tide of the conversation, inserting knowing nods whenever he felt the conversation called for it as Brandon continued trying to find ways to ask about the young woman in the elevator.

As he was starting to run out of items to discuss, Virginia walked in the room wearing a half-shirt and daisy duke shorts. The wiggling of her bum made the cut off straggling strings look like tassels on an ample-bosomed pole dancer. She didn't even look in Brandon's direction. Her attention was squarely focused on Michael.

"Where is your ex?" she demanded." She has to pass my approval before she presents today."

Michael stood up, towering over Virginia, clearly asserting his authority. Brandon's presence was forgotten for the moment. His voice was like ice. "She has to do no such thing. I am still in charge here."

Virginia crossed her arms over her red plaid shirt. The outfit she wore was more appropriate for a teenager just leaving school than for a grown woman in a business environment. Her voice was petulant. "Why doesn't she? You put me in charge of fundraising, didn't you?"

Brandon ignored the argument, giving Virginia a side glance, checking out what she freely displayed. It wasn't a rude leering stare, just a brief checking in.

He nodded as if she had just said "I am happy and doing just fine."

The bottom of her ponytail swung right to left, brushing the top of her well toned tuchus cheeks. He laughed when Virginia jumped as she finally noticed his presence in the worn leather arm chair.

"Oh! Brandon. How are you?" She barely looked up at him as she counted her allotment of cash for the day. "Nice seeing you," she said as she exited without even bothering to wait for his reply. Clearly, she had important business to take care of at a few high-end shopping boutiques. To hasten her departure, Brandon stood and opened the door for her.

Michael frowned as she left the room. "That girl can run through money."

Brandon knew the truth of that statement all too well. He followed behind his former girlfriend a few minutes later and chuckled. "She says beauty isn't cheap."

He bumped into Rose, sending her new employee papers flying every which direction. "I am so sorry," he said to her, flashing his most charming smile. "Let me help you get those together."

"No, no, it's okay." Rose's eyes were fastened onto him. She hardly seemed to notice the papers. He was used to that. It happened a lot. He bent down anyway and scooped up the scattered papers, sweeping them up like an organizing broom before handing them back to her.

* * * *

Michael's visitor was even more handsome up close than he'd been from her desk. The dark hair and sparkling, water blue eyes as clear as the bay waters twinkling in the sun captivated her. The man was gorgeous. Strike that. Dear God, he was fine.

The last paper had a laminated photo, identifying the person, their title, and the company of employment. Rose hardly noticed. She gazed at the gorgeous male hand that was offering her the paper in awe, her entire purpose for coming over to Michael's office forgotten.

She wondered what it was her sister had done to get two men in the last twenty-four hours. Did she start with words or physical contact? She would love to be as forward as Haillie.

Backtracking for a moment, she wondered how it was she could be jealous of a shut-in. She remembered the way it used to be. Haillie always landed on her feet, smelling like vanilla, the scent that scientists say men like the most.

Behind Rose and this man, Michael glanced down at the dissheveled stack clutched to Rose's chest. He eyed the photo on the paper and asked. "Did your sister call to say she'd made it home with my son?"

Rose only vaguely realized that Michael was speaking to her. "No, not yet." She sidestepped him, trying to move to the space where the two men had vacated. She remembered that Michael had called the man Brandon.

Brandon stepped back to allow her room to pass. Still trying to channel her sister, she gave him an obvious and steamy once over. He watched her walk by with interest, but it was not the type she'd been hoping to see. His pupils following her did not go unnoticed, though, so she added a little sashay. Brandon followed her into the office.

Chapter 11

_"Da. . . sh. . ." Liam looked down at his ex-half-stepmother twice removed, counting the pending nuptials. She had just beat him twice in the video game. He allowed himself to be killed.

He wanted to complain, but the strategy they had developed was his primarily and he was the stupid one. Filling up his water, he wondered why she had stopped being crazy. What made her leave the house?

Of course, his mother would say she was battier than the cul-de-sac of a nocturnal avian abode in a deep cave. Liam slurped down an orange soda with a slice of pizza. The pepperoni was oily and delicious. This was terrible food for a flu, even if it was made-up ailment.

An extra grand to the school nurse's assistant and she would give you any symptoms at any time for the next six months. It was a good enterprise. She had a good service, including scheduling the sick days for you so it wouldn't be too obvious.

Then again, the LPN was fresh out of junior college, so she had sympathy for the youthful pangs of distress. Her only rule was that a fake illness could not be used for midterms or final exams. Quizzes were an annoyance, so they were permissible.

No matter how crazy Auntie Haillie was, Liam knew she could be counted on to keep any secret. The funny part was that only he seemed to notice her tendency to keep her mouth shut. After, of course, she cleared her mouth of excess viddles.

She crossed her legs and sat on the floor in front of the controller. Unpausing the game, she moved her avatar on the screen, readying it to terminate any perceived problems on the screen.

"On your left."

She screamed and inadvertently hopped off the beige carpet while hitting the button to release a spray of bullets, striking three assailants. Time flew by for Lia as he snacked on the pizza crust along with random snack food his favorite stepmom, the former Mrs Prescott now known as Auntie Haillie, placed in front of him.

As ten p.m. rolled around, the two gamers knew they should call it quits but, knowing no one expected much out of them for the next day, they decided to power through without letting up, well past either of their bed times.

****

Placing her fork across the second course, Lisa signaled to the waiter she was done. The chatter of other couples conversations around her filled their awkward silences. It had been awhile since either of them had decided to try dating.

For him, it was a record setting seven days. For her, it had been sixteen long, lonely years. Both had an in-home tryst, hence the seven days, but they hadn't been out to share their time and conversation with anyone within the decade.

"So we talked about work, right?" he asked Lisa.

She twirled the stem of the wine glass between her forefinger and thumb. The red liquid sloshed up to the brim and almost spilled over while she meditated on work. Did she want to talk about her job? If they didn't talk about work, what would they chat about?

She picked up her glass and sipped. Forcing herself to relax, she slouched down a little bit in the chair and began answering the question that caused her the largest amount of stress all day.

"The new lady is a know-it-all." There was a lot of venom in her voice. Hatred was oozing from her words like slime on a kid's network gameshow. "But she has done this for awhile, so I guess she has some know how."

She lifted the wine glass again and swallowed down the velvety red alcohol, along with her enmities, and added, "But we are still friendly. It is a job after all."

A forced attempt at mirth escaped her lips.

****

He didn't want to be inconsiderate to her, so he passed on commenting about the new hire. Besides, she seemed angrier than necessary about the newest addition to the team's executive level offices.

"I guess work isn't the best topic." He tried to laugh off the serious hiccup in the conversational progress before switching topics. "Since I am striking out on the social part of this date, may I ask what you want to talk about?"

"I have never heard that question before." The surprise in her voice was clear and he could practically see her flipping through the mental files of possible topics hanging in the cerebral cortex. At last, her mental fingers pinched the tab on a mutual folder as she spoke. "How are your children?"

"Which set? 'Experienced' is a name that really applies to me!" He joked. To his relief, Lisa laughed along with him, clutching the table cloth.

"It applies to me, too." Lisa said.

Inwardly, he congratulated himself on finding a way to break the ice. " I don't think anyone around that table can deny that."

Lisa smiled in agreement. He watched as the tension visibly slid from her shoulders down her back and exited her body as she placed the wine glass on the table and released her grasp.

****

Lisa decided she could handle this date. Backtracking in the mental progression, she renamed it 'dining with a male friend.' That label sounded funny. She felt that 'dining with a male friend' was too close to explaining the type of step she had taken.

Her thoughts drifted back to earlier that evening, when her cell rang incessantly from the passenger seat of her minivan. Unwilling to continue driving with the silence and the time to meditate on the pending life changes hovering over herself and her son, she broke the law and picked up the phone on it's umpteenth ring. She remembered praying it wasn't her mother as she greeted the caller.

The smooth, sexy voice that came back both exhilarated her and made her sit rigid against the back of the driver seat's upright cushion. Cautiously, she listened as the caller eloquently requested her presence at his home.

There wasn't a time she could remember that man stumbling over his words. Even the first line out of his mouth flowed like the refreshing waters of a babbling brooks.

His words were not as inviting as the experience itself would be. The man came with his own ambience. His opening line was simple.

She was so caught up in their past even as her caller laid new groundwork over the potholes of love he had caused. His stride is what caught her off balance the first time. She thought about that as she drove and almost swerved.

His long blue suit-clad pants smoothly glided up to her like a stallion galloping across a beach. There was a collective gasp as he neared.

He didn't present a smile like most of the men that approached her. She could feel her inwards go into the semi-solid state of jelly when he spoke. with soft words of gravity. "I strive to be an honest man." He flashed a smile in her direction. "Honestly, I would like to buy you a drink."

Moments ticked off the clock and she did not respond so he filled in the blanks. "What will you be drinking?"

He wasn't pushy or aggressive with the second question. His syntax was a nudge in his direction. It was a suggestion she followed up on after she twisted the diamond ring that adorned the hand lying under the table off and listened for it to tumble. To clarify, she wasn't married nor was she truly engaged in her own mind.

Lisa was number sixteen in the tried and now the failing fiancée position for Mrs.Prescott the third. As her lips spoke her order, her mind answered her girlfriends' seven queries when her limitless credit card hit the table. The eighth girlfriend couldn't be bought. She would have to be persuaded, but that is what sisters are for.

"Sixteen attempts will not me a bride make." Lisa's sister didn't object when she left the VIP section with the little-known but incredibly confident producer. The smoke of mistakes past cleared up, catapulting her forward into the clarity of seventeen years worth of single mom hassles.

"Sweetheart." The pitch of the speakers sang out, "Are you still there?"

Lisa smiled. "Yeah, I'm here."

"Well." he waited for a response, then hung up. She answered him with an earful of dial tone. He wanted to try again, so he did. This time she listened.

His offer never changed over the last seventeen years. Her RSVP's varied widely. Tonight, a night in a house on the poshest side of town didn't sound too bad. Champagne from Champagne, France paired with a jacuzzi and some late night skinny dipping in an Infinity pool overlooking the city, followed by breakfast with free range organic farm eggs, and no Liam? That was a prescription she was eager to fill.

"Where?" she asked, giving in to her impulses.

He gave out the address while she pulled the vehicle to the side of the road and jotted it down on the back of the receipt. She turned the paper list of items over and shook her head.

Each item reminded her of a responsibility that wasn't going to get done tonight. Super value generic laundry cleaner, floor cleaner, vacuum bags, ham and cheese, raw materials for lasagna like ricotta and no bake noodles. Yup, none of that was getting done tonight.

She signaled to re-enter traffic on the barren suburban road. After nine thirty no one ventured out unless there were emergencies. Convenience stores were almost the only thing open. She passed a local family run one on her way out of attainable normalcy on her way to the unattainable evening for most. While exiting off the highway, her heart nearly skipped a beat thinking about the lump sum he had given her last time they reminisced.

He blubbered about his missed opportunities to be a father to Liam. He could have stepped up. The tearful, snot nosed blowing, Hennessy fueled tangent went on for an hour last time while Lisa sat perfectly still, clasping the sheets to her throat and grabbing a cheese cutter at her side, just in case.

For her patience, but really more of his guilt, he gave her twenty thousand dollars out of the emergency spending fund. His words echoed around the foyer bouncing off the marble everything.

"I can give him what he can't get from you." Michael told her as he had pushed the cash across the table. "You take the money." He bent down to push the stack of mixed bills to her, falling forward from his own inertia. The money disappeared into her purse quicker than his cognac before his vision could return.

It would have been funny watching his circular body lightly tap the floor. Instead, she heard him loudly smack the natural stone floor and then lay motionless. She feared his death. Her concern was short lived. Soft snores soon escaped his throat.

Her excitement for the lavish evening diminished when her current dinner date rang her mobile. Uncertainty filled every capillary but that was the result of sitting at the dinner table with a developer thrice divorced and visibly nervous. He was trying too hard and failing. It made her feel like she was on her first date back in middle school at the lunch table picnicking in the outside courtyard.

A light kiss landed on her forehead at the end of dinner. She looked down at her watch. There was still time to drink French sparkling wine and enjoy breakfast if he hadn't found someone else to fill her spot. Her hand patted down her leg to the strap of the purse she left lying on the floor.

She plucked it up and was about to put forth the effort to find her phone when she glanced over the table that held the ruins of an enjoyable dinner. A smile stretched across her face. They had eaten through two desserts, shared each other's entrees, laughed about their stupid juvenile mistakes, and ordered a second round of appetizers to start dinner over since they had been so nervous during the first one.

Street lights in the distance spread their beams across the two, bathing them in the soft light, washing away the years of experience making her look as novice in love as her heart was. Their parting outside the restaurant was brief but their longings for the conversation of the dinner table grew as they walked toward their vehicles.

****

Two communities over from where Lisa's humble van pulled into the drive, Michael opened the bills along with a ten-year-old gift he kept tucked away in his desk drawer from his first wife, Elena. Slicing through the vanilla paper with the twenty four karat yellow gold letter opener left a gaping hole for its contents to slip out onto the dark rustic oak table top.

The paper was folded in three equal parts with the simple heading Mastercard and a number at the bottom equaling a middle management year's earnings. His fingers went to his brow, wiping away the fond memories of his financially prudent wife. Scanning over the sums in the accounts, he reminded himself of her beauty. Beautiful things are very expensive.

Most of his friends had no idea how much they spent. All of their transactions were handled by an accounting firm and wealth managers. Since his retirement, his goal was to follow his grandmother's example by performing all the financial tasks his small fortune required to look after it. The exception to the rule being taxes.

Trifling with the IRS was unwise unless professionally trained. He sat back listening to the African imported fan's blades making a swooshing sound as they sliced through the air; his hand rested comfortably on the leather lounge chair. The sound reminded him of the ocean vacation he and his fiancée took last month.

A sigh escaped his lips. The hammock he remembered was going to and fro in the breeze like a baby's swing. That was just what he needed, he boomingly declared as the numbers scrolled down the front of his daydream. Pinching the bridge of his glasses, the data stream dried up and he fell asleep.

Tomorrow would prove to be an interesting day.

Chapter 12

Locking onto a lump she wasn't sure was part of the funhouse effect of the reflective surface or if it was something her personal trainer would have to stretch, run, and low impact rep off of her. If it was the latter, and what she prayed it wasn't, then he would remove it with the skill of an experienced surgeon.

Completely engrossed in what could be the beginning of a love handle, she didn't notice the pucker in the carpet and tripped, lunging her forehead toward the gleaming chrome of the closed elevator doors. *How mortifying* she remembered thinking.

Midair, a muscular arm curled around her from behind, suspending her in the middle of a potentially embarrassing snafu. Currently she was caught between mortification and warmth from an area that had not pulsed like that in a while.

"Are you okay?" the bass voice with a surprisingly soothing undertone filled the air with its melody.

He could sing a gaseous teething toddler to sleep with the mellow sound of his vocals. How was she to respond to someone with warm securing arms and a voice that floated you to bed? She could turn and look at him, but that angelic chiseled face with those eyes, would cause her to call into work sick and . . . that thought trailed off and was replaced by concern on how much time had passed since he caught her.

Had the doors closed? She panicked. If they had, she had taken too long to answer his question and unravel herself from her gasp. Any longer than fifteen seconds without protest, thanks, or movement to steady herself on her feet without his assistance could be misunderstood.

The Adonis opened his mouth to ask her if she was ready for him to let her go, but before either of them could form the words to express gratitude or a second helping of concern, his pinky twitched.

His pinky's innocent knee-jerk reaction caressed the apex of her mountainous "DDD" dorsal plane. If there had been an onlooker, they would have noticed well before this moment what unanimously dawned upon them both. This had been a happy accident that could easily turn into a moment that was so much more. Rose's face felt flushed. He gently swooped her back onto her feet.

This was an accident on his part and an oversight on hers. He hurriedly released his grasp with no warning and Rose crumpled to the ground like ice under a hot water faucet. She lay heaped on the floor like a gelatinous mess covered in the stylish vintage clothing scattered about her.

Her thoughts scrambled in an effort to correct what was starting to be a bumbling mess of a morning commute...and they hadn't even left the building. That thought elicited a chuckle from Rose. She mumbled, her voice carrying a few decibels above the acceptable connotation of a mumble, "Well don't that beat all…. He is fine, available, and nice. I, of course, mess it up by falling. "

By the time she got to the part about falling, she noticed his pearly white perfect teeth smiling down at her.

"I'm sorry, so sorry, sorry I say. .." she stopped talking, giving her stuttering thoughts time to clear and her tongue a chance to form words other than, "Good God, you are hot." She didn't want to be stuck in the bumbling idiot female club before she officially knew his name.

His hand extended to hers, meeting her in the jelloish mess she envisioned in her mind. She could easily imagine what the situation must appear from the perspective of any onlookers. Accepting his hand and glancing around the elevator, she found herself reassured. There was no one else in this elevator.

His cheeks reddened when his words startled her as he quickly apologized. "I didn't mean to." She stared at his hand briefly and then at the triple D's. His eyes darted back over to the scene he was truly apologetic for. " I am really sorry."

She accepted the hand as a peace offering, but couldn't help noticing how soft it was. She was getting a hint of a masculine scent. It made her think of cowboys, ranches, lassos, and real men.

"Thank you." Her hand interlocked with his, palm to palm, and he anchored her as she stood. "Thank you again. I am in you debt."

"Dinner?" he said it so quickly she thought she had mistaken her hearing.

Hoping she was hearing what she wanted to hear she responded. "Name. First. Maybe?" The elevator lurched to life after her one word mash ups.

"Was that a sentence or a multi-syllable guess?" He turned to face the door and press a number.

"More like babble." After yesterday, the lanyard and that gentleman, she was not going to trust the words floating about in her frontal lobe.

She moved back from the front of the elevator, still watching the smooth way his broad shoulders moved from the inertia of the elevator going descending two floors and then lurching to a stop.

How could this man have such a melodic tone to his movements and his voice, but seem so masculine? What was she to say to him to continue the conversation? She really wanted to continue talking with him, but she would let it stand. Letting the stagnant verbal what if's stand between them created a stench in her nostrils.

What would Haillie do? She thought and then finger tapped him on the shoulder.

"Would you like to do lunch instead of dinner?" Her eyes swept over his face, stopping to notice his cheekbones. She wondered what those crystal clear blue eyes were hiding.

What was he thinking of her at this moment? Then again, did any of it matter? She was fairly certain he had asked her about dinner. She cringed as a sudden thought crept into her mind. *He could have just been joking. Should she ask him if he was joking?*

Reviewing her thoughts, she wondered. *Would asking about it being a joke not make it funny or was that just weird? Whatever she was going to say, she better say it soon because the silence was becoming awkward.*

"Umm, I Couldn't..." He started to say. Her mind desperate, a thought flickered to life *WWHD?* It darted across her mind, urging her to take life by the cajones. She decided that was just what she would do. She squeezed the girls together until they almost popped out of the v-neck blouse. "Why wait for dinner, for what you could have at lunch?"

Gorgeous and gentlemen like, he tried not to look at the temptation of the golden brown overstuffed potpies steaming fresh from the oven. His eyes were landing on the dull scenery surrounding them like a fly buzzing away from magazine sized death swings.

Okay, maybe that isn't what Haillie would have done. Quite possibly, that was a little too much. Maybe that was offering him a buffet instead of a taste testing. A voice whispered in the back of her mind. *What do I do next?* She was panicking, hoping not to let the opportunity go, desperate to find the next trick to pull out her magic hat when the doors popped open and a elderly lady joined them.

Scanning them both, she shuffled to the unoccupied side. Her lips never parted, but that first ocular encounter had said it all.

"Hmmm." Would have been how she summarized the two. "Hope he says yes?"

To Rose's mortification she recognized that the older lady with her pill box hat cocked to the side and a devious glint in the side of her eye. Rose had met her before on the elevator and in the lobby.

The older woman was always secretly amused. Rose didn't like that about her. All she wanted to know was *What on earth was so funny all the time? Was there a makeshift peep show going to be added to a list of daily things to giggle over?*

Right as she was certain the vintage dressed lady with the respectable two inch blue velvet shoes adorned with shoe clips older than both the younger riders' ages put together was nothing more than an unpleasant menace, the wooden cane with a petite crystal ball fell to the floor.

"Oooh, my..." The older lady's voice spoke with a twinge of desperation. "I can't bend down and get that."

The Adonis bent down to get it for her. The eldest occupant's eyes roved about over his taut figure. He had a slim waist line, a tight tookus and broad shoulders. The complexion wasn't bad, either.

* * * *

Lifting her gaze, she looked at the very shapely young lady across from her. That young lady's eyes were enjoying the view as well. She remembered seeing this girl around the lobby.

She was always busy and never with someone. *That was it,* the older lady thought to herself, *that young man would do nicely for her.*

"Thank you, kind sir." She said when he gave her the cane.

Instinctively he hovered around the lady, inching ever closer with his arms at the ready in case she would fall or her cane would take a return trip to the floor.

"Young man." The pillbox hat lady put on her shakiest elderly voice and addressed him, "I don't believe we have had the pleasure."

She stuck her hand out as if to shake his. He overreacted and tried to steady her, causing her to tip back and forth.

"Well, this isn't much of a pleasure." She joked as he tried to correct his mistake.

"I'm sorry, I'm sorry, I'm sorry." Came in rapid succession as worry over breaking one of her fragile osteoporosis riddled bones when she fell jogged about in his head.

"Young chap, I think I've got it from here." She advised as the elevator descended another floor.

"If any one needs help, it is the pretty little thing over there."

She pointed to Rose and that bemused smile reappeared on her face. That smile she always wore.

"You should ask a hot number like that to dinner or breakfast even, because once she leaves this elevator, someone else is assuredly going to snatch her up." She looked at him and surmised his uncertainty.

She humphed in a disapproving tone. "That is what's wrong with young men today. They see bosoms like that and think they should ask her for drinks. My own great grandson does the same. You don't ask that out for drinks. You ask her to the closest meal you haven't eaten yet."

The gentlemen swiveled his head to see a thoroughly embarrassed Rose staring down at the floor. The old woman ignored her discomfort as she pressed on toward victory. "Sonny, what meal haven't you eaten?"

His face was a bright red. "Lunch."

She turned her attention to Rose. "He wants to ask you to.."

"Lunch" He provided.

The older woman noticed the girl's eyes widening until they were practically round. "Why? I thought you said you couldn't..."

His mouth dropped open for a moment and then he closed it. "I have an appointment, but I just realized I can reschedule. That appointment can take place anytime, but lunch with a woman as beautiful and confident as you are doesn't happen everyday."

The old woman cackled with glee. "Nice job sonny. If you didn't ask her to lunch, I was going to ask you." She laughed and slowly shuffled out the elevator door toward the lobby and the car service waiting at the curb.

Smoothing the sides of her skirts, she dusted off her strut. Wiggling from left to right, the man stood there watching the show until the emergency buzzer rang on the elevator.

She heard the ringing and the temptation to turn around began building. She resisted the urge.

* * * *

The elevator doors closed behind the older woman, leaving the younger couple once more alone together. "Okay." Rose reassured herself. This was really happening.

Elevator music, Mozart, poured thorough the speakers drowning out any and all happily surfacing memories. As the elevator doors sprang open, her gaze skimmed over the tops of three rows of cubicles.

She wondered who would have thought stuffing people into half-cloth urban walls was a good idea. Everyone here frenziedly working to move to the career suburbia complete with golf weekends, and long leisurely lunches. The office territory sure did look greener.

Rose intentionally stared at the ground-in dirt on the carpet. She was certain at one time it was the grey color the developers intentioned. Now it was dusty brown all the way through. Each fleck of terrain her co-workers had trekked in was fascinating enough to demand her full attention.

Distraction like this could have her in the boss's office if she looked up. She followed the trail to her desk where she set up for her uninterrupted, hopefully she thought, workday. Laptop turned on? Check. Three sharpened pencils, three felt tip or rolling ball point pens? Check. She went down her list for the next fifteen minutes. By that time it was 9 am. Time to start the work day.

Being a casual non-profit, where most of the board was absent, the staff trickled in. Ironically, those receiving biweekly paychecks started arriving before the volunteers.

This time of year, the volunteers were thicker than ants readying for fall. They hummed about, nearly bumping into each other. Watching them was like car gazing on Hwy 95 south of the mouth of an exit lane. The inevitable collision was going to happen.

Rose's desk was the third door to the left of the chairman's suite. Enormous windows and a French door combination shut him off from the rest of his staff. If the offices were real estate, then his place was a Mansion. Few hoped, or even aspired, to hold as much as a chair in that abode.

She shuffled piles of paperwork that seemed to have grown overnight. Piles, as a description, was an understatement of the worst kind. Mountains of papers met her every morning like a work hangover from the intoxication of daily success. Coffee was her answer to the stacks' silent interrogation and it's link to adequacy peer reviews.

Stirring the super coffee, she gazed off into space as if she sat atop the duo peaks. There was so much to contemplate, so many scales to balance, all of which had nothing to do with her job. As she began a regime of deep breathing to restore her peace of mind she heard a voice that sent her hurtling down the side of that mountain, bopping her head on every pebble below as she tumbled.

If her inner painful cause of distraction would just stay closer to the break room/ lounge area until 11 a.m, she could get some work done without taking the time to smother or stoke the fires of anger that would inevitably start when Haillie walked through the door.

She was properly chuffed. Her sister had a job and had bested her demonic ex- to get it. Of course, she was skipping the bit about Haillie returning to Michael's outstretched arms while his fiancée was out shopping yesterday.

Rose had to admit she could see how the make out session was sweet revenge. That revenge, sweet as it might be, was going to have repercussions. That was the part Rose was fearful of ever since Haille's chat yesterday night.

Chapter 13

Virginia work an hour earlier than her husband-to-be. Since sleep was an elusive bugger that night, she decided to go for a jog. Six in the morning was as good a time as any.

Whipping the covers off her lean runner-toned legs, she cursed the chill from her future husband's side of the room. She added it to a list of things that would change once they said 'I do.' From memory she crossed the coal black room to her dresser and yanked out running pants and a pair of socks before putting them on as quietly as possible. Bending down and reaching to the left, she found and then slipped on and laced her tennis shoes.

The crisp morning air not yet ruined by pollution should soothe her anxious body, allowing her to slip back into the welcome warmth of the down comforter and, with any luck, reclaim her missing four hours of beauty rest.

The cool morning breezes lightly caressed her bare face and encircled her shock absorbing trainers. One foot in front of another made contact with the pavement creating a rhythmic light thud. The sound wrapped her in familiarity and she felt the desire for a peaceful rest creep up on her like a lost cat slinking back through its door after an evening out. She pushed ahead for another two blocks.

Light drizzle dissipated as the sun's yellow glow began to fill the sky. Steam rose from the pavement and dew clung to the blades of grass, causing the lawns to sparkle like a chandelier weighed down by crystals. Inhaling the freshness of the day, she let the possibilities the day offered soak into her while she stood in front of the home she had once shared with Brandon when she still wore his ring around her finger.

Wiping the sweat away, she drew a rushed breath, turned around, and began the three mile trek with Brandon skipping through her thoughts. She decided she would dress, shower, and come into the office early. Since Micheal would be using the west wing of the house, she would use the south east side for a long relaxing bath. Possibly she could soak away the thoughts that were penetrating all her synapses, sparking ideas and recollections like stains on her grey matter.

****

Michael sipped hot coffee from the coffee lounge in the kitchen area. Association with all those working with Experienced People was important to him. Watching the masses checking in and drearily trudging to their cubicles, then gathering together for water cooler chats before fleeing the building by five or later, eager with excitement to be anywhere but there, reminded him regretfully of his corporate days.

He wished for the distractions of that life periodically. Watching from prime secular office real estate was lonely. Micheal appreciated the mornings when he was included and it warmed what was left of a heart.

As usual there was an exception to the rule. Rose's head popped up over the grey carpeted half walls and overhead compartments similar to an airplane and their eyes met. Foe against foe, they stared at and acknowledged each other with a nod.

Neither would acknowledge that their morning ritual was more of a challenge than a greeting. Michael walked away from Rose's challenge in full retreat to his office and the protection of the frail framed secretary without a second look in her direction.

The phone rang and he picked it up. "Mr. Prescott? Your son, Liam, has not arrived at school. We thought you ought to know."

Michael gritted his teeth. He should have known better than to trust Liam to Haillie's care. Where was that woman anyway?

****

The rude, insistent ring of her cell phone woke Haillie at 8 am that next morning. She reached for the phone and put on her best friendly smile. "Hello, Elegant Events. This is…"

The man's voice stunned her. "Hi. This is Micheal."

Shell shock was quickly replaced by a tempest of fury that she quickly held back, putting a lid on the squall of emotions, in order to calm herself enough to make a civil conversation possible.

Michael's voice was even, dangerously so. "Liam. Where is he? Where are you?" She recognized it from years earlier. "Why isn't he at school?" he demanded with a low growl. This was his warning shot.

Whispering barely above a level that was audible, her head pounding, she told him about the doctor's visit and the progression of the sniffles.

***

Michael's lips flattened against the tirade of names he wanted to pelt her with. He was going to be civil for a while longer, but if she didn't begin talking, he glanced at his clock on the left corner of the glistening clean desktop, in the next thirty ticks of the seconds hand, he was not going to be responsible for what came next.

Tightening the dike against the flood balking against the barrier threating to crack and break through, he clenched his teeth as she defended herself against his question.

"Liam is ill." Haillie's voice morphed into Lisa's mom voice. Michael instinctively sat up and absent mindedly switched to a more respectful tone.

His mind cleared. He understood the words. "Liam is ill."

He mulled it over a bit. If Lisa had made this call, accepting her verdict would be natural, but Haillie knew nothing of motherhood. How could she possibly make that judgement call?

"Call Lisa and ask her if he should miss a day at school."

***

Haillie started doodling on the notepad she kept beside the bd. Circles within circles swirled in a spiral on top of her notes. Pen marks changed the three to an eight and the nine to a zero. "I'll call Lisa about the boy," she dutifully promised before Michael hung up the phone.

Last night, she promised Lisa she would care for Liam. At two in the morning, she told Liam he wouldn't have to go to school. Haillie took

Michael's advice into consideration after hanging up the phone.

Operating on just six hours of sleep, she lost the battle with her inner child and decided it wasn't worth the fight. She would ship Liam off to his private school a few hours late. That should fulfill her promise to care for Liam.

She called for a car to arrive at ten a.m. Now fully awake, she turned her attention to work. There were a few venues to put on her short list and scout out before she met the female board members. She knew of a couple of decor places in the vicinity and decided she should give them a once over in person.

This was her first statement as a reborn professional to a changing landscape of companies. She turned on her tablet and began listlessly browsing web pages filled with floral arrangements, tableware, furniture, and lighting.

She picked up her cellphone and texted Liam three times. She would do it again after her morning cup of Earl Grey had finished boiling and was properly steeped.

She pulled a mug out of the cupboard that was six inches taller than her grasp. She chuckled about that. They had remodeled the kitchen to fit Michael's height needs. It was peculiar how, once she fell in love, she often forgot to think about herself.

Everything in her life had revolved around Michael. What time would he be home? What did he want for dinner? What was he going to wear tomorrow? The list went on and on.

On autopilot, she poured the steaming hot liquid into an old chipped mug left over from her single girl days. Plucking the tea bag out she opened the trash can lid and tossed it into the rubbish bin, but her thoughts stayed singularly on Michael and how Virginia would fare under his demands. Her assessment gave the next Mrs. Willam Prescott a 40% score for potentially maintaining the household.

Then again, it had been ten years since she had to cope with him. Did his gut busting laughs still make him look like a fit Santa clause, especially when he grew his winter beard? She sipped her tea and pondered the past for a bit longer before disturbing her houseguest.

She called the third firm down on the search engine page as well as three of their references. Turning her attention back to her notes, she dialed the interior decor firm dialing the last two digits as eight nine. The receptionist answered the other end. "Hello?"

Haillie smiled, allowing warmth to ooze from her voice into the phone. "Hi I'm from Elegant Events. Do you have an appointment available today between three and five? If not today, maybe some other time this week?"

Staring at herself for a second in a mirror attached to a colorless wall, she practiced expressing the range of emotions they rehearsed yesterday in acting class while saying her script by rote. She heard the woman's voice reply."Yes, we have a wide open schedule between three and five."

"Perfect. I'll be there at 3." She told the receptionist and then waited for a confirmation for her appointment.

****

As Jill the receptionist spoke to the woman on the other line, she contemplated the reason for this lady wanting an appointment. Visitors to this sector of the floor were unusual, and definitely not to the boss's office.

Normally, she would be stricter than Peter at the pearly gates, but the woman had called on his personal number. There was a lot of leeway in what she could allow on this number. Whoever was on the other side of this conversation knew him well.

"What's your name?" she turned back to the computer screen and typed Ms. Prescott. While she typed a devilish smirk curled her lips in an upward arch at the perspective of his former fiancée walking through those doors.

She knew that he might change his open door policy for his personal lines if that woman came waltzing into his offices. She finished the task of typing her name into the personal time slot, blocking out the two hours between three to five p.m. She knew that it would take at least that long. Instantaneously the appointment alerted him via text and his email accounts.

****

Grabbing the handle of the sunshine yellow taxi, Brandon escorted his plain Jane girlfriend of two months into the back seat. Gingerly, he pecked her forehead and flipped his phone over to examine the new alert to discover two text messages about a new appointment. He shook his head.

Up until then, he had every intention of cooking dinner as a belated, and formerly forgotten, eight week anniversary. She may be plain, but she deserved every indulgence he could give her because she saved babies' lives. Her career as a pediatric cardiac surgeon kept her busy and traveling.

When he looked at her each morning, he felt special. Through all that was available to her she had chosen him. A saint had chosen him.

****

Rose immediately regretted locking eyes with him. Her conscience was eating at her as she logged in and plugged in the last of last week's employee insurance information.

****

Urgently knocking on the door with both fists, Haillie hoped to rouse her stepson. Nine-thirty arrived much quicker than she thought it would, and there was still a lot to do to prepare him, if her memory served her right.

Then again, it had been a few years since she did this. He was seven years old the last time. Did she still have to sing the body song for bath time?

She answered herself. *Of course not*. He was seventeen and he didn't smell like an ogre, so she assumed he knew the song by heart now. If he would just wake up. The car would be here in twenty minutes. "Liam. Get up!"

A half groggy, mumbling, practically snorting Liam hissed an answer with the cover still over his head. "Go Away!"

This was not what Haillie needed. "I can't. I called the car service."

The thought of pulling up to his school in a car with a proper driver, like some of the more wealthy snits that made fun of him, should get his butt up. One day without the scooter might repair some of the self-esteem damage his father was hell bent on inflicting on the boy.

What was wrong with that man? She mused to herself. Through the door she could hear the shuffling about and his door opened as she turned her back on it.

"What time does it get here?" he asked, darting toward the bathroom.

"Twenty minutes." she yelled to the lean bodied blur closing the door. The shower turned on and the phone that fell out of Liam's pocket, lying on the floor jumping and convulsing across the hardwood.

It was impolite to answer other people's phones, but he was a minor, that rule didn't apply to him the phone was on the last vibrating ring. Scooping up the phone, she ran her finger along the dots imitating the gestures she had watched Liam do yesterday.

The screen brightened and the accept or deny button requested attention. Haillie pressed accept without looking at the caller's name. "Hello?"

"Lee!" the deep voice answered. "Man! What are you doing today?"

Haillie knew the voice belonged to a young man, not from it's sound but from the pace. There was a laid back way he spoke. No need to hurry ,like he knew death had other things to do besides calling at his doors.

Without thinking Haillie answered the question. "Nothing."

She could practically hear the grin in the voice. "Dude, we should hang."

She decided it was time to get the boy's attention. "This Is Ms.Prescott."

There was an audible gasp, and then the boy hung up. She stared at the phone in her hand, wondering what that was all about. The phone rang again with the same number. Hailie answered again. "Hi."

"Ms. Prescott?" The youthful voice took on a solemn tone to add maturity. It was clear he wanted her to think of him as suitable, maybe even as an equal to her former marital partner. She half smiled at the idea of him calling her, then remembered that this wasn't her phone.

Liam's mobile had rung and not her own. She let the recognition of this information darken the clouds of hope over the boy's perceived appreciation of her femininity. She held her breath and it abated.

****

James quietly listened to each breath Hailie inhaled and exhaled. He would recognize that voice anywhere.

His nerves were frayed like a thread at the hem. One word would yank it and a few others would free themselves. James didn't want to pull the string and drop the bottom out.

He steeled himself, scraping an edge of fear off the top. The ore of true courage flexed in his voice. "I wasn't expecting you to answer Liam's phone."

Her words were stiff and halting, as if she were worried about how they would sound. "He dropped it."

James held back a chuckle. He doubted Liam would appreciate the invasion of privacy. So, you picked it up and answered it?"

She didn't answer him, responding with a question of her own instead. "Do you want me to take a message for Liam?"

James smiled. "No, but you can take a message for yourself."

A light hearted laugh escaped her throat and caressed his eardrums, encouraging him to speak up. "You have a pen?"

She sounded curious. "Yup."

He moved ahead bravely. "Make sure you write this down: James, I know I am speaking about myself in the third person," he added, "Six o'clock. Dinner at the pub on third. I'll be there waiting until eight. Did you get all of that?"

"I'll read it back to you." She repeated what he said verbatim.

"Make sure Ms.Prescott gets this message." He pushed his luck. "Tell her it's a matter of the heart."

****

Haillie's lips curled up in a bright smile as she heard the last part of the caller's message. She'd gone from wanting to laugh at the audacity of

Liam's teenage friend to realizing the offer was coming from intimately familiar territory: James.

Ian's young, lean teenage form shot past her down the hallway to the guest room, knocking her right shoulder back toward the wall where their family picture hung.

She frowned at the rudeness of it. "Are you going to say excuse me?"

Her attention returned to the phone as "Excuse me" purred across the phone line. He mixed in bass to his voice like the oak flavoring in a mature wine. She sipped on the thoughts his voice conjured up in her head.

The nose of the wine soured in her mouth. It wasn't as appealing to her as when she first uncorked the bottle yesterday. The bouquet lost numerous petals. Whether she was going to meet him tonight was still up for debate, but a morning egg white omelette would be wonderful.

Could she do breakfast? Could she counter his offer for a pub dinner? For a cafe breakfast? Bakery breakfast? Not a coffee shoppe meal? Yummm! Yumm!

She heard him say something. "I'm going to hang up now."

"Yes." Suddenly, she changed her mind. She didn't want to let the exhilaration of his phone call dissipate yet "No."

She beamed on the inside at his juvenile dialogue. It was an honest admonition. His actions and dialogue did fall into the arena of sophomoric, but she didn't care. "I'll hang up, James."

He sounded disappointed. "Must you?"

She was about to counter his offer of another minute to communicate until her phone rang. Reluctantly, she ended the call unceremoniously without saying goodbye to James.

Cracking the guest room door open just enough to fit the slim sleek body of Liam's mobile through, she tossed it with enough force for it to make it to the bed without seeing any underage tidbits while balancing her own phone.

* * *

"Jill, what can you tell me about this appointment?" Brandon asked as he showed her his cell phone. The 3 o'clock appointment was just minutes away.

Jill looked up in surprise. "She called on your private line and asked for an appointment. I didn't ask why."

"It says Ms Prescott? Do you know the woman's first name?" Looking at the text and the type of meeting that had been added, he was certain he didn't know her, but if she had his personal emergency appointment number, he must have given it to her.

Jill's eyebrows raised. "I assumed it was Virginia."

Brandon glanced at her. "No. Virginia isn't yet Mrs. Prescott. This must be someone else."

Jill frowned. "I'm sorry. I didn't think…"

Brandon watched as a woman exited a town car in front of his building. Smoke from the exhaust billowed around her. She coughed as loudly as an early stage tuberculosis patient, clearing six inches around her on the sidewalk thick with bodies as if she were Moses parting the Red Sea.

Brandon froze, flushing in embarrassment, suddenly recognizing her. Images of the body beneath those clothes standing in all its morning glory on her doorstep came unbidden to mind. That was immediately followed by a memory of the encounter in the elevator. He felt a familiar tug against his pants as his member decided to execute a sudden salute to her.

He turned on his heel and walked into his office. "Tell her I'm running late. I'll let you know when I'm ready to see her." The last thing he needed was to greet her in that state.

Chapter 14

"Liam!" Haillie yelled, although he was right behind her. Her volume made him flinch.

The open box of golden mini baked wheat rings exploded like a volcano then softly rained down around them covering every surface in breakfast food. Haillie looked around at her kitchen.

She ignored the mess. "The cereal is two years old. I wouldn't eat that." She slid off the stool and stomped away, grabbing up her cell phone from the counter as she went. "If we hurry up, we can stop and pick up breakfast before I drop you off at school." She yelled over her shoulder.

Her fuzzy socks slid across the hardwood floors and she pitter pattered up the stairs out of earshot. Her fingers flew across the keypad, her eyes scanning through the list of contacts for his name.

He picked up on the third ring. She was on the upstairs landing by then. There was no chance of Liam overhearing her up there.

"Haillie." The way James said her name sent shivers down her spine.

She smiled. "I was calling to invite you to breakfast with Liam and me. I know it is last minute."

She continued rambling in an effort to cover over what had just dawned upon her. This was the second time talking to him in an hour, and she was asking for a second date. She sounded desperate and old.

Was it cool to ask someone out over the phone? Should she have texted him instead? She decided that a half octave deeper would make her sound nonchalant. "It's like whatev's if u can't."

* * *

James checked off his to do list mentally while weighing the inconvenient breakfast invitation he just received against the ten thirty prescription run he would have to make and the one o' clock shift he was due to take.

James hung his head and shook it. His finances hadn't bothered him before. Now their failings were like the sun in a mid July sky. Whether he was with her in person or on the phone, she made him keenly aware of his deficiencies without even trying. "I'll try and make it." They hung up.

* * *

Haillie sprinted down the stairs, screaming for Liam to grab his bags and be ready for the car. It would arrive in five minutes she repeated over and over again. She snatched up her purse off an end table at the end of the stairs. She searched by the door where her keys resided and cursed herself for using a car service again.

This wouldn't be a problem if she were just willing to drive, but leaving the house was difficult enough. The thought of getting behind the wheel again was more than she could handle.

"Liam, come on. Leave the cereal. I'll clean it up when I get home." Liam did as he was told. The two of them were out of the door and at the curb when the car pulled up outside her home.

Liam held the door for Haillie. She slid in and Liam followed. The driver closed the door and they were off to breakfast.

Liam bolted into the local café with his crisp two hundred dollar bills. He ordered enough food to feed a horse and a farm at full capacity. Haillie picked a table near the back of the restaurant. She didn't want to be seen.

Liam joined her, explaining the orders he made and joyfully discussing the challenges of the video game from the night before. "I can't believe you blew your avatar up juggling those grenades."

Haillie poked him in the ribs. "I know how to play. I just didn't want to play the next level, so I did the only honorable thing I could do. I juggled myself to death."

James walked in the door dressed in jeans this time. They fit him snugly in all the right places. She noticed his pectorals were emphasized beneath the shirt he was wearing.

He cut a fine figure for a parking lot attendant. Pins and needles made her heart flutter and other parts flutter for him. He walked over to their table. "It turns out I had some time." His eyes never left Haillie's. She blushed under his gaze. She was so thankful her melanin hid her feelings.

"Have a seat." She pointed at the empty chair next to Liam. "Liam ordered." She opened her hand, counting the change she had left over. "$199.18 worth of food."

He pulled the chair out and sat. Haillie listened as Liam and James fell into easy conversation as they waited for the food to arrive. James periodically looked up and shot her a promising smile.

She lowered her gaze, struggling to hide the leftover energy from yesterday's emotional power surges fueled by the pent-up sexual frustrations of long years of undesired abstinence. He looked back up at her, diverting a quizzical gaze from his hard boiled eggs and sprout toast.

Liam's constant barrage of Role Playing Game insights faded into the background as her eyes gleamed, basking in the warmth of James's obvious desire.

* * *

James found himself musing over the notion of Haillie Avery. He couldn't deny she would look great in white. Truthfully, she would look great in anything.

Mentally, he gave himself a shake to clear his head. He was rushing things. His thoughts were like an attention-starved three year old.

He tried to keep in mind the advice his friends had given him when he discussed their date over drinks at the bar that previous evening. He'd been careful to leave out the part about everything that took place after breakfast and before his 1 pm shift had started.

A friend of his from the art department leaned in. "You went out with the former Mrs Prescott? Seriously? Is she still hot?"

"Oh, she's hot alright. I just want to know if you think she's really into me or is she just blowing off steam."

One of the other attendants from the garage, a perpetually single guy, shook his head. "You guys just met. Give yourself time to test drive a few more vehicles before you settle on one."

James took that advice with a grain of salt. He didn't want to be perpetually single. He wasn't interested in "test driving" every model that came through the door. He just wanted to be sure that the car he was interested in was going to be a good fit for him. That was all.

A friend of his from the finance department whistled. "The Haillie Prescott? That's who you went out with? That woman's been on page six of the business section more than once. She's got an impressive list of accomplishments, in addition to an impressive physique."

James knew Haillie was both loved and scorned by their overlapping acquaintances, but that was a fact he was keeping to himself. A sneaking suspicion told him if she knew the truth about him, there would never be anything permanent between them.

* * *

A cool breeze from outside distracted Haillie from her thoughts about yesterday. A chic New Yorker type dressed in designer shoes wearing a trim trench that stubbornly refused to be belted stepped inside the door as if she'd just stepped out of the pages of a magazine.

Women like this were the bane of an average woman's existence. Women that couldn't pull off the glossy hot looks of a woman like that could blame Photoshop and make excuses until a woman like this wiped all the 'buts' away like an eraser with one swipe.

Hailie continued to muse about the lady as she took a seat at the next table. She was all that Haillie wanted to be again, wrapped up in the proper packaging, outlined by the one hundred and twenty pound benchmark Haillie was struggling to accomplish.

Her mind floated backwards, recalling the woman she used to be and how she wore power, responsibility, and stress like a finely tailored pants suit. She could develop, produce, and destroy concepts, socialites, and employees without raising her voice or her finger. All she'd needed was a phone.

"Where are you?" He whispered into her ear, tickling her skin. His words swirled around in her mind a bit before they became audible discernible utterances.

Fighting back urges to tangle herself up in him again, she simply answered. "No where important."

He rubbed her shoulder and started to massage the muscles that were bunched into an angry mound directly below her shoulder blades. "I would still like to know, if you don't mind sharing."

"I was just thinking that I should have been at work." She melted into the pleasures of the massage, then remembered that she still had Liam with her. She frowned as she looked around for the boy. "Where's Liam?"

"He went to the bathroom." He wielded his knuckles in circles loosening the tension in her back. "He'll be right back."

She sighed and turned to look at James. He was hot. He was young. And, she reminded herself, he was poor. What could he possibly do for her aside from the obvious? She tapped his hand lightly, signaling that she wanted him to stop.

He looked hurt. "You want me to stop? Why?"

She reached for the only excuse she could think of that made sense. "Liam will be back at any moment."

It was a lame excuse, and it also wasn't true. The truth was that she was done. She had to be done with him. She'd had her fling, she'd had her fun, but he was bound to be a liability to her efforts to climb back up the social ladder.

Liam stepped out of the bathroom with his backpack slung over one shoulder. He had a natural bounce in his step. It looked like the type of pep his father would have had at that age, she guessed, based on the picture he had shown her of Michael at his age.

Micheal was a fine specimen of a man, one that aged like cheese. He was smooth with a sharp, dangerous edge to the emotions but that edge of danger was what made being with Michael so exhilarating.

"Are you thinking about him?" James asked in a whisper, moving back to his side across the table.

Liam approached them. James purposely lowered his head to meet her gaze before Liam sat down and he asked again. "Are you thinking about him? Is that why you look so sad?"

Haillie chose not to answer the loaded questions he had just carelessly regurgitated onto the table. They weren't at that level yet. She was not about to share intimate detailed emotional information. Instead, she chose the easy path of answering the obvious longing Liam had to skip another day of school for video games.

Liam sat down. "No." She answered.

"No what?" Liam asked. His head swiveled between the two grown ups, clearly wondering if he'd interrupted something.

Haillie clarified her meaning. "No about you hooking school for a marathon gaming day. "

Liam's smile slid halfway down his face. "I really don't want to go." His voice carried a pleading tone.

Haillie pulled his chair away from the table and put her arm around his shoulder.. "I promised your dad and your mom."

He got down off the stool and started toward the door. "I thought you weren't afraid of them."

Haillie smiled instead of reacting to his sarcasm. Teenagers could be such sarcastic little buggers.

James dropped back to join Liam and started in on his dream bike. "Hog or crotch rocket?"

Haillie smirked and quickened her pace toward the car idling by the curb. The back door swung open and the three climbed into the back leather interior Lincoln.

Haillie recited the address to Liam's school. The driver shut the door and they pulled away from the curb and out into traffic.

Chapter 15

Lisa slid her black T-shirt over her head. Emblazoned across the front was her place of employment . She had worked her way up to manager, but since someone seemed to always be out, she still had to put that shirt on and show up to fill the gap.

They paid her twice her old pay to do the same menial labor plus manage the other employees. She counted herself lucky in one way: She'd made it to management. Managing was a dream come true.

Laughter seeped through cracks in her general disappointment with life. She found herself smiling as thoughts of yesterday bubbled to the surface. He was brown and beautiful on the inside.

Lacing up her tennis shoes, she found herself audibly chuckling. The sound made her jump, but she liked the way it sounded in her mind and how it tickled her insides like the bubbles in champagne.

* * *

Haillie was done with her morning checklist and her tryst. She was glowing. She just hoped no one else noticed her unrelenting smile as she swung open the doors to her ex's office suites.

"You're late." His secretary whispered tersely.

Haillie was unwilling to step away from the warming flames of being wanted and the lingering heat that lent her face a fluorescent afterglow. She pretended she hadn't heard. "Is he in his office?"

The secretary practically snarled a reply. "Of course. Lisa is there also."

Haillie let her insolent tone slide because she had the work of three people and the stamina for only one. The swooshing of her boho skirt flared the ruffled edges. They danced around her ankles as she passed the desk.

Grabbing the door handle she swung the door open with a hangover worthy loud crashing. "Hello, Lisa. How was your day?"

* * *

Lisa reflected on the evening before and the extra four hours sleep she'd been able to enjoy because of this woman. She did a three sixty in attitude. Her response was civil. "It was wonderful."

* * *

Micheal stood watching the two women with his mouth ajar. Lisa had used the word wonderful. He couldn't think of a single time he'd heard her described anything as such. She seemed genuine in her reply.

He listened as Lisa returned the inquiry. "How about yours, Haillie? Did Liam behave himself?"

Haillie nodded before adding,"Yes. He got to school late this morning."

As if suddenly remembering what she had told Lisa last night, she explained, "His health improved in the morning."

Micheal's head turned from one lady to the other while they engaged in civil conversation.

Neither of them exchanged a single hostility, engaged in enflamed brief conversation, or delivered the occasional blow to the self-esteem that brought one or both of them to tears.

Why had they changed? The conversation he'd had with Rose came to mind suddenly. That was it. Haillie was seeing someone, or someones, since Rose had implied there was more than one man involved.

His jealousy reared its head. He became irritated. "What are you doing here?"

Both women turned to look at him, as if surprised to find him standing in his own office. "What do you mean?" Their voices came together in unison.

Micheal touched the intimidatingly large wooden desk to make sure it was still between him and his shocked ex's. It was there. It just seemed miniature right then because their combined disappointment filled the room.

Lisa put a hand on her hip "I called her. You have a problem with that?"

He realized too late that he'd made a terrible mistake. Lisa pointed a finger in his direction and took a breath, preparing to unleash decades worth of pent up frustrations. "Why do you try to run our lives? We may have slept with you or, in her case, may have been stupid enough to marry you, but that doesn't mean you own us, or tell us what to do."

His face darkened. He found himself winded and used his hands support the majority of his body weight on the desk that seemed to be decreasing in size with every word that Lisa spoke. "Liam is my son! I have the final say!"

That was his second mistake. Lisa's eyes crackled with dangerous energy, daring him to keep going. "I gave birth to him. He is my son. You didn't even want anything to do with him. You wouldn't even have a son if not for me."

That stung. He lobbed the only thing he could find to grasp at her. His financial superiority. "Why don't you try raising him on your income? Try sending him to that expensive private school on that pittance you call a paycheck."

He plopped down in the oversized leather chair as if hoping the desk would defend him against Lisa's anger. Haillie stepped back, as if trying to get out of the way of any fall out from the direction this conversation had taken.

This was their court and they volleyed the verbal tennis ball across that net at speeds high enough to maim or kill. Serving up insult after insult, they would wear down all protective barriers until all that was left was their raw emotions scraping against each other,making high pitched shrieking noises that one's ears could hardly bear.

* * *

Scooping up her purse, Haillie started creeping backward moving slowly toward the door. In the background, she could hear them going at each other.

"Your mother was a scrawny, two bit ..." She could hear Lisa's voice through the solid wooden door as it clicked shut.

Haillie exhaled. She had held her breath while inside for fear of them hearing her retreat and drafting her into the ongoing war of the baby mama drama.

Letting go of the handle one finger at a time, she stepped outside the door and eased away from it like there was a napping baby inside.

"What are you sneaking away from?" Haillie heard the secretary ask over her right shoulder. She jumped. A gasp escaped as the door her pinky was attached to swung open, dragging half her body along for the ride.

"And ..." Lisa trailed off as her motherhood milk producing sized cleavage smacked into Haillie's half bent over head. This provided an odd counterbalance, allowing Haillie to remain upright instead of face down on the floor.

"Sorry." She garbled, her voice muffled between the cleavage valley as she worked to extricate herself.

Lisa made a noise of disgust and pivoted once more to face Michael. "And your trifling second wife. . " she began her tirade again.

Haillie actually felt bad for Michael. It looked like he was losing this battle. The thought shot though her neural pathways, etching a smile across her face. This wasn't such a bad morning.

A voice spoke behind her, causing her to turn quickly toward the hallway. "I think she was talking about you..." Rose stated matter of factly.

Haillie couldn't help but agree. "I am his only second wife."

Rose paused, as if thinking about it. "...unless you count his mistress."

Haillie hardly needed that reminder. "Don't start."

She gave her sister a once over. Rose's hair was a natural wavy hair that boho girls spend numerous nights twisting and braiding to attain. Her eyes weren't spectacular but had a bubbly inviting warmth. Anybody could see that if they talked to this girl, they were sure to have fun.

Rose rolled her eyes. "Are you re-styling my clothes again in your head?"

Haillie shook her head. "Nope. You look great today. Something is different."

Rose stood there in the spacious foyer with the on-edge secretary. Haillie waited for her sister's next words. None were given.

She pressed Rose for an explanation. "What has changed?"

Rose's guilty expression told her she was right. Haillie decided she would let her sister have her moment of privacy. They would have time to get to the bottom of it later. She had more important things to handle. With a wave of her hand she pushed the entire subject out of her mind. "I don't know, but whatever it is it looks good on you."

* * *

Rose knew was being swept away like an annoying bit of dirt on a clean surface. She was okay with that if there was something more serious or attractive on Haillie's mind. Just a few more seconds of silence and Haillie would crack.

"May I help you?" The annoyed high pitch voice asked the ladies. The secretary gave them both a glare to go with the words in case they didn't understand they were loitering on sacred ground.

Rose didn't acknowledge the words that were still hanging in the air. She was too distracted thinking about the events of the morning and wondering if she should tell Haillie.

"She was talking to us!" Haillie interjected into Rose's thoughts about her day.

Rose looked at the stick figure behind the desk and shrugged. "She can't fire us, so she might as well be talking to a wall."

Haillie frowned, suddenly looking more intently at her. "This isn't like you. What's wrong?"

Rose immediately felt bad. "Nothing. I guess I'm on edge, that's all."

Haillie's face took on a guilty look as she asked, "Is it because I got the job here? "

They left the corridor, heading toward the cubicle where the mountains of paperwork Rose had yet to scale waited in a temp office with a view that Rose had sacrificed to make sure Haillie felt accepted.

Rose gave her sister a reassuring pat on the back. "Nope, since you got here Micheal has been flustered and forgetful. We should all be thanking you."

Haillie gave her sister a meaningful look. "So is it me?"

Rose thought about that. It could be her sister that was causing all the anxiety, but the question was why? Micheal was over her and Haillie was doing her job. It couldn't be her presence alone.

Could it be the ease with which life was accepting her? She didn't have time to think about this stupidity. She decided to answer her sister's earlier question.

In what she hoped was an off-handed manner, she said,"I met someone this morning."

Haillie squealed and gripped her sister's shoulder. "Where? When? How? What time? Again where? Is that what is different? "

There was a mischievous glint in her eye, but Rose offered no words.

Haillie pouted. "Tsk, tsk. You really aren't going to tell me? I tell you everything."

Rose shrugged. "Some things I want to keep private."

The ladies arrived at the foot of Rose's twin paper mountain peaks rising from the desk of her cubicle.

Haillie looked at Mount Paperwork and then back at her sister. "You need help with that?"

Rose sighed. "Yeah, but don't worry about it. It's that time of year. We hire a bunch of interns and new blood in the spring. It's not as bad as it looks." She felt the familiar sense of dismay that came over her every time she looked at the paperwork.

Haillie poked her. "Your face says differently."

"Face, did you just betray me?" Rose joked, pointing at her oval shaped physiognomy.

Haillie's back was turned to her. Rose adjusted the chair, scooting it back and forth until it was the right distance from her desk. An awkward silence lulled the conversation, then Haillie asked, " Who did you meet?"

Rose laughed lightly. "I'm not telling. I want to see if it works out."

Looking like a toddler about to snatch a goodie snack from a high place, Haillie asked about his number.

Rose shrugged. "It's probably on the business card he gave me." She swiveled in her chair, sipping coffee from her teddy bear mug. It was her Linus blanket for work. She was mesmerized by the ripples in the liquid and the curling steam escaping the surface.

Haillie started chanting. "Name! Name! Name!"

Rose shushed her. "Calm down. You're jumping around like you're on a trampoline."

Haillie shook her head. "I'll calm down when you give him a call and then come back from lunch with him with stories that make me blush and giggle."

Rose turned around to start pounding away at the keyboard, entering the data in perfunctory swipes. Papers seemed to float from the pile and fall in place in front of her. The typing with its annoying speedy click-clacking would drive Haillie up the wall, that is if she wasn't hypnotized by the efficiency.

Rose was scanning, analyzing, and processing. This was her domain. She was cynical and logical when at work. She dealt with things the way they were. Rather than joining Haillie on her clouds of hopes, she rolled up her sleeves and went to work with her to make them come true.

* * *

Haillie was determined not to let Rose miss this opportunity. "Give me that card."

Rose didn't look up. "I'm not giving it to you."

Haillie crossed her arms over her chest. "Yes. You are. I'll make the call for you if you don't make it now."

Rose sighed and fished the card out of her purse, then handed it over to Haillie. "I'm going to regret this."

The business card showed the face of a gorgeous Adonis smiling back at her. "Nice one, little sister. He's a lawyer and smoking hot on top of it."

Rose looked up at Haillie for the briefest moment. "Really? A lawyer?"

Haillie nodded as she reached for the phone. Dialing the number on the card, she listened to the roster of employees' names for his extension before pressing the digits 8259.

She felt her heart race. Rose could be going on a date this afternoon. Rose's life largely revolved around two things: Haillie and Everyday People. That was something Haillie was determined to change.

She met Rose's eyes looking at her from the reflection on the computer screen. "I bet you it isn't his number."

Rose, Haillie could tell, was trying to temper her excitement. Haillie stuck her tongue out at her. The phone connected.

"Hello." Haillie said putting her finger over her smiling red stained lips.

"Hello." A smooth baritone male voice replied.

"You meet a lady named Rose today, and you gave her your business card when you left this morning...." She let her voice trail off, hoping he would remember. With some guys, giving out a business card meant absolutely nothing. For the right guy, giving out a business card wasn't something he did all the time.

There was a short pause on the phone. His voice sounded guarded when he answered her. "Who is this?"

Haillie didn't want to embarrass Rose by making him think she needed her big sister to call in a date for her. She thought fast. "This is Haillie,

Rose's secretary. She wanted me to arrange a time for the two of you to have lunch together...."

Another awkward pause arose before he spoke. "Is Rose available? I'd really rather speak to her myself, if you don't mind…"

* * *

Rose watched as Haillie held out the phone to her, her hand over the mouth piece. "He says he'd rather speak to you."

Rose's hand animated itself and grabbed the phone from Haillie. "This is Rose. I apologize for my intern receptionist. She was supposed to call, not chat forever."

His voice was smooth as a glass of the finest whiskey and just the way she remembered it from the elevator. "It's fine. I just would rather things stay between the two of us...if you know what I mean.."

Rose blushed. "I wanted to accept your offer of lunch, but we never did say when or where we were meeting. "

Rose's shoulder pressed the phone to her ear and she held it there. "What about 1 o'clock at the White Rose Lounge? I'll buy."

The White Rose Lounge was a posh restaurant on the north side of town. It was the kind of place where a single plate cost a third of her weekly salary, the kind of place a girl like Rose could never afford to eat. "I'll see you there."

She almost added "I can't wait," but decided that would be a little too much. She didn't want to sound desperate or overly eager.

She hung up the phone and spun around in her chair, tilting her head back to look up at the ceiling. She felt breathless with excitement. It was happening. It was really happening! Haillie whispered behind her. "Does that hurt your neck?"

"What happened!?" Haillie started shaking Rose like a cocktail.

Rose's hand flapped up and down as she shooed Haillie away. She popped her sister on the nose one time playfully. "I'm going to get whiplash if you don't stop."

Haillie backed up and waited in the corner of her cubicle tapping her foot. She paused her assault. "Well?" She dragged out the syllable for effect.

Rose grinned. "I have a one o'clock lunch appointment. With the Adonis. At the White Rose Lounge!"

Haillie's mouth dropped open and then her face lit up like a Christmas tree as the two of them squealed with glee. "Seriously?'

Rose nodded. "Seriously."

Hailliee's hand rose up and Rose gave her a high five before swiveling back around to her work. "High-fives? Those are so old."

Haillie shook her head."It is not old as long as I am not."

Rose teased her. "May I point your attention to my earlier description."

Haillie was already heading down the hall. "If I'm old, you're old, too." The words floated over the top of the carpeted grey half wall as Haillie headed toward the makeshift office that had been set up for the duration of her stay.

Chapter 16

The bright sun that filled Haillies' office gleamed, temporarily blinding her. She wondered if she was becoming a victim of office politics with the appointment of this office. It didn't matter if she was or was not, she was there to do a job.
Settling into her chair, she prepared herself for said work.

Three post it notes were stuck on her desk. Two were callbacks she needed to make. One of them she had scheduled already, she just needed to find someone from the board to accompany her so she could get quick approval.

Holding the third note in her hand, she felt a tingle run up her arm. The note simply said to "Call me." A number was scribbled at the bottom.

At first glance, she assumed it was James. The number was familiar, but since she had not dialed James' number this morning, she couldn't be certain. A feeling of dread coursed through her veins. The little voice in her head told her not to dial, but a sense of adventure that she hadn't felt in more than a dozen years spurred her to pick up the phone.

* * *

Brandon heard the phone ring three times. He looked at the number before excusing himself from the water cooler chat. Fearful Haillie would hang up, he answered before he left the crowd. "Hello! Hello!"

"Hello?" The tone sounded cautious and yet curious at the same time. He was hoping she would remember him.

"Just hold on one minute, Haillie." Practically jogging over to his office, he closed the door behind him so as not to be overheard.

He closed the door and tried to catch his breath. He suddenly felt nervous, as if he were back in junior high trying to work up the courage to ask Amy Ecklestein out to the Christmas dance all over again. "Hi. Sorry for the wait. We met in the elevator yesterday. You gave me your card."

He did not mention the meeting before the meeting, when he'd come across her standing on her front porch in all her morning glory, but an image of her body came to mind and he found himself breathless for a whole different reason.

* * *

Haillie sat patiently doodling, swiveling from right to left in her chair. Faint footsteps could be heard on the other side of the phone. He was audibly trying to catch his breath,and he was nervously rushing the words. "We met in the elevator yesterday. You gave me your card."

She met a lot of people in elevators. She had no idea who this might be. He didn't need to know that his name and face had escaped her memory. "Yes, I remember. You. What can I do for you, sir? "

He spoke the magic words. "Ms. Rose suggested I use your company for my open house."

She perked up and the swiveling stopped. She dropped her thumbs onto the flat surface of the desktop and remained still. She had a second client in two days?

This was happening fast. This was amazing. She had been silent for the duration of her thoughtful cheering. She squeezed in one more question before thinking about her next words. "What are you looking to achieve with this event?"

She continued without waiting for her client to respond, too excited about the prospect of new business to mind her manners. "Do you have a tentative date? What type of clientele do you want to attract and do you know if you want a theme?"

She fumbled around, looking for a pencil in her empty drawers, then on the-pristine floor, she did the blind grab and sift at the bottom of her purse until she found a pencil and a piece of paper.

He had been talking for thirty seconds, before she found a utensil to write down what he was saying. She half formed letters in a hurry to catch up with his answers. Why had she asked so many questions? One at a time would have been a better option. She would store that away for later.

The nervousness was gone as the man got down to business. "I want a cross section of people there. I am aiming for the artsy and financially well-endowed. If you could get some up-and-comers, that would be a bonus."

She listened steadily, storing information and writing what he said a paragraph ago. She wanted to ask him to back up and explain the tsunami of words, but she didn't want to seem incompetent. She's promised herself she would catch up soon. That stray thought made her forget what he just said

She flipped through the venues she used during past successful events.There were a few she knew of that might be able to accommodate his mixed crowd and please them. They weren't as chic as he probably wanted, but she was sure he could be persuaded.

"I think something classy would be best." His words were like lightning, breaking through the creative storm that was going on in her mind. They trashed everything she'd been picturing.

He sounded concerned when his next question came through. "Do you know any place like that?"

She was going to need more time to find the right place for this event. With the cool of someone beyond and above it all, too chill to let her own life experience weigh her down, her response rolled off her tongue without hesitation. "I know a few."

She could practically hear the relief in his voice as he exhaled. "Thank you. You have no idea. This is the third firm I've contacted. Ms. Rose recommended you highly, and I know how exceptional she is at finding support staff and contractors."

She made a mental note to treat her sister to lunch if this deal went through. Excited to close the deal before it either escaped or turned sour, she put on a smile. Snatching whatever she could get was a point of wisdom she learned at the bottom floor of her last venture.

She spoke calmly, as if this didn't matter to her at all. "I'd like to set up a day and time to meet so we can go over the details. I want to be sure I understand your needs and can meet them within the budget you've allotted."

After several moments of back-and-forth, he agreed to a rendezvous the day before the gala opening. It was the only day he was available. She hung up the phone feeling giddy with excitement.

Nervousness pelted her belly with concerns and problems, causing hibernating butterflies to rise and tickle her self-esteem until it was something laughable in her own mind. '

A creative tempest flashed up again and again. This time, she was determined to ride out the waves of ideas. Grabbing her pencil, she surfed the crest freely writing a list of grandiose possibilities for both her clients. Time ticked away.

* * *

Lisa still in the office prime realty district had tired of being horn locked in battle with the sole resident of the area. Waving the white flag was becoming as appetizing an option as eating the

breakfast she skipped to be here on time.
Grumbling filled the room.

Her belly had a point it wished to contribute and
it didn't involve her ex-lover. Visibly she cringed
at the height of making her son with him. Oh,
the joys of being young and dumb,she thought.

Her smile made him furious. Pink and bright red
flushed his face making the color of flames
portrayed in artwork. His voice was booming
through the room with his doubts about Liam's
paternity.

Rehashing the same argument no matter how
loud the volume was a boring battlefield to both
combatants. This battle was running low on
ammunition. All they were waiting for now was
the surrender.

"You could have been with. . ." He started.

" Isn't it your turn to surrender?" She drolled.

He sat down, took a long breath in, and
exasperatedly announced "That was a lot."
At that moment, Virginia turned the door handle.

Lisa looked the size two girl over. "Unlike that." She said with a smile, rising from the chair.

His eyes twinkled with laughter, and he nodded to Lisa as a display of respect. She had kicked him while he was down, but he appreciated the sardonic humor.

"Unlike what?" Virginia questioned while scanning over the rows of numbers on a paper at the top of the piles lying on his desk.

Micheal's voice changed. It was similar to how he used to speak to Liam as a toddler, when he was the apple of Michael' eye. "Sweetie, put that down. It's not important."

Lisa felt a tear. Her hand went up to wipe it away, but she blinked it back in time. Although she was not about to admit it to him, he had touched her heart. The door clinked behind her and she armored up to face the reason they were arguing.

****

A light rapping on the door awakened Haillie to the real world. She had been dancing to a stringed quartet on a raised stage under the stars of an observatory. This was the place. She had said that about the last three places. "Come in."

Lisa stepped in the office. She did an oversized wave. The circle covered the span of area from her face to her torso. She did it twice for emphasis on good will.
Haillie's smile brightened to express her acceptance of the peace offering.

" Hey. Did you win?" Haillie knew this was safe ground to build a working relationship.

"I got my shots in." Lisa gave her a sideways glance.

" any injuries?" Haillie raised an eyebrow.

"His pride took a few hits." Lisa shrugged and plopped herself down in the chair across from her. She folded her legs at the knee and relaxed.

"Make yourself at home." She welcomed her with a bag of unopened in her lap. Lisa sized up the office.

She opened the bag and fished around for three red pieces. "Did you sleep with the boss...for this office?"

She snorted. "Yup for a few years."

They shared a laugh on that one. At the conclusion when they were wiping tears and rubbing their aching sides.

Haillie got around to asking why she was there. "So what brings you here?"

"I am supposed to be the representative from the board." Lisa looked her in the eyes.
Haillie's face was crestfallen. She was hoping for Virginia the easy, yes girl. "Oh, I am happy you are coming along." Her statement was a weak attempt at best to cover her disappointment.

Lisa gave her a sly smile. "He was going to send cheerleader Virginia with you. I didn't think you wanted a pep rally. I was pretty sure you wanted a decision partner."

When Lisa put it that way she was happy to have her as a shopping companion. Lisa had experience with this and she knew the board members. Those she couldn't honestly speak for she had the charisma and fortitude to influence. They looked at each other and knew that between the two of them, whatever they decided would stand up to any vote. They smiled at each other.

The buzzing of the alarm on her phone told her she had forgotten part of her day. Daydreaming, staring out of the window, she grabbed the phone behind her on the particle board desktop and bought it up to eye level.

It was the alarm for the afternoon appointment. Ten minutes were all she had to prepare. On the scale of difficulties she faced, this meeting didn't make a dent. She was hoping she remembered the format from the decorations meeting correctly. She felt she was oversimplifying the process.

Pulling up her checklist of ideas, she bounced some of them off Lisa. Lisa listened patiently, either nodding or shaking her head as indication of her opinions.

****

"You do have creativity." Lisa mused as she checked her watch. Forty five minutes until she had to leave. Trying to relax, she eased into the back seat of the car and put her head against the leather head rest.

She wondered for half-a-second how Haillie could afford car service. Shrugging her shoulders, she let go of the thought and the animosity that would be coupled with such thinking.

"You have a good life." She blurted out the words, half-surprising herself as the temperature adjusted to comfort them in the back of the car. "How does he know what you like?" She grabbed a bottle of fancy named water and a piece of the chocolate.

Haillie was looking through her purse in a transparent effort to clean it. "They have my preferences written down on a client card."

Lisa lifted her head from its resting spot to stare at her, curiosity boring through the silence.

Haillie seemed to anticipate Lisa's unasked question. "The list is dark organic chocolates, light natural spring water from upstate New York, and fruits in the evening. Champagne is barely ever in here. This state outlawed drinking in the car."

Lisa shook her head. "Nice to know. I'll spend my next refund check on that."

Haillie looked up and arched an eyebrow. Her face scrunched up. "What was it you were going to ask?"

"How much do you get in alimony?" Lisa felt bad about asking and shrunk down in the car, raising her arms to cover all her vital organs.

Something sparked in Haillie's eyes. "Nothing." Haillie spat the word at her. "You kinda ruined it for all of us."

Lisa's arms came uncurled and she leaned forward a bit. "What on earth do you mean?"

****

Haillie stared out the window. The woman next to her had no right to access the emotions that had sprung up in her. She watched the building go from dots to full sized and back to dots in the rear window until her voice was even and she could swallow down the past ordeal. There had been so much turmoil then, so much crying, she couldn't remember living through those days.

"After you, he made sure that we don't get anything. He helped me with my struggling business after we were married. At first I was so grateful for the help, I didn't realize that slowly but surely his help meant that everything I had, including my offices, were technically his. It was all considered community property and up for grabs. The prenuptial made sure he was the only one doing the grabbing." Her voice was low and she struggled to keep the bitterness out of it.

A decade later, she thought she should have surpassed the emotional stimuli from this sore spot in her life, but it was as red and raw as the day she'd first figured out how badly he'd betrayed her. He'd taken everything from her. Everything that truly mattered, and with it, her confidence and self-esteem.

He'd left her with almost nothing, except the house, but living in that house was like being trapped in a kind of mental purgatory. She couldn't be with him and she couldn't forget him. She was surrounded by constant reminders of him, of what they'd had, and of who she'd been before everything went wrong.

Haillie hadn't turned around to look at Lisa. She was too caught up in the moment. "He asked, before he proposed, if I would ever use his child as a pawn to bleed money out of him."

For the first time, she locked eyes with Lisa after wiping her eyes and cheeks dry. Anger was surging and sparking within her. She wanted to spit them out of her mouth like lightning in a storm "He compares us all to you. He assumes we're all carbon copies of you."

****

Lisa closed her eyes and rested her head against the seat again. She closed her eyes and listened to Haillie's whining like it was background noise in the city outside the floating Lincoln. She had heard it before.

A steady ticking noise invaded the silence, interrupting the storm brewing between them, and demanding an answer. Lisa contemplated what to do with the revealing emotional oil spill Haillie had left on her doorstep.

Lisa's head bumped up against the roof as the car ran over a deep pothole. Haillie managed the unexpected change in inertia with experience.

"Are you going to say something? I just ..." Lisa trailed off as the top of her head made contact with the ceiling. "just, just ..." She stammered and her words got caught up in her throat.

Staring at the buildings again, Haillie hid a snicker at the insensitive t-shirt clad female's run-in with the ceiling.

Lisa desperately wanted to put this behind them both. She gave Haillie a rueful smile. "was it as funny as I imagined it looked?" She was desperate to deflect the embarrassing episode.

"Yes." Haillie collapsed under the strain of holding in the laughter. Lisa joined in with Haillie. A good chuckle was worth it. Hyena pitched shrieks of joy strung together like a loosely woven rope and became maddeningly rapid in succession. Tears streamed down her cheeks as the small incident became a movie premiere big comedic event for Lisa.

Haillie wiped tears from her eyes and looked at Lisa. "It wasn't that bad."

Lisa could appreciate Haillie's attempts to console her as she rubbed her head. "I'm sure it looks and feels worse than it is."

Haillie couldn't finish her sentence without giving in to another fit of laughter. "I'm sorry, but I think it's a little humorous, I'll stop laughing."

Lisa deigned to look embarrassed. She got over the prideful streak she was holding onto to keep a wall between the two former Prescott lovers. Lisa's T-shirt clad hand jutted out to do the unexpected. She offered her hand to Haillie.

"It's fine." Lisa mumbled, a pinch of annoyance sprinkled on top of the last word.

The scenery changed to an up-and-coming neighborhood. They left behind the sleek look that an excess of money and the sudden achievement of worldly success could buy. Lisa glanced at her watch to whittle away the idle seconds as the car pulled to the curb.

Lisa didn't recognize the neighborhood. "Where are we?" She stepped out of the car, taking a look around before glancing back over at Haillie.

Haillie gave her a reassuring smile. "My top choice for a venue. They agreed to see us this morning."

Lisa's mind was racing with words to describe the lecherous thief. "Oh," was all she managed. This woman had stolen her attention, her support, and now the job that gave her status in the community. Lisa trailed Haillies slingback Burberry clad feet, examining the woman's pencil skirt with Old glam.

She had to admit the girl knew what she was doing and was flourishing as a person in the position. They walked inside and Lisa wanted to discredit the place, but when she look around at the natural oak beams in the ceiling and the floor-to-ceiling windows overlooking a rooftop pool which was landscaped to look like a lakeside view, she knew why her head had betrayed her jealousy and sided against Michael in the vote. "This place is amazing.How did you find it?"

Haillie gave Lisa a conspiratorial smile. "It's a good friend's private banquet spot. This is part of his residence."

Lisa's eyebrows went up in surprise and she looked at Haillie with new eyes. "Wow. You know people like this?"

Haillie shrugged in an obvious attempt at modesty. "I had my own business before I met Michael. I called one of the connections I developed through that business this morning, and he said yes."

Lisa felt a begrudging respect for Haillie. She'd always thought the woman was a conniving little gold digger who had ridden to success on Michael's coattails. That's exactly how the story played out whenever Michael told it. However, she was starting to see that there was a lot more to Haillie and her relationship with Michael than she'd realized.

****

Haillie thought about the quick cryptic conversation she had with the private benefactor during the car ride to breakfast with Liam and his inquisitive inquests as to the identity of the person on the other end. Her staunch silence made him press more. Even with the distractions, she had negotiated this place for a weekend.

Haillie took a moment to examine her handiwork. This place was a fantasy amongst the woods. Her connection, Taylor, was an architect. His actress wife had wanted Shakespeare's A Midsummer Night's Dream. What she got was so much better. Snapping out of her reverie about the world Taylor had created there, she focused on angling for board approval.

"Lisa." Her heels click-clacked across the spacious open room "Over here we will have the entrance. From there,there, and there." She pointed to six spots in the ceiling which were made to support theatrical performers as they glided through the sky or to showcase an entertainer's grand entrance. "We have the possibility of aerial entertainment."

She directed her attention to an area on the opposite side of the space. "None of this is etched in stone" she prefaced before beginning to describe her vision. "Our signature cocktail could be served here. I'm thinking lotus juice."

Lisa listened patiently and nodded for the first few minutes like an obedient puppy, but ten minutes after the Ariel dancers, she was thinking and imagining with her. This space would be amazing. "You have an eye for this." She conceded.

Pride surged in Haillie's chest. If she'd won over Lisa, she'd won over the hardest board member over. Lisa turned to her abruptly. "Now that we've dreamed together, let's talk facts. What is a place like this going to cost us?"

She could tell that Lisa was prepared to reject it, to find fault with it, and to destroy the dream before it had a chance to be born. Haillie wasn't about to let that happen. "The place is free to us. As I said, I called in a favor."

Haillie pulled her phone out of her purse and started up the signature app. "All you have to do is sign and approve, and the place can be ours."

They both ran their finger over the line labeled signature in the formation of the letters that spell out their names. A tap on the word send at the bottom of the page and they had accomplished step one of the process. Haillie resisted the urge to openly celebrate her victory.

Lisa checked her watch, evidently anxious to be sure the remnants of time left was enough for the next stop. "I've got a little more time, but that's all I can spare. I have errands I need to run before work."

Haillie's mind revisited happier days as she looked around. A smile that she didn't feel like explaining to Lisa tugged at her lips as they left the building and entered the elevator. She hoped Lisa hadn't noticed.

****

Something about the place had changed Haillie's mood. Lisa didn't know what it was, but the woman's step was lighter and she was carrying herself with more confidence. There was a joy that seemed to radiate from her.

Lisa assumed that the preparation for the party was the cause. She was thrilled she could be part of Haillie's recovery. She could easily imagine Haillie as the powerful negotiator, an image that was slowly replacing the evil boardroom witch Michael had portrayed her as being.

One of the most inspiring parts of working for Everyday People was seeing the life return to the hopeless faces of the people that came to them. She loved being part of that transformation, and she felt a familiar longing to see Haillie return to her former glory. She could see the woman's potential starting to sprout and knew what role she wanted to play in helping bring about that transformation. It wasn't the part she was currently playing. Things would have to change.

The driver popped out the driver's side door and hurried around the car to open the passenger's door for them both. "Ladies." He greeted them.

Haillie gave him a warm smile as she got inside the compartment. "We'll be going to 5227 Autumn drive."

The driver gave a smart nod and then confirmed. "That's across town, right?"

Haillie nodded. "Yes."

Lisa got in and scooted behind the driver's seat. Fastening the seatbelt, she informed Haillie she wouldn't be accompanying her to the next place. "You have impeccable taste. You don't need me there. Whatever you sign off on will be okay."

She was rewarded by seeing Haillie's face light up like a sixteen year old who had just been given the keys to a new convertible sports car, a license, and a date Friday night with the hottest guy in school. Lisa knew she'd made the right decision.

"Thank you. I'll let you know what we get." Tapping to get the driver's attention went unheard so Haillie texted him the new address. They were on the way back to the office.

****

"Hey, leaving early again? Where are you off to today? Is there a mid-day club?" Rose's tone was teasing, but she was tired of seeing this girl get paid to do nothing.

Virginia was packing her oversized handbag for a leisurely luncheon with a friend that had just returned from two years in France as Rose walked past her cubicle. "Don't start with me."

Virginia's usually bubbly personality wasn't present. Even her outfit was deflated. Something had taken the air out of Micheal's doll. Rose wanted to snoop into the inner workings of what looked like a possible depressed Virginia, but waved off the urge. "Drink yourself happy."

Virginia gave her a fake giggle and the stiffest smile she'd ever seen. "Two shots of tequila."

****

Virginia was aware that what she'd said didn't make sense, but nobody expected her to. They all thought she was an empty-headed, barely competent living Barbie doll, a toy for Michael's amusement.

This was becoming more evident every day Haillie marched around that office, disgruntling her fiancé with her efficient, effortless comfort in a leadership position. No one wanted to admit it, but the workplace had changed in the little bit of time she was present. Micheal was either scared of Haillie, or still in love with her, and Virginia was feeling the pressure to evolve.

Hoisting her purse off the floor, she decided to change her plans. She was going to go back to the house with Tracey, the single triplet. They would have their drinks at his residence right outside the city limits.

But first, there was a detour she needed to make. Three times, the plain girl with the off-the-rack department stores outfit asked, in a forceful monotone, "Who do you want to see?"

When she refused to answer and simply continued to stand there, as if willing him to come down that elevator and see her, the polite questioning gave way to more intrusive questions followed by a veiled threat. "Do I need to call security?"

The receptionist was now next to her, putting her hand on Virginia's shoulder. Ma'am was replaced by, "Lady, are you okay?"

Virginia was not okay. She was standing in the middle of the lobby, dressed to the nines, her make up impeccable, and she hadn't moved from the spot for five minutes. She stood there, rooted to the spot, watching the busy worker bees gathering pollen pay checks from her ex-fiancé.

She found her voice. "I'd like to see him."

The receptionist stopped tapping her on the shoulder. Her voice changed from soft tones of annoyance to honey laced charm "Darlin', who would you like to see?"

Virginia slid her sunglasses down her nose to reveal her eyes. She was most famous for their unusual shade of blue. "Do you know who I am?"

Recognition dawned in the receptionist's eyes and on her face. "Of course I know who you are."

Virginia was glad. She didn't want to waste time explaining. "Tell him to use an emergency block of his time and that I'm not taking no as an answer."

The plain girl broke land speed records as she moved back to her desk and picked up the phone to get him on the line. This was the best gossip of the fiscal year. Two rings chimed before the Executive Assistant outside his suite picked up.

"Brandon's desk..."

The receptionist didn't wait for the woman to finish. "There is a Virginia that needs to see Brandon urgently. "

The assistant put up the standard roadblock. "Brandon isn't free right now. I believe he's in a meeting."

The receptionist was used to this. She rebutted the statement with one sentence. "She said to use his emergency family time for this."

****

Delores, Brandon's Executive Assistant and primary gatekeeper, squirmed uncomfortably in her seat. How did the receptionist know about his emergency time? Was Brandon sleeping with that girl? She hoped not.

Wait - hadn't the receptionist said a woman wanted to see him? She checked the time, making sure that the time for the woman named Prescott hadn't yet arrived. She wanted to witness him meeting the Prescott woman. She breathed a sigh of relief.

There was still an hour until that meeting, so she pushed the conference button on her phone, opening a line to Brandon's office. "Brandon, there's a lady that would like to see you. She said she wanted to use emergency family time."

"Send her in." His voice was calm, but she'd have paid good money to be a fly on the wall for this meeting.

****

Virginia stuck her nose in the air as she passed both the receptionist and the executive assistant's desk. The door clicked behind her and the place was quiet. Brandon sat in his sleek chair looking as handsome as his figure would allow, his eyes scanning her face for an area of emotional injury.

Sunshine poured in through the windows, bathing his office in warm sunbeams that soaked the interior with beaming glows of innovation and youth. She couldn't help but compare it to the dark somber atmosphere created by the heavy drapes that blocked the light from entering Michael's domain.

She wanted to stand there until she became part of the light again. She'd forgotten how much she missed it. There was space to breathe, to flow, and to be herself here. The rules she was running from didn't apply in this space. Anyone could make up their own if they were productive.

Brandon waited patiently for her to speak. He got up and pulled two chairs up so they could face one another, but out of the view of any prying eyes that might walk by. The seats he chose were equal in beauty, style, and comfort. He didn't stay locked behind his desk as Michael did when she sought him out in his office, as if he were a king and she were a mere courtier there to beg his favor.

She accepted the seat, and he sat down after her. He was so close to her she could see his five o' clock shadow coming in strong. His dominant high cheekbones and square chin paired with a button nose combined to make him look imposing, yet gentle. Caring Brandon, she thought. She was ready .

****

She looked down at her hands. "I don't know what I'm doing."

He reached across and cupped her hands in his, petting them as he reassured her. "That's perfectly normal."

"I'm engaged. Well, I was ..." She trailed off, then composed herself and - over compensating - she added, "No, I am."

His eyes didn't leave hers. "Okay." He nodded. "You are trying to make up your mind. That is acceptable."

She became agitated by those words. "No." Her pitch rose defensively. "I'm not trying to make up my mind. I know what I want."

His expression didn't change. "Good." He firmly nodded this time. " Good. You are being decisive."

She broke down into a sob as tears started to drizzle onto her lap. "Love wasn't as hard with you. It didn't play tricks on me."

There was the slightest hint of self-satisfaction that touched the smile which stretched across his face. "Yes. It was."

"No." She protested," It was you, me, and our emotions."

He shrugged. "Feelings are hard things for logical men. Most men deal well with numbers. They make sense. You can write them down, add them up, check to make sure you've got it right. There's no guess work. You either have the answer or you don't. Emotions aren't like that. You can't write your emotions down, add up the columns, and get a sum total that gives you a definitive, unwavering answer about what to do next."

She frowned. "But…Women can do that. We can put the pros and the cons on paper. Just seeing the information spelled out that way helps us sort things out."

He opened his mouth to respond and she stopped him dead in his tracks, capturing his still speaking lips and roughly shoving her tongue into his mouth. It was mouth rape. He hadn't asked for this or given his consent to it, but she was confident he wasn't going to press charges on such a delightful surprise.

When she released him, she whispered " Pro."

He drew back and stared at her. His cheeks were flushed and she could sense that he was angry at her for what she'd done. She realized she'd crossed a line she shouldn't have. "Pro or not, I'm sorry for that. They were so pink and I just had to..."

She bit her lip and looked at the floor, glancing back up at him from beneath her thick lashes, in perfect imitation of an adorable four-year-old caught with her hand in the cookie jar.

They say there in silence. She watched his left eyebrow settle down to take its normal place on his face. His eyebrow rose when he was trying to suppress a large irritation. It had to be an immediate threat. She kept going. "I didn't mean to do that. I know about the pediatric cardiac surgeon, and I have no intention of trying to butt in there. You are happy. I am happy, and I'm happy for you."

****

Brandon struggled to gain control over his temper. He reminded himself of what he knew from their years together. She tended to act out when she felt cornered.

He took a deep breath, calming himself, and said what he knew he needed to say. "The kiss was nice. Like a postcard from the past." He touched his lips. "I know something is wrong. Really wrong. I want to help you, but I will wait until you are ready to share."

They sat there, looking at each other. She leaned forward numerous times to try another kiss, but each time he held a finger to her lips and shook his head. He wasn't here for a make out session. She recoiled and the silence resumed as the sunlight poured down on them both while she let sparing tears drop down to form dots on the fabric of her skirt.

Finally, she heaved a sigh. "I'm tired of sharing him."

He jumped on the words. "How so?"

Her eyes were filled with hurt as she spoke. "Haillie is his ex-wife, Lisa is his baby mama, Liam is his son and I'm his fiancée, his little play thing with all the right decorative curves."

She freed her hands and stood up from the chair, walking past him to look out the window at the people on the sidewalks below. "I'm last. I'm stupid. I'm a joke to his former sister-in-law." Her rant continued. "I'm a joke to myself as well."

The full storm of tears rolled in as she turned back to him. "What am I doing?"

Brandon was asking the same thing, but for a very different reason. He found himself staring at her backside with yearning. It had been awhile since he had touched a slender, proportional butt.

The girls with personality were a blast to talk to and he knew those were the enduring qualities that made long-term relationships work, but that kiss reminded him of everything he'd been missing since she left. He knew about her early morning job from his previous neighbors. He guessed noone told her that he'd moved closer to the city to be near his current girlfriend.

"I mean really?" She turned to face him. He saw the dark streaks of mascara running along the basins dredged on her cheeks.

He came to her with tissues. "I never thought you were a joke. I still don't."

He dabbed at her tears tracks while she babbled. "They all know who and what they are. Rose is an advocate, Haillie a fighter, Lisa a survivor, Liam is making the best of everything. I'm just some puppy allowed to play at the grown up's table and fed scraps of whatever Micheal has left over after they're through with him. "

She buried her face in Brandon's broad shoulder. Her breath was warm against his neck, her chest inviting. "I swear he loves her."

He began stroking her hair, as if she were a cat with the fur up on its back, "You have his ring, therefore you have his heart."

She gave a short, bitter laugh. "His heart? It's not his heart that's connected to me. Try lower."

He closed his eyes and reached for a lie he hoped would soothe her and reassure her. He just hoped she couldn't tell he was lying. "Sweetheart, I know Micheal. He wouldn't be marrying you unless his heart was involved."

She looked up at him and, with all seriousness, asked, "Can I sleep with you for old times sake? Please?"

His groin was definitely giving a yes vote to her proposition, but he knew that this invitation was poison. That was one apple he wasn't about to bite into ever again. The last time had nearly killed him.

He kissed her forehead, then whispered into her ear, "Just because I'm in an open relationship doesn't mean you are. Besides, my girlfriend would be mad, to say the least."

Wiping her tears, she smiled up at him. "What good is an open relationship if she won't let you enjoy it?"

Brandon pulled back leaving her at arms distance. "Too many strings attached for me."

She sighed and put her head back on his chest. "You are right." They stood that way for a long moment. "What about Sky's French beau?"

Brandon made a noise of disgust. "What about him?"

She opened her purse, searching for her makeup bag. "I was wondering what he was like."

Brandon wrinkled his nose. "He's an annoying, pompous ass. What else would you expect? He's a frenchman."

She pulled out a compact and began to dab at the mascara that had traced the path of her tears onto her cheeks. "Like Sky? She doesn't seem to mind if you're mad about her boy toys."

Brandon sighed. "It's different. I have no concerns that she's going to leave me for him, for one thing. I don't like him, but she does, and that's enough for me."

Virginia finished fixing her makeup and stood up. His intuition warned him she was rushing back to status quo. His heart broke for her. "You don't have to be okay. You have legit concerns."

Her back straightened and she gave him a smile he recognized as her war face. "I'm fine. I will do what Miss Rose said and drink myself happy." She shrugged. "I'm marrying him and I'll still be wealthy."

Brandon sat back down in his chair. "The reason we broke up."

She puckered her lips at the mirror, then shut the compact. Her response was glib, but cold. "Women like numbers, too. We like things that can be added up in columns."

The laugh he gave her was weak, and she joined him in it before turning the knob, readying for her departure to the car waiting down below.

He leaned forward to look her in the eyes. "Come see me whenever you need to talk."

Smiling like a mouse that outsmarted the trap and got the cheese she slyly asked "Nothing else?"

His groin once again voted "YES!" but his mind took control. "No." His voice was firm and clear.

The door shut behind her.

****

Rose watched the second hands inch by each tick. She could swear they were getting slower, to the point she was sure she was in a time stasis.

She wanted the afternoon to hasten its step. Instead, the piles of work seemed to be the only thing that wasn't static. She was absolutely positive she could watch them grow.

She secretly laughed all morning at how her sister had made this lunch come to fruition. Her waiting was about to be rewarded in twenty more ticks. The mini-coo coo clock sang its giddy songs.

Buried beneath the papers, the sound was mostly diluted, otherwise she was sure her pretty chill coworkers wouldn't be so understanding about the noisy racket on the top of every hour. Chiming and ringing intertwined, rising to such a crescendo those on the right and left took notice. "Sssh" came over the half wall on both sides.

Hoping to stop the ringing of the office phone, she answered with a swift, "Hello?"

"I'm in the lobby." Adonis said "I'm a little early, but I thought you wouldn't mind."

She stuffed her things into her purse without thought or concern. Adonis had showed up early to fetch her. She was giddy with delight.

Chapter 17

Haillie's toes tapped against the marble flooring of the owner's waiting area. She looked around at the sparsely decorated modern space, and became preoccupied with her phone again.

The administrative assistant tapped her on the shoulder. "He will see you in about ten minutes,Ms.Prescott."

She quickly glanced up. "Thank you." Those words were accompanied by a troublesome feeling that she had missed an obvious piece of information. Her alarm went off and she gave up playing her word game.

Preparation began. She reviewed her list of needs for the venue. She wanted ice sculpted tables with a very stylish and relaxing Hookah lounge area, along with a topiary maze. The lounge would be in the middle of the puzzle.

Real plants would be best, but the clean up when overly thirsty guests or people high on O2 water vapors came amorously stumbling back to the main attendee area always made such a mess. She toyed with the idea of adding an indoor slide to provide an authentic authentic sophomoric feel throughout the celebration. That was over the top, but she did have a flair for extravagance.

For the first time she looked up at the sign she'd passed in front of the office space. Where she was sitting was not where she should have been. How did she end up here? While she was sitting there inputting the information she'd searched for this morning during her fevered race to accomplish her self-imposed list, she realized she must have misdialed.

She wondered if she could leave stealthily without any eyes seeing her. Haillie bent down and gathered her stuff together, put it in her purse, and stood up ready to leave.

~ ~ ~ ~ ~

The receptionist had waited all morning for this moment. Ms. Prescott had arrived. There was no way in Gehenna she was going to let her leave. There was drama waiting to unfold and she was going to be there, front and center, when the fireworks erupted.

No one, not even Ms Prescott, was going to steal this moment. The week had been so boring. This was the most excitement she'd seen since Brandon's new girlfriend made him an honest man. More like a boring man.

"Excuse me." She spoke up as Haillie turned toward the exit. "He's coming right out."

It was a bold faced lie, but whatever it took to get a hint of spice back in her life was good enough a reason to say the line she fed everyone, from business men to socialites.

~ ~ ~ ~ ~

Surfacing for the first time in three hours, Brandon strolled down the corridor toward the open tiled area adjacent to his office suite. Confident strides purposefully covered the distance between his office door and Ms. Prescott, who now had her back turned.

He cleared his throat so he wouldn't startle her before speaking. "I believe we had an appointment at a different location for another time."

Something between a scoff and a chuckle escaped. She clasped a hand over her mouth.

She stood there just as radiant as she was the day before when she was attired in the full glory of nothing but her birthday suit. Her eyes widened slightly and she seemed to be looking for an exit, but his curiosity was peaked and he wasn't going to offer her one. He led the way toward his office as if he'd been expecting her all along.

~ ~ ~ ~ ~

As Haillie followed him toward his office, she felt the start of a panic attack. It was for certain there was no air coming into her lungs. Trying to take deep breaths and relax herself, she could hear her audible efforts. She was sure she sounded like a laborious train pulling a load uphill.

He would think she never saw the inside of a gym with the way she was huffing and puffing like this. A wafting of his cologne caught her attention and, surprisingly, helped to calm her down.

Returning to a serene mind she faced the real challenge in front of her: Explaining why she was sitting in his waiting room for no plausible reason. Honesty would make her out to be an idiot incapable of handling business for the new client she hadn't signed yet.

He was talking about how nice it was to see her again. He hadn't yet expressed what was clearly bumping around in his mind the question she didn't wish to answer.

Turning the knob on the door he opened it and invited her to sit in a chair to the left. It was an art piece more than a comfortable place to rest the bum. She adjusted herself in the chair until she could find a spot with a minimal form of comfort.

His leanly toned sleek muscles were presently outlined by the dark colored suit he wore, and he was just as dashing as she remembered. His hair was gelled to perfection and his blue irises pierced hers, searching her face like an interrogation lamp.

~ ~ ~ ~ ~

Brandon folded his hands carefully on top of the desk across from her, taking in an eyeful of what attracted him before and attempted to push away the stray thoughts currently tempting him. " As I said before this is an unexpected"

He paused for a moment before continuing, as if to make his meaning clear. "Visit. Not undesired, but unexpected." He smiled at her, hoping to reassure her, and leaned forward slightly. "What can I do for you?"

A very becoming blush was creeping up her neckline and face. "Yes," she began squirming in her seat in a way that made his breath catch just the slightest bit in his throat. He couldn't take his eyes off her.

"After yesterday…" she looked down at her hands for a brief moment and then looked back up at him. Her words came out in a rush as if she couldn't stop them. "I had a busy morning stepping in as a single mother and I made a clerical error and ended up here."

He felt the slightest twinge of disappointment at discovering her visit was a mistake and not something she'd planned. He wondered how she'd gotten his private number, but supposed that it was truly possible it was just a misdial.

She slowed down as she approached the finish line for her story. "I'm upset I'm going to accomplish less today, but this isn't a terrible coincidence."

He couldn't have agreed more. "We might as well make the most of it." He stood up and offered her his hand. "Madame, est-ce que vous déjeunez avec moi?"

The smile that slowly spread itself across her face made it worth asking. "Oui."

Brandon stepped out from the behind the desk, kissed her hand and tucked her arm gently in his, and led her out to share a meal.

****

Rose's eyes cut to the man in the driver seat directing the car. She was mentally screaming and doing back flips. She was midway through a full routine with her pom poms waving high when he turned onto the highway, heading out of the city.

Her excitement turned to nervousness. "I can't take a long lunch."

The man gave her a reassuring smile. "You'll be back. I promise."

The car pulled into an underground garage. They descended through three stories of exotic Italian muscle cars until they made it to a parking spot with his name on it. "Trent" was spray painted between two white lines in gold block lettering. He squeezed his Audi sedan into the spot. He cut the engine, unlocked the doors, and stepped out to open hers.

She was now on alert. "Where are we going?"

He offered his hand. "Do you trust me?"

She accepted the hand and followed his lead. "That depends." She hesitated for a moment and pulled back before they entered the door to the stairs. "Are you a serial killer?"

Taken aback, he chuckled when he saw she was joking. "No. You think your neighbor is a criminal? Besides, would I tell you I were if I actually were a serial killer?"

"You might be. Maybe you would tell me you were just to throw me off." She jested as they stepped onto the elevator.

A slow grin spread across his face that enhanced the slight dimples in his cheeks and made him look even more impossibly handsome. "I could be a lot of things."

She coyly asked "And what might they be besides a man who helps the elderly and can get bullied into a date by a lady who looks like she is in her eighties."

He winked at her. "Hopefully a gentleman in your eyes."

She returned his smile. "Well, so far I see just that."

He gave her a jesting maniacal laugh. "I have you fooled! My plan is working."

She shook her head. "See? I am going back to the serial killer notion."

Trent opened the doors to a restaurant with the most incredible view of the city. Rose took in the restaurant. The floor-to-ceiling to floor windows in lightly dusted smoked glass gave the skyscrapers an air of mystery much like the Adonis she was standing next to. It was all too much.

She found a lump of fat on her side this morning. She lacked so much, but this is what Trevor believed she needed to be impressed. This is what Virginia deserved, what someone like Micheal would give a woman like Virginia because he knew she would only accept this level of beauty.

She stood there in silence, doubting her abilities to accept such an outlandish gift. Rose's mouth dropped open. "This is expensive. You can't take me here on a first date." She felt incredibly underdressed for the location.

Trent shrugged. "Why can't I? I'm supposed to be impressing you. Is this not impressive?"

Rose looked up at him. "Yes, but too much. It makes a girl wonder what you're hiding." She winced at how blunt her own words sounded to her ears and hoped he wouldn't be angry with her.

His fingers encroached upon hers as he took her hand and led her to a table. She looked around nervously, expecting to be stopped at any moment. "Don't we have to wait for the Maitre D?"

He gave her that winning smile of his. "Not when you booked the restaurant for an hour."

How was all this for her? She wasn't a princess. She didn't have courage. "What?"

His eyes lingered on her face. "I want to get to know you, and I don't want to be distracted. Now, pick your table."

In her entire life, no man had ever treated her like this. She wandered toward a table under her preferred street artist and then, directly, changed her mind. Instead she shot across the restaurant to the table next to a baby grand piano.

She wondered, if it was only for an hour, what were the chances he could afford a pianist? She wasn't sure what the rent out rates were for a restaurant like this. Haillie would know. Haillie would know what to do in this situation.

She searched for another seat. "Umm, I can't decide? I never have these options."

He raised her hand to his lips and kissed it gently. "Let's take the guesswork out of it. We can have lunch under the painting and I'll play the piano while you eat dessert."

She shivered slightly at the feel of his touch on her hand. She could hardly breathe. "A sensible solution."

He pulled out the chair for her. "I try." She began to sit then shot back up, nearly knocking his head back with the top of her head.

Rose felt a swell of panic. She didn't belong here. She didn't belong with him. If she spent an hour with him, he'd figure that out soon enough. "I can't accept this. I am a sandwich and soda type of girl. I thank you, but this is just too much."

Trevor didn't let go of her hand. His voice was soothing. "We'll order a sandwich."

She shook her head, nearly in tears. "It's not the food. It is the place and the effort. I only got your phone number this morning and you put all this together?"

He gave her a winning smile. "If you stay, I'll tell you the unimpressive truth."

She mulled over this. Her foot turned aside to leave multiple times, but his pleading eyes reeled her in. "Okay, I'll stay. But only if you come clean before I sit."

Trevor laughed. "Fine. My buddy opens the restaurant. He told me to come in two hours early when they close down for dinner and we will have the place to ourselves. He is in the back with a three man crew to help me out. I knew Ms. Mabel would want me to do my best."

Rose was suddenly confused. "Who is Ms. Mabel?"

Trevor raised an eyebrow. "The pillbox lady,"

She sat in the waiting chair, her fears allayed. "Oh."

The tension in his shoulders seemed to go out and he visibly relaxed. She was immediately sorry for stressing him out. He was being so good to her, and she must seem unappreciative. "So you'll stay?"

She gave him a small smile. "If your friend can make a killer pastrami sandwich."

Trevor laughed. "I'm sure he can."

Rose nodded. "Then, I'm staying."

Trevor sat down across from her. "There is a caveat. We'll have to help clean up."

"I can handle cleaning." She laughed. "Now tell me about you."

Chapter 18

Brandon pressed the button for the top floor. They rode in silence to the roof access and climbed the stairs to an open terrace area. Trees, bushes, plants, and flowers stretched out in a carpet that seemed to go as far as the eye could see and made the roof look vast. The greenery and colorful buds flawlessly meshed into the brilliant blue sky. In the middle of this oasis of nature sat their lunch.

Haillie gasped. "I'm speechless."

Brandon looked at her. " I am going to assume that is a good thing."

Haillie nodded. "Yes, it is so far."

Brandon chuckled. "What do I have to do to keep you in awe?"

Haillie looked up at him and raised an eyebrow. "Be an amazing date."

His pearly whites dazzled. "I might be able to handle that. " He confidently poured the wine, careful not to spill any on the fine linen tablecloth that covered the wooden legs and solid varnished top of the table.

Haillie shook her head. "You are sure of yourself." She smiled as she picked up her glass.

He winked impudently. "I've got to be, or else who will be?"

She smirked at him over the rim of the crystal. "Maybe you're right." Haillie said.

He added nothing else, and sipped the beverage whilst arranging their picnic to be more palatable to the eyes therefore whetting their appetite.

"This was your idea?" Haillie laughed, tilting her head back at the maximum volume level allowed in such a posh restaurant.

He tilted his head and gave her a lopsided smile. "It was my invitation you accepted."

Hailliee took a sip as she pondered this. "Why did you offer it?"

He shrugged. "You were there. I needed a break from what was on my table, and I wanted to vet you before I gave you my grand openings. Currently, the receptionist you met handles those affairs. It is an overwhelming amount of work for her, and not part of her responsibilities. She's done the best she can, and it is a position I have overlooked filling, but when you showed up, I grabbed the opportunity and was happily surprised."

There were many ways that statement could have been interpreted. Haillie wondered at exactly which of those interpretations he intended.

* * *

Brandon felt a twinge of guilt as he sat down across from the beautiful woman in front of him. At this exact moment, his girlfriend was in surgery working to repair an infant's heart.

She was literally holding the child's future in her skilled, steady hands while he was having lunch and a few laughs with a woman he'd wanted to get to know since he first laid eyes on her.

Was he being disrespectful of his relationship with his girlfriend? He wasn't doing anything with Haillie besides having a conversation about business, yet he felt as guilty as if he'd done a whole lot more than talk to her.

If his girlfriend asked, he could honestly tell her he'd had a business lunch with a prospective contractor. That would be the truth. Yet he knew if he said those words, it was going to feel like a lie.

He groaned inwardly. This must be what purgatory felt like: so close to heaven, yet unable to enjoy it, tormented by guilt.

Haillie wrapped up their lunch with a handshake. Brandon's eyes glistened with sparks of intense desire hidden beneath the depths of those dark blue irises. His dilated pupils punctuated the gushing run on sentences he wanted to say about her, but he kept those to himself. Instead, he offered a mutual agreement of respect. " I look forward to working with you in the future."

* * *

Haillie blushed under his stare, her body responding to the subconscious chemistry, but she kept her voice steady as she responded. "I do, too. I mean, for work. I do hope you will come to the charity gala."

Brandon was on his feet and around the table to assist her with her chair. He leaned in from behind as she stood there, his breath baiting her ears to listen to his mesmerizing voice in that sensational tone. "I already have an invite. Now I have a reason to show up."

She felt a slight shiver run up her spine and gave a low chuckle. "Don't forget your checkbook, Experienced People is a good charity."

He smiled as he escorted her back down to his office. "Have a nice day."

She waved as she headed out the door and into the sunlight. "I will."

* * *

Rose tilted her head back and laughed before placing the wine glass back on the table cloth.

The Adonis corked the bottle and wrapped up the picnic, putting it back in the basket. "Did you have a good time?"

She smiled. "I did. We should do it again sometime." She raised an eyebrow as she looked at him. "Soon?"

He glanced over his shoulder at her puckered pink fat lips. The confident smile on her face was reward enough for all he'd done. He bent down so close to those lips he could feel her breath on his face. "We most certainly will."

His next words were lost in the delicious taste of her lips. He resurfaced for air a full minute later. He pulled away reluctantly, his hands searching for the napkin to his right on the table to wipe the lip gloss off his lips, and thought about returning for a second helping.

Rose snickered "If you're looking for the napkin, you knocked that over about thirty seconds ago."

He gave her a half-smile. "I guess that takes care of packing it up."

He scooped the scattered remainders of their wondrous lunch up off the pavement and tossed them into the trash. Scooting her chair back, Rose readied herself to leave.

Trevor gave her a pout. "You're done with me already. I feel used. You kiss and run."

She smirked "Maybe, but I can't leave till you drive me. I rode with you, remember?"

He walked six paces away from the setup to a miniature house camouflaged in ivy vines. He handed her a broom. "You want to help sweep? It'll go faster if you do."

"With a broom?"she accepted the cleaning utensil and began sweeping their rubbish into a pile.

He watched her domestic display and was humbled that someone as beautiful as she was would stoop down to cleaning, especially since he was jesting about sweeping. Watching her made him work harder.

His shirt had a moist sheen of perspiration around his rolled up sleeves that stopped at his elbow, and he tucked in his collar.

They chatted merrily as they tidied up, exchanging life experiences, mutual past experiences, and common desires. Discovering common desires and a shared, resolute determination for accomplishing their goals, they finished the cleaning and replaced the tools where they found them in the little shed.

It didn't look like a shed to her anymore. It reminded her of a quaint cottage on the side of a country enclave amongst the urban cement wilderness. The sorrow of leaving such a peaceful place drew a sigh from her as they entered the elevator for the descent back to the hustle and bustle of ordinary life.

Like Cinderella, her time at the ball was over and she would now have to go back to the drudgery of her everyday life. Fortunately, unlike Cinderella, she wouldn't have to wait for him to find a shoe and then search a whole kingdom full of feet to find her again.

* * *

Micheal's fork hovered over the salad Virginia bought him. Forest green coloring of the arugula and spinach stared back at him with disdain for his taste bud's longings. Steak, French fries, and chimichangas were on a list of about thirty other things he desired to eat. Top of that list? "Ribs."

He mumbled to himself. "Ribs slathered in barbecue sauce accompanied by a side of coleslaw, maybe French fries." He nodded. "Definitely French fries."

If he recalled correctly, he had m&m's stashed away in the top right filing cabinet. Supporting his weight on the oak arm of the chairs, he strained to get up. He wheezed a bit as he felt his biceps spasm in open rebellion against the physical exertion.

Thinking back to his last trip to the gym he did feel sluggish on the treadmill. Midway to the filing cabinet, he tapped his tummy and pinched his arm. There was more than an acceptable amount of body fat, so he begrudgingly dragged himself back to the Arugula and olive oil in a BPA free plastic bowl.

Why was it that every time he opened the lid he swore he was standing in a field. He almost wanted to start singing "the hills are alive." There was so much greenery. With chagrin, he forced himself to emulsify the grassy assortment of nutrients while trying desperately to convince himself it was a steak.

Fifteen minutes into a meal he would rather drink than chew, his secretary dropped off the early invitees list.

* * *

"Yesterday, I went to Brandon's house. Not by choice." Virginia was eating lunch with Tracey, the middle of the triplets. She was considered to be the ordinary one, despite being stunning to most people, and it left her insecure. That insecurity made her eager for attention, which is why Virginia chose her as her lunch companion.

They sat together in the front window of the cliche organic cafe for the upper crust, displaying their thrifty facade by buying fourteen dollar salads. It was a place to observe the pretty people as they grazed on the vegetation of choice while cheerily involving themselves in light chatter and the perfect amount of laughter.

Virginia was not there for people watching. She was there because she wanted to dish about her own life to the one person she knew had no life of her own and didn't know anyone that she could use to leverage the information in a meaningful way.

As if on cue, Tracey looked up at Virginia. "Did you say Brandon?"

Virginia awaited an oral chastising from Tracey and squinted to block the words from hitting her soft spots. "Yes."

Tracey dropped her silver coated eating utensil. She leaned forward and placed her hand to the left side of her mouth to shield the troublesome content of her message. "Does Michael know about your visit?"

Virginia felt suddenly impatient at the juvenile manner in which Tracey was behaving. "Tracey, really with the fifth grade secrecy mode? Of course he doesn't know."

They silently ate a few bites before Virginia looked at Tracey. "Do you know if he is dating?"

Tracey didn't look up, focusing instead on stabbing a mandarin orange. "Yes."

Virginia's impatience grew. Barely able to contain herself, she pushed back in her seat and rolled her eyes. "Which one is it? Yes, he's seeing someone or Yes, you know but he isn't seeing someone?"

Clearly irritated, Tracey's eyes narrowed. She practically spat the words at her. "Yes, he's seeing someone."

Both their heads swiveled toward the curb so as not to look at each other after this disappointing revelation. Tracey's eyes widened as they wandered away to the outside scenery, as if she couldn't believe what she was seeing, and Virginia's turned to see what it was that she was staring at out of curiosity. She felt a flash of anger as she recognized Haillie and Brandon, walking arm in arm.

Tracey gushed, "This is the reason I eat here. Everyone is bound to show up!" She scrambled for her phone, obviously intending to document the sight.

"No! No!" Virginia practically screamed, swatting the phone out of Tracey's hand and toward the floor.

Tracey glared at Virginia as she reached for her phone. "You could have broken it!"

Virginia shrugged. "But I didn't. Besides, I would just buy you another one."

Tracey's eyes narrowed in speculation. There was clear suspicion in her voice. "Why shouldn't I have taken the picture?"

Virginia sat back in disgust. "Because it's useless. Micheal hates her, she is dating the parking garage attendant, and Brandon's hand would be at the small of her back if he were interested."

Tracey stared at them as they continued down the sidewalk. "Why are they together? That's so weird. I bet his girlfriend wouldn't agree with you."

"So!" Virginia didn't want to think about Haillie and Brandon anymore. She shrugged her shoulders nonchalantly as if she could shrug off the images. "Tell me more about his girlfriend. Is she cute or is she one of those beasts he's been dating lately?"

Tracey's lips tugged down in a frown. It was clear she didn't want to talk about this, but Virginia was buying lunch and Tracey understood how the game was played. "She looks like the other two after you."

Virginia was relieved. He couldn't seriously be interested in those women. No man would want to spend a lifetime staring at those faces when they could have someone like her. She waved the notion of them away with a flick of her hand. "They mean nothing to him."

Silence grew between them. Tracey concentrated on her salad while Virginia studied the colorful collage of foliage on her plate. Eventually, though, she couldn't take it anymore. "What does the troll do?"

Tracey shrugged. "She's a pediatric cardio surgeon. I think that means she does baby aerobics or something."

Virginia rolled her eyes. "Another smart one. I'll just get rid of her like the other two. Then, he'll be available again."

Tracey looked up. "Not if he's with Haillie."

Virginia coughed suddenly, spewing minced green tidbits onto Tracey's creamy complexion. Tracey looked like she had puke green chicken pox dotting her face. Virginia felt like she was going to be sick. "Sorry. I think I've had enough. Let's get you a new shirt and a facial."

Tracey bit her lip. "I think I should get back to work. Michael doesn't like it when I'm late."

Virginia placed cash down on the check and looked the girl over. "Not until I at least replace the shirt you just ruined. I'll tell Michael you were helping me with important business for Everyday People. He won't blame you for being late then."

Tracey's face lit up and a huge smile stretched across her face. "You'd do that for me?"

Virginia cooed. "Of course, what are friends for?"

Keeping Tracey loyal to her ensured that she always had access to the nitty gritty details of Michael's calendar and anything else he entrusted to the secretarial pool. It also meant she could trust Tracey to keep her little secrets from Michael. She didn't mind if that loyalty cost her a few grand every time they went out to lunch. It was Michael's money, anyway.

* * *

Tracey slid back into her chair at her station feeling refreshed and relaxed after her facial and wearing a brand new Gucci tunic top that was worth a month's salary, courtesy of her BFF Virginia. She checked her email and noticed the urgent request from Michael for the friends and family list to be delivered.

She walked into his office with a smile. "This is the preliminary list of board members, their families, and the friends they want included."

She'd been feeling cheeky after lunch, so she'd added the names, "Ms Virginia Winston & Mr Brandon Bradford Ayers Benton the III" with an RSVP "yes" as a couple.

* * *

Michael's eyes bulged as he saw the name of his fiancee being linked with her former beau on the RSVP guest list. He stabbed his fork into the pile of vegetation on the plate in front of him.

What was that young pup trying to pull? Infuriated, he picked up the desk phone, jamming his fingers into the rubbery buttons with force enough to push them through to the other side.

The phone rang three times before Brandon's secretary picked up. "Hello, Brandon Benton's office, how may I help you?"

Michael struggled to contain the anger that threatened to boil out of him. "This is Michael Prescott from Everyday People calling for Brandon. I need some information from him about his recent donation to our fund."

The secretary's voice was cool. "Of course, sir. Let me see if he's available."

* * *

"Mr Benton, Michael Prescott's on the phone for you. He says its about your donation…" She stopped speaking, obviously waiting for Brandon's response.

Brandon could not imagine what Michael's problem was. He shook his head and picked up. "Mr. Prescott, how may I help you?"

He turned to face the view he paid a small fortune to rent from Michael, the same man who was his former fiance's current beau. He sighed to himself as he shook his head. "Oh, the tangled webs we weave."

* * *

"Are you coming to our gala this year?" Michael asked as he toyed with the lone tomato the artisan establishment put in as a garnish when they made his lunch. He decided to take a direct approach with this issue.

Brandon's voice on the other end of the line was vacant of any emotion, save an apparent curiosity. "Yes, Sir. I enjoy your charity and it is an advantageous networking opportunity. Plus, it truly changes lives at a time when it is most necessary."

Michael couldn't argue with what Brandon said but it still seemed puzzling to him that she'd placed his name on the guest list as an RSVP yes with her as his companion.

"Did you come last year?" He didn't remember seeing Brandon there. If Brandon was a new invitee, there might be cause for real concern. Was Viriginia considering going back to Brandon?

Brandon seemed shocked. "Yes. I have attended every gala your organization has held, and I'm looking forward to this one."

Michael felt suddenly ashamed. Quite likely, Virginia invited him as her guest every year. Part of her job was getting wealthy donors like Brandon to invest in their work. Fear had made him forget this blatant and enduring truth. How coud he forget that? "We look forward to seeing you again. It was just that your name was missing from the list and considering your…"

Brandon filled in the blanks helpfully. "Family's friendship and constant support." Michael winced at the reminder of how important the support of the Benton family was to his organization, and how little he could afford the loss of that income.

He could hear the smile in Brandon's voice. "I'll be there with bells on my toes."

Michael attempted a jest in return. "Formal attire, Mr. Benton, not costume." He felt suddenly ashamed at his reaction and hung up.

* * *

Brandon shook his head in bewilderment at the conversation that had just ensued. He honestly worried about the older man's mental health. He seemed off lately.

He returned to reading the short biography of one Haillie Prescott. She accomplished a lifetime worth of achievements in the six years before her self-isolation following the spectacularly messy divorce from Michael.

His smile widened and he leaned back in his chair, suddenly connecting the dots between the frantic phone call and the lunch date he'd had with Haillie. Somehow word had gotten around to Michael that he'd spent his lunch with the old dog's ex and it had ruffled his fur.

He knew it was best not to pursue Haillie, but she was magnificent without even trying to be. It was innate to her to be above whatever stuff was happening around her and to come out crisp, smelling like roses, with her grace and dignity intact no matter what happened.

If he were honest with himself, he knew he fell for her the moment she first laughed. There was one small problem: he loved his girlfriend.

The thought of proposing to his girlfriend, Sky, didn't physically make him Ill, but ever since Haillie stirred the first groaning of his discontent, it also didn't sit right with him. Sky deserved better than to be committed to a man who couldn't fully give his heart to her.

"I should let her go. It's the right thing to do. It's the fair thing to do." But letting Sky go when he wasn't sure yet of how things stood with Haillie meant risking being left all alone all over again, and that was something he couldn't bring himself to do. Not yet.

Still, he wondered if this was what it had been like for Virginia when she met Michael. Had she stayed with Brandon as long as she had until she was sure of Michael's affections? Had he been her fall back plan in case that romance hadn't worked? It was a bitter pill to swallow to acknowledge that he was anything like his ex-fiance.

****

Haillie opened her eyes after a five minute nap in the back of the town car. They were still stuck in traffic. She checked her e-mail and planned to make pointless phone calls to fill the gap, staving off boredom with work. She scanned the electronic mail box full of junk, trashing everything except the response she'd received to the event census she sent out to the company.

Scrolling through names, she found herself stopping multiple times at the Brandon Bradford Avery Benton the Third. A dreamy smile stretched itself across her face as she thought about lunch that afternoon.

Dignity and vanity muscled their way past the pearly gates of her dreams. *"You cannot go falling for the same guy that saw your fat butt naked just two days ago,"* the two of them scolded her. *"Besides doesn't he have a girlfriend?"*

Her heart put its hands firmly over her ears and shushed the two killjoys. Grinning from ear to ear, she thought to herself *"I have a crush"* and laughed. She felt like a school girl all over again.

"Are you okay back there?" the driver asked.

"Yes," she glanced down at her watch. It was three o'clock. "Just take me home. I have to be there for Liam."

She half expected Liam to call today with a cocka mamey excuse for another day off so he could play video games. She guessed that she wasn't the cool auntie after all. She didn't have a break up, so there was no reason for a half gallon of ice cream to be screaming her name.

The ringing phone broke her free fall into self wallowing. Appreciation for the mental change of venue filled her with each ring, focusing her mind on fruits instead of frozen dairy sweetness.

"Hello." She mumbled mid-vision of mental fruity goodness.

James's voice interrupted her fruit filled revereries. "Hello, how are you? I saw you this morning. I was just checking in to see how your day went."

She felt suddenly and inexplicably guilty, as if she'd been caught with her hand in the cookie jar. "Everything went well."

He hesitated for a moment. "I didn't see you in the garage today."

She glanced out the window. "I have car service. It is a perk of owning the company that employs me."

They laughed. His voice took on a teasing note. "How is Liam? Has his illness progressed? Will he recover?"

She chuckled. "I haven't heard anything, so no news is good news, I hope?"

She was cautious about hoping for anything, especially when it came to Liam. Liam had too many people involved in his life for her to have a stable enough place to hope for information about his well being.

There was a momentary silence, as if James were waiting for her to say something. When she didn't, he took the lead. "I know you have to work, but I heard you landed another account. I wanted to offer my congrats with a bottle of wine, let's say, maybe around nine this evening."

She grinned. She definitely wouldn't mind a little company. "That all depends on Liam's health."

James's voice kept a casual tone. "If he is home, we'll have wine and since I hear you are good at the RPG you got him last winter, we'll play on teams."

Haillie liked the sound of that. Casual, no commitments, just a little fun. "We don't need him to play. Shall we be a duo against the world tonight?"

James lowered his voice slightly. "As long as I can bring the wine."

Excited, she concurred, "Yes."

Her heart jumped with excitement. He was not good for her. He was a hot-bodied youthful distraction. Definitely not the one for her, but he was fun, and he was young. He was exactly what she needed to soothe her vanity and restore her confidence.

She had lunch with the one earlier. She absently smiled as memories of lunch with Brandon this afternoon came to mind.

Mentally, she compared images of the two men. She felt a guilty pleasure steal over her at the notion of James doing the same over a bottle of wine after a competitive evening of gaming. She couldn't believe that she was even considering a third date with James within twenty four hours.

She knew she was going to end up breaking that boy's heart. But that was a problem for another day. Tonight, she was going to thoroughly enjoy all the energetic attentions that love starved puppy could lavish on her.

****

"Anything for you." James complied without a single fight. He didn't have guts, gelatinous or otherwise, to slosh together for a semblance of courage when it came to her.

It was ironic, considering how much courage he'd mustered just that morning after overhearing her phone call this morning on their ride into work. He had called in a favor on the favor she called in to see the venue she loved.

That favor was going to cost him dearly. He'd just indebted himself to the portion of his life he had to keep from her. He felt so stupid for cashing in those chips to make this happen for her. After just two dates with Ms. Prescott, he was already acting like a love sick puppy and he knew it.

She could have demanded anything of him, and he would have done whatever she asked. His spirits lifted at the notion of seeing her later with a bottle of wine and no Liam.

Maybe she would talk about the exclusive venue she'd booked with hooks for the aerial entertainers, and he could revel in the joy of knowing he made that happen. It would be his little secret.

The line went dead on his evening and his conversation. He was texting Haillie before the dialogue was completed and postponing the glass of wine.

****

"What do you mean he left early?" Haillie stared at the school receptionist. She couldn't ascertain if it was a genuine sickness or just another skipping attempt without more information.

The woman was obviously uncomfortable. "Miss….Prescott." The lady blushed. "You are permitted to have information about Liam on a case-by-case basis only with written permission from his parents or a guardian."

Haillie understood. She had given up any and all rights to a parental status when she deadbolted and locked the door on her house and didn't open it again for ten years, but it still irked her. "Fine. I'll call his mother. She can fax over her permission."

She walked off, concentrating on anything but the woman's last syllables. She knew this wouldn't be a problem for long. Both Lisa and Michael were as eager for her to pick Liam up as she was to do it.

She took just five steps in the direction of her open town car door when she received a phone call from Michael. "I'm so glad you called."

Michael's voice sounded strangely smug. "We are congregating this evening to go over your full pitch. You will, of course, be expected to attend."

She felt like she'd been sucker punched in the gut. The contract she'd signed required that she must have flexible availability and be wholly committed to the event. There was no way to back out of this without losing the contract.

She felt suddenly angry. "You picked up Liam from school didn't you?"

He'd sent her here to cheat her of time she needed to prepare that presentation. "I'm sorry. It must have slipped my mind. Liam had an early appointment at the doctor's office."

His voice sounded anything but contrite. She restrained herself from a sudden urge to curse at Michael as she shut the car door. She contented herself with slamming the car door as the driver jogged around the car and tucked himself behind the wheel.

"Where to, ma'm?" He shut the driver door tightly and looked to her for verification.

"We're going back to the office," she announced above the external city noises.

Frowning into the reflective surface of her aviator sunglasses, she reminisced about the peaceful solitude of the last ten years before she'd allowed her sister Rose to convince her to return to the land of the living before her company was as dead as her social life had been. That time was becoming more paradisaic by the moment.

As they pulled away from the curb of the school and into the flow of traffic, though, Haillie damned the flow of self-pity and became a cerebral creature of logic once again. Her misstep this morning that led to a private meeting with Brandon meant she couldn't check off the venue decor as she'd planned.

She was going to need liquor. To keep the budget small, she would suggest a rail bar or wine and beer option. This morning, she was thinking of a signature cocktail for the event. A lightbulb went off in her head as she thought of the perfect bartender, someone reliable she'd worked with at previous events. She just hoped they were still in the business. She made a mental note to call them right away.

It was a weekday, so most of the DJ's she knew should be available. A full painted canvas picture started coming together in her mind. It was going to be a crowd-pleasing presentation for all, if she could get some help. She started to hit the speed dial to ring up Rose, but she thought better of using her sister for this.

This had to be professional, and that meant she had to do it alone. Otherwise, she would call in the Calvary, Candy and Justin, associate members of her firm. They, along with the senior coordinator, had kept the business going profitably so she could keep paying the bills. Unfortunately, with Haillie in seclusion, they just hadn't had the social connections to keep getting the big events that kept their firm's name in the papers.

Besides that weekend, her firm had two events: a cocktail party for the local zoo and a country themed wedding in urban surroundings. They had their hands full. This was her burden to bear. She signed her name on the dotted line and accepted the job for herself, not for the firm.

Dialing with lightning speed, she crossed her fingers and connected to Lisa's phone. Skipping the cordial greetings, she introduced herself in a way she was confident would get Lisa's attention. "Would you like to stick it to Micahel?"

"Of course I would." Lisa was elbow deep in flour pastry and greasy fried foods. The heavy scent of coffee clung to the polo fabric she wore. She patted down some biscuits before checking on the rolls rising in the bowl nearby. "How are you planning to do it?"

Haillie's voice was filled with a heady combination of determination, resentment, and sadistic glee. "I need you to help me finish a full presentation for the event. Michael is demanding I present it all tonight by 7 pm. This is a ploy to terminate my contract."

Lisa suddenly understood why Haillie was calling. She laughed. "Everyone expected the two of you would have a tumultuous time working together." She covered the bulging mound of dough again, allowing it to continue rising.

"He's being impetuous trying to get you fired this early. No one's going to go along with him. He should know that." She wasn't worried. Michael often threw temper tantrums that went nowhere and did nothing except allow him to blow off steam. They were usually more for show than anything else.

Haillie didn't sound reassured. "What if I can be proven incompetent? Doesn't the chair have permission to fire me in that case?"

Lisa waved over a fellow employee. She pointed toward the stainless steel bowl containing the growing lump of bread and whispered, "Take care of this."

Turning back to the phone conversation, she consoled Hailee. "You were almost done when I left you this afternoon. What did you have left? Flowers, food, entertainment, and decor?"

Lisa walked back toward the office, taking a seat on a piano stool and listening for the soft click of the lock while Haillie drolled on about her worries over her contract's cancellation. "What do you want me to do?"

She heard Haillie take a deep breath. "You have access to decorations and food right?"

Lisa reluctantly agreed. "Yes."

Haillie's words came out in a rush. "Can you do the place up with a few examples of what we discussed today?"

Lisa shook her head. "There's not enough time."

Haillie pleaded with her. "If you do this, I will owe you. Big time. Do you like your current job?"

The answer to that one was a no brainer. "No."

Haillie made her an offer Lisa never dreamed she would ever be made. "I have a vacancy since I'll be out of the office often. If you want the job, it's yours."

Lisa spun around taking in the office's four walls and the sole drab calendar that was two years out of date. This office was the size of a flea bag. If she could come through for Haillie tonight, she could secure herself an office with enough space to stretch her legs without touching the dull blue hue of the painted walls. Work might become more bearable

This was the undeniable chance of a lifetime,

and Lisa was not stupid. She was going to take it. "What does it pay?"

Haillie's words were music to her ears. "I promise it will be more than double whatever you're making where you are and it will come with full health, dental, and eye care benefits. Plus, it comes with an office with a triple set of bay windows. Make it happen for me, and I'll let you have your pick."

Lisa readily said "Yes." Jotting down a note to explain her reason for leaving she was done here. No more double shifts and swing schedules.

No more late nights and being on her feet all day. She was done with that. "I'll bring the papers for employment and the contract with the tax forms tonight, is that okay?"

Haillie agreed. "Yeah. Sure."

Lisa pulled up a website and began entering in her credit card number for thirty day free rental purchases from the rent-a-center. She called Pinkie, her cousin, who worked at a moving company to go pick the stuff up. Her next call was to Mo, the store manager. He happily filled out the forms for her so everything would be ready for pick up and signature upon arrival.

Waving goodbye to her co-workers, she informed her boss that she would not be closing tonight and pushed the shop door open. Evening air caressed her face, and brought a smile to her lips. Her new found freedom tasted sweet.

****

Rose walked in the door when Lisa called. "Are you coming tonight?"

Rose was exhausted. "I'll be there. I'm just stopping to change clothes. What I don't understand is what's so important? Why is Michael calling this meeting tonight?"

Lisa paused. "Haillie didn't tell you?"

Rose stopped in her tracks. "Tell me what?"

Lisa took a deep breath. "Michael's forcing Haillie to give a full presentation for the Gala tonight. If she doesn't present, he can legally cancel her contract."

Rose felt a measure of anger she'd not felt since she'd first learned about Michael's affair more than ten years ago. She'd just gotten Haillie out of her self-imposed dungeon and back to life. She was not about to let Michael snatch that away from her sister. "Thanks for letting me know."

Chapter 19

Michael stood in the doorway of the conference room gleefully surveying the plot where he would bury his former wife's career. She couldn't Phoenix her way out of this one. He thumbed the key in his pocket that he'd thoughtfully wrapped for her.

His gift was a new door with an electronic key to the brownstone so she could be secure with her therapist when she returned to her three level agoraphobic den. He would get her out of her own world and sociable again in about a year, just in time to watch him commit to a monogamous lifetime with Virginia, so she could feel special.

A revisit to Haillie's sheets would be just what he needed by then. She would be a woman with sense to chat to before he headed home to Virginia. A secondary thought slipped into mental focus. He would have her master bathroom remodeled since he would be showering there.

A twinge of guilt pricked him, but it was Virginia's idea to run her out of the office and watch her business fall apart. His fiancee might be an infant, but she was an infant with sharp teeth who was good at sinking those teeth into other people's lives and ripping them apart.

He was beaming after the useful relationship time they'd spent together after lunch. Nodding in agreement with the devious twist on their plan, he turned off the light and started back toward his dinner with his golf buddies.

****

Haillie came crashing through the door in a dead heat sprint, racing against time. Time, as always, had an early lead but Haillie was confident she could beat the clock. It was unlikely since there were only thirty ticks of the minute hand between her and unemployment.

Dashing into the bedroom to grab a fresh garment for her presentation and some emergency twinkle lights from the bottom of the closet in a box to the left of the shoes she was going to wear, she gathered a few more necessities.

She snatched up two vases off the kitchen counter that could hold the weight of the center pieces and a box for the vases. Yanking the clothing off the hanger with such force that some of the inferior plastic ones snapped in half.

She gathered up her clothing and started down the stairs where she received a shock. "Liam! What the . . .? Does your mom. . . ? Where did you ...?"

A powder blue dress shirt hung from a hanger slung over his right khaki pocket. His hair was tossed to the side and his smile played off his puppy dog eyes. He answered her with a pout. "Are you going to finish any of those questions, or is this reverse Jeopardy?"

Haillie didn't have time for this. "Don't be sardonic. It isn't attractive. Liam, what are you doing here?" She shoved the square cardboard object holding the two vases into Liam's free arm. The other hand held the single backpack strap on his left shoulder. "Take that." She demanded, knocking him back a step.

He gave her an insolent salute. "Yes ma'am." He walked out the door, carrying the box to the open trunk of the idling town car. "Anything else or can I get in?"

She didn't have time to answer him. Skipping and leaping over steps to shave milliseconds off the time, she tucked and rolled her way into the vehicle, not bothering to wait for the door to shut behind her. She slammed it closed and screamed, "Drive! Drive! Drive."

Burning rubber and screeching tires announced their entrance into traffic. The driver sped, obliterating obstacles with hairpin turns that demonstrated his skilled driving.

Haillie clutched tightly the handles on the side of the car. "Don't kill us." She wailed as her small shears hand trimmed the flowers and arranged them in the vases. The stems of one of the snowball plants were layered over plain carnations, baby breath, and white roses she had the house cleaner pluck off the shelf at the local grocery store two days ago.

If she couldn't get a florist to do a centerpiece, she could throw one together. She just hoped it fooled everyone for an hour or two.

The car came hurtling into the garage, barely stopping for the gate, slamming on brakes at the door for the stairs. Tumbling out of the car, with her arms full, she secured the vase firmly in the hand of her reluctant helper.

James opened the gate without checking the occupants, but now that he could see who it was he was taken back. "Haillie!" His voice echoed through the lower level.

She turned around to see James jogging toward the trio. Out of breath, he filled them in on a vital piece of information: Michael locked the place up tight and would not be back for another twenty minutes or so.

Tears of frustration glinted in the corner of Haillie's eyes. "So you are telling me he is going to be late to the meeting he called on a technicality he added to my contract?"

James grimaced. "Yes."

The air seemed to go out of Haillie. She signaled Liam to stuff the boxes back in the trunk. She was through.

James extended a cord and a ring loaded down with keys. He shook them to get her attention. "But I could let you in the building."

"Thanks. Give me a hug!" She ordered and he followed her instructions.

"Liam with me" he instructed "We have to hustle."

The boys and the driver started hauling the things up to the conference room. James was a continuous cheerleader, pepping the guys up and verbally quickening their stride.

Haillie accepted James's offer to do the job of pushing the button to open the gates for any other guests. The cars with the catered food and ordered plates showed up. Haillie's hand hovered over the grimy green button encased in metal around its circular figure.

Three vehicles dropped off scrumptious dishes with the instructions to tell the guys at the entrance know it goes into the kitchen. By the time Lisa showed up with her truck and crew of fifteen, Haillie was swapping kisses with James while reading her incoming text saying: "We have no staff available."

When she started this, expecting perfection was not on her mind. She was just figuring out how to plug the holes in the boat of her sinking career. Now that things were coming together, though, she wanted perfection. Picturing how she would smear Micheal's face in his miscalculation of her resourcefulness was powering her to do the impossible.

****

The long face Haillie wore as she scuffled toward the concrete sidewalk to go upstairs caught James's attention. He wanted to fix whatever was killing the triumphant spirit she just had, but he had to let out the cars that came in and allow access to the ones beeping at him to get into the place. The importance of the steady flow in and exit of traffic was a crucial part of keeping her operation moving smoothly.

When he got a moment, he would call her to see what had gone wrong, but as the minutes ticked by, the desire became overwhelming. He picked up the phone. "Hey, what's wrong?"

He intermittently pressed the button allowing the gate to open or close while waiting for her answer. Her voice sounded so defeated when she finally answered him. "I need waiters to really make it pop."

James knew exactly who to contact. "I'll take care of that. Ask Lisa if she'll switch jobs with me until I can get this taken care of for you." He hoped his confidence would cheer her up.

She sounded hopeful, but skeptical at the same time. "How do you propose to get that done? Who do you know?"

He knew she was secretly beating herself up over this, and it was such a trivial matter. "Go upstairs and finish up." He smiled at her over the phone, hoping it would come through in his voice. He was trying to keep her spirits up.

****

Haillie jogged up the stairs. The furnishings Lisa was unloading were in the elevator and there was no room for her to fit. Sweat dripped off her chin and a sheen formed on her face. She cursed herself for the lack of exercise just as she caught a second wind on the third floor.

The rhythmic huffing and puffing was the instrumental beat her feet patted to as she climbed the stairs. Exiting the dark dungeon cavern corner the building designers stuck the stairs in, Haillie looked around at the chaise, chair, and couch lining the hallway.

She started yelling orders down the corridor and the crew flew into action rearranging the office quarters. The couch went into the conference room against the farthest tan colored wall. The chaise was placed against the adjoining wall. Haillie draped mosquito netting around the chair, creating a small sheer alcove as she mingled strands of the twinkle lights from her closet within the bundles of sheer fabric and spaced large electronic candles as mood lighting.

The conference table was pushed to the side and Lisa brought in the rolling chairs with the help of the crew down the hall from Haillie's office. Haillie had a quick word about how to fit all those chairs in her matchbox office area with Lisa and then shared her vision for the presentation space.

The team under her management got to work bringing her vision to life. Standing back, Haillie observed and appraised the skill of her new hire. If there were any inadequacies in Lisa's skills, she wanted to make note of them and pass them along to the senior coordinator.

This was the least she could do , since she had been running the place for the last ten years and now Haillie had not only taken over but hired someone without her counsel. Tomorrow was not going to be a good staff relations day. Pushing these stray thoughts out of her head, she proceeded with the preparations.

****

James had finished up his preliminary role and made a quick call he regretted making to explain the truthfulness of a rumor that would drag him back kicking and screaming to a lifestyle he abhorred.

Doom's bell tolled once ...,twice...,thrice..; he was about to hang up when a disheveled voice that was barely alert after a hurried awakening spoke. "What do you want? It's past my bedtime."

Desperation rose as he spoke. "I need some help with a dinner party. May I use your account and charge it to you? It's a culinary emergency. I have to impress Ms.Prescott."

The voice on the other end of the line perked up like they'd just had three shots of espresso. "Why certainly, son. I'll have your mom make the call."

He could hear his father shaking his wife of thirty years awake. "Ms Prescott, dear! Our son is dating Ms Prescott." The pride in his father's voice was unmistakable and James felt a growing knot in the pit of his stomach. He knew very well which Ms Prescott his father assumed he was dating, and his mother was going to be terribly disappointed when she uncovered the truth.

His mother picked up the phone. "Where do I send them?"

He gave her the address of his place of employment by rote. He could tell from the sound of her voice she wanted an explanation. Concern entered her voice. "I'm assuming you have something amazing in mind. Do not cut corners when courting Ms.Prescott."

He suppressed the urge to reach through the phone and strangle her. He did not have time for this. "Believe me, I'm not cutting any corners. Just make sure they are here on time. It's crucial to my plans for the evening. Thanks, Mom. Bye!"

He was going to owe them big time now. It was only a matter of when they would call in that debt due in full. He cringed at the thought, but hoped that perhaps they would forget.

Either way, he couldn't wait to tell Haillie the good news. He would deal with his mother's disappointment over helping the "wrong" Ms Prescott when the time came.

****

Haillie was frantically affixing the high quality plastic lightweight chandelier to the ceiling when the phone rang. She picked up, fearing for the worst, and was pleasantly surprised to hear James say the magic words. "Help is on the way. You'll have everything you need."

She exhaled. Ever since the moment she'd realized what she was missing it had been eating away at her. Any creative glitch needled at her. It could all be the difference between keeping her contract and losing it, and she could not afford to lose it.

Relieved by his news, she got back to work. It was much easier to go over the plans for any last-minute details that needed to be attended to when her mind was peaceful and calm. She rolled a chair to the door of the room she'd fixed up and sat looking back at the festive elegance that her tasteful touches and Lisa's hard work had created.

A small sigh of satisfaction resonated through her body and out of her lips. Everything was accomplished. There was no way the board could find fault with her work tonight.

The elevator door opened as her lips shut. Three men and a woman walked out dressed in monkey suits with full tails. They looked around the office before spotting the room with a soft glow emanating from it and made a beeline in her direction.

Haillie gave them a bright smile and delivered preliminary instructions for their evening. They lined up along the counter in the coffee break room, trays at the ready, prepared to serve the moment she gave the command.

The first to arrive was a construction worker covered in dust so thick it turned the denim fabric of his jeans tan. A trail of sawdust and drywall particles followed in his wake. His booming hello, accompanied by a hardy smack on the back, was a welcome to either the beginning of her happiest ever after or a new low in her career. She wasn't sure which.

She showed him to a wooden chair around the covered, decorated conference table, then sat down to ask him about his day. He rambled happily on until the bulk of the expected guests rolled into the room. Rose was the last to arrive. She pulled Haillie to the nearest corner.

Her eyebrows were raised. "You did this with two hours notice?" Rose swept her up into her arms and squeezed her. Whispering in her ear with a few tears falling she mumbled, "I'm so proud of you."

****

Rose patted her sister on the back, "They can't scream about nepotism after seeing this. You went above and beyond."

She reached out for another hug. "This is amazing." She gazed about at the marvelous soft touches around the room. It was a garden of opposites her eyes were taking in. Haillie had completed a miracle.

Lisa tapped Haillie to get her attention. "We make a good team. Do I get the job?"

Haillie raised an eyebrow. "Do I look like Michael to you? If I promise you a job, you get a job." She laughed to soften things a bit. "You did incredible work today helping me to pull this together."

Haillie was confused by Lisa 's distrustful comments until Lisa gave her a sideways look. "You were observing me like a boss with a pink slip in mind. I know the look. I have worn it many times myself."

Haillie nodded. "You caught me. I was observing how you handled the stress, but not to take your job before you even began. I wanted to see how much training you would need so I could advise my team, but you are good, exceptionally skilled at supervision and organization with a sharp designer's eye."

****

Lisa blushed and thanked Haillie before beating a hasty retreat out of sight for a phone call. She had to check on Liam. He was old enough to care for himself, but the mischief he could get himself into while she was absent was worse than an unsupervised toddler.

She entered the digits and waited. Heavy bass laced rhythmic beats bounced through the air. The other members of the board were milling about with jaw dropping expressions. They did not hear the melody playing, but Lisa's ears perked up. That ring tone was suspiciously close by.

Her eyes sought out the source, knowing that Liam would not be far from it. She watched

Liam flip his phone over. He stood beside the DJ, getting a detailed lesson in beat synchronization. His face looked the happiest she'd seen him in a long while.

She knew he didn't want to take her call, but Lisa was more than a little unhappy that he wouldn't consider it might be something important. The DJ was bopping his head to the beat of an early release pop song, an exclusive track only he could play for the crowd.

Lisa tapped Liam on the shoulder. He whirled around, clearly irritated, until he realized it was his mother standing there. "Ms Haillie said I could come and help her with the music."

Lisa sighed heavily. "Did you finish your homework for the evening?"

Liam rolled his eyes. "Yeah, Mom. I did the homework already. Can I get back to work on the music?"

A slow ballad replaced the throbbing, bass-laden beat. "You have ten minutes to get your homework for each subject and show me what you've done."

Liam groaned. "Mom, please can't we just focus on the important stuff for tonight?" Lisa glared at him. "School is the important stuff. You get good grades in school, you get into a good college, and you don't have to wind up like me. I don't want you to ever have to work as hard as I do to make ends meet, and you know you can't count on your father to be there for you."

She watched Liam stomp off toward his backpack as the DJ played the next song. He had no idea how good he had it. No idea at all.Lisa thought.

****

Rose sought out her sister once more, armed with a brand new concern. She excused herself from the small group of four that were standing around her and grabbed her sister as she passed. "Hey did you think about your presentation? Where are you going to set it up?"

Haillie gestured at everything she'd put together over the last few hours. "This is my presentation."

Rose stared at her. "You are going to need the numbers for the charity night, and those numbers have to match the budget. None of the work you've done will matter a single iota if you go over budget by as much as a penny."

Haillie handed her a drink and patted her back. "Don't worry. I have all the numbers and the receipts for this." The blood drained from her sister's face and her eyes widened. Concern crept in, replacing her confidence. "I don't have charts. Am I going to need charts?"

Just that fast, Haillie went from calm and collected to frazzled and on the verge of a panic attack. Rose recognized the symptoms.

Haillie looked over at her. "The clothes? Did you remember the clothes for Lisa? If she's going to be an employee, she's got to look the part."

Rose gave her sister what she hoped was a reassuring smile. "It's all in the hall closet next to the break room."

Rose watched as her sister marched down the hall, pausing just long enough to instruct her culinary soldiers to go forth and conquer the tastebuds of the guests in the room." She returned with the bag of clothes, which she handed off to Lisa.

Lisa's voice was filled with a surprising amount of enthusiasm as she accepted Haillie's offering. Rose wondered what Haillie had offered the woman to bring about such a remarkable change in attitude. "Thank you so much, Haillie. You won't regret it."

Rose could only hope that Lisa was right about that. For Haillie's sake.

****

Virginia sat in the back of the chauffeured Mercedes ruminating over her role in the little plan that Micheal cooked up. She was as trusted and twice as devious as Haillie.

Her eyes narrowed as she thought of her rival. First, she'd caught Michael's eyes, and now it seemed she was stealing Brandon away, too? Of course, that last part wasn't a certainty and it didn't bother her quite as much as the obvious problems she was causing with Michael, but it was further proof that the witch had to go.

She'd made a mistake in siding with the board on hiring her in the first place. She'd thought that having Haillie around would make Michael appreciate her more. He'd always spoken about her with loathing and disdain.

She hadn't understood it back then. She'd felt sorry for the poor woman. She'd seemed so weak willed and harmless, stuck like some old maid, wasting away in that cheap brownstone cottage of hers.

Virginia still couldn't figure out what had happened. The Haillie that showed up to work at Everyday People was not that same woman. This Haillie was charismatic, confident, and seemed to win over everyone she met. Even Tracey, her loyal ally in her battles against Michael, seemed taken by her.

A smug smile of satisfaction crossed her lips as she thought about Haillie being banished from the halls of Everyday People in abject disgrace. It would be the end of her company and the end of her career. A few choice words in the right ears and Virginia would make sure Haillie was never able to secure another contract from anyone who mattered ever again.

She would banish that little nobody back to her crumbling cottage and Michael would be hers again. Brandon would continue to be her little side plaything that she took out whenever Michael needed a reminder of how desirable she was and how easy it was for her to find a lover that wasn't nearly twice her age. The fact that Brandon had money enough to almost match Michael's was a bonus. It meant he would take that threat seriously instead of just cutting her off.

****

Micheal couldn't take his eyes off Virginia, especially when she was in her element. Usually he found her witty, conniving activities stimulating. When he first heard the plan, he thought it was too simplistic and direct. There was no way the Haillie he knew wouldn't step up and exceed expectations when faced with this sort of challenge.

After Virginia gave her a long list of Haillie's shortcomings, her lack of contacts, and cast doubts about her abilities after such a prolonged absence, though, he was swayed. There was a part of him that hoped Virginia would have to eat her words and bow to Haillie's will, if only because he chafed under the heels of Virginia's slender stilletos that seemed to have him so thoroughly under her control.

He wasn't ready to acknowledge the flicker of a flame that rose up at the thought of Haillie's slender waist and voluminous backside. The woman he'd fallen in love with more than 14 years ago was returning from the brownstone grave where he'd buried her after their divorce.

Her presence haunted him, taunting him with images of what they'd once been. He wasn't ready for that. He needed to put her back in the ground, bury her back in that townhouse where their marriage had breathed its last breath, before he forgot and made a mistake he couldn't undo.

He was sure that the woman to his left was much stronger than the woman in his office and if she succeeded tonight, Haillie would be destroyed. She would disappear from the office and he could go back to hating her for the weak thing she was. Their car pulled up to the curb and the driver got out to open the door. James waved at them from the gate.

****

"In consideration of your generous donations, the Experienced People Charitable Foundation invites you to enjoy a sneak peek of this year's gala on behalf of our new event coordinator, Haillie Prescott. The festivities begin at 7 pm sharp."

Brandon read the text message and raised an eyebrow. He knew for a fact that Virginia was not the formal events coordinator for the charity. Normally, he wouldn't have considered going to something Virginia had thrown together, but the thought of an opportunity to spend time in close proximity to Haillie brought a smile to his lips. He sent a text "yes" as quickly as his wifi connection would allow him.

He felt a moment of guilt as he thought about Sky. He'd promised they would stay in tonight and spend time together. She wasn't home yet.

Temptation tugged at his heart. He promised himself that he wouldn't stay long, just long enough to show Haillie his support and make his presence known. He didn't feel like cooking anyway. That was one thing he missed about Virginia: she could cook up a mean omelette. It was the only dish her nanny taught her.

He wrote a hasty note to Sky, explaining his absence, pocketed his keys, and headed toward the garage. Twenty minutes later, Brandon watched from the parking garage as Michael opened the door for Virginia. He cut the motor to his Maybach and reflected on how much Virginia had changed over the years.

Back when he was dating her, she never minded playing a game of horseshoes or tossing back a few beers with the guys. She'd been just as at home in a pair of jeans and a concert t-shirt as she was in the Prada and Gucci she tended to sport these days.

He missed their friendship more than he missed her body. She'd been a dynamite pool hustler with a mean right hook and a wicked sense of humor. She'd been his best friend.

That woman had disappeared with Michael coming back into her life. Virginia was all polite nods and polished waves these days. Her hair, her makeup, and her nails were all as perfect as her clothing and shoes. Nothing was out of place.

He felt sure that Michael had never seen the real Virginia. He pitied the man. He didn't know what he was missing. As painful as it was to have lost Virginia to Michael, he realized she'd done him a favor. She'd set him free to find someone real, someone he could depend on to always be there for him, someone who would be content with him just the way he was.

****

Haillie exited the event to check on the first round of appetizers to be passed out to the guests. They looked adorable in their mini cupcake liners. It wasn't five star quality for sure, but it was something.

Her next stop: Dinner. She moved across the kitchen to talk to the chef, who was arguing animatedly with a server. "Plates, idiota! Where are the plates to dish all this food onto?"

Haillie's heart stopped. Had Lisa remembered the food but forgotten something as basic as plates and utensils? Surely not. A mad dash through the cupboards should produce a solution.

She scrounged up just enough plates of the same size and color to serve the board and breathed a sigh of relief. Twenty plates for less than twenty guests. They weren't ideal, but they would do.

The search was fruitful but took up a good chunk of her time. She was confident Lisa could handle things from here. She needed to be out there glad handing board members and making sure the h'ors d'oeuvres didn't run out.

"Lisa!" She called as she walked out of the kitchen and down the hallway, searching for her new assistant. To her horror and surprise, when she came back into the party room, the crowd numbered in the thirties and was climbing.

Among the crowd she recognized several notable event bloggers and a sparse sprinkling of journalists, along with a handful of key donors. Haillie wanted to scream. The plastic plates and dinnerware would suffice for board members, but was in no way going to impress these new additions.

****

Virginia extended her arm as she walked toward the elevators as a way of telling Michael to get his old bones moving. She had places to be. Namely, inside, reaping the rewards of her mental labors.

Brandon stepped up to join them. She gave the necessary polite wave, as if a certain kiss that she'd shared with him that morning had never happened at all. She absently wondered where his girlfriend was.

The three stepped onto the elevator and Virginia pushed the button to the boardroom floor. She spotted Haillie standing there outside the softly lit meeting room and quickly enveloped her in a hug. It was the best position to slip the knife into her back.

"Sweetie!" She cooed. "I thought you might appreciate some exposure. I invited a few people over to join us, along with some of our friends who will take all the right pictures for you. I hope you don't mind. It'll be great publicity for the charity. I know that the gossip scene isn't going to want to miss the Former and Future Mrs Prescott throwing a little get together."

She could feel Haillie tense in her arms and released her, keeping a benevolent smile on her face as she slipped an arm around Haillie's shoulder and turned her to face the journalist who was, even now, aiming his camera their direction.

****

A sickening feeling of dread ate away at Haillie's stomach. It was the feeling of inevitable doom. She wasn't prepared for extra guests. There might be dinner enough for forty if they scaled down the portions, but there was not enough flatware for that many guests.

She was going to look like she was unprepared. The event bloggers wouldn't care that she'd been set up. They wouldn't take pity on her for being betrayed. All they would see was the sloppy presentation. Her business, her credibility, would be ruined.

There might be a 24-hour convenience store she could buy a few sets of dishes from, but that would take time she didn't have, and while the quality would be better than the plates she had and plastic cutlery, it would still raise eyebrows. The donors and event bloggers were used to being served on fine china.

She forced a smile to her lips when Virginia turned her toward the camera of one particularly obnoxious blogger. She'd gotten used to playing pretend as the spouse of Michael Prescott. Eyes were always on them, and there was never an opportunity to let her guard down and just be herself. She didn't miss that life, she realized suddenly.

Thinking about that life, she remembered a wedding gift Michael particularly loved. He'd left it in his office for use during special occasions and luncheons with donors. It was a set of gold rimmed porcelain dishes, a box of antique silverware, and crystal water goblets to match. Everything she needed to save this situation was down the hall in Michael's office. All she had to do to get to it was get the key from Michael. Her mind drew her attention to a more pressing, quite literally, problem: Michael's warm hand on the small of her back, his lips ever so softly whispering in her ear. She took a step to the side, hoping to remove the hand, and felt it still there. She was sufficiently distracted by the erotic feel of the whispered words that she didn't even hear what they were saying.

She became aware of Michael staring at her as if she were a daft cow. He smiled at the audience in front of them and cleared his throat, beginning again. "This is my wife, Haillie Prescott."

She raised an eyebrow and noted Virginia's smile beginning to fade. She wondered if Michael realized his Freudian slip was showing. Should she correct the record or let it pass? She didn't have time to think it over. A response was expected.

"It's truly a pleasure. I do apologize for being distracted earlier. It's a challenge to both keep an eye on things and socialize." She gave them a broad smile she hoped would keep any questions they might have at bay.

The heads in front of her bobbed in understanding. "So what do you think of what I said?" One of them asked.

She smiled and nodded. "I'm sure Michael can tell you more about it than I can." She unhooked herself from Michael's grasp. "I'll just be a minute."

His unexpected kiss on her forehead and orders to hurry back sparked something deep within her. She gave him a brief smile as a light long extinguished turned itself on in her lighthouse of romance.

It wasn't a warm, welcoming light. It was a light warning her of the jagged rocks hiding beneath the warm currents now skimming over the tops of the turbulent issues that caused their break up.

****

Michael moved into position without thought and kissed her forehead, agreeing she should hasten her return trip to his side. It was like old times. Haillie was like an appendage, a part of him that he commanded, moving with grace and answering without coaching. He was confident she would hold him up and support whatever move he chose to make.

As he watched Haillie saunter off to take care of whatever business she needed to attend to, he mentally compared her to Virginia. A frown replaced the smile and he felt himself tense.

None of those things could be said about Virginia. She was a child, and he was constantly needing to direct her like a parent. She couldn't be trusted to act on her own, let alone hold him up or support him when he needed it.

Micheal felt a sudden pang of regret for his part in this and considered warning Haillie about Virginia's planned climax to the evening. Was there a way to warn her without implicating himself?

****

Brandon entered the thirty four person gathering behind Virginia. He watched her embrace Haillie and say something to her. Haillie's face drained of color but she plastered a smile on her face and turned to face the room. He wondered what it was Virginia had said.

He didn't fail to notice Michael's hand on the small of Haillie's back, or the way he called her his "wife" instead of his "ex-wife." He could tell by the sour look on Virginia's face that she hadn't failed to notice these things either.

He waited until the frenzy of picture taking was through and Haillie had departed before approaching Virginia. He vigorously shook her hand and gave her a hug. "You did a great job here. I"m impressed that you did all this for Haillie."

Her forced laugh might sound genuine to ears that hadn't spent significant amounts of time in her company, but he recognized it as a laugh for the audience that surrounded her. She was not happy about the situation. "As I was telling these gentlemen," she swept her hand in a semi-circle to encompass the five men whose gazes were on her, "Good deeds begin at home."

They nodded in agreement as if she'd invented the phrase. He gave her a pat on the back and went off in search of Haillie. As he moved toward the doorway, he instead found himself nudged aside by Michael. Irritated, he decided that causing a scene would not do her any favors.

****

Rose's eyes lit up as Trevor, the Adonis from her building, entered the room right before Michael presented Haillie for an impromptu speech. She wanted to jet over to him, but respect for her sister kept her rooted to the spot where she stood, listening intently to every word Haillie spoke without blinking.

Her eyes, however, never left him. He was smartly dressed and, although his feet were firmly planted on the floor, she could tell he wasn't paying attention to the bland speech. His eyes were searching the faces in the crowd, as if he were looking for something. A sudden thought crossed her mind. Maybe he wasn't searching for something. Maybe he was searching for someone. Maybe he was here, looking for her. That thought was immediately followed by another. How would he know she worked here?

Come to think of it, how was he here at all? Was he a donor? She'd attended all the galas they'd ever held. She was pretty sure she would have remembered that face if he'd ever been to one before. Then again, not all of the donors attended the past year's galas. Maybe he was a new donor.

That must be it. He couldn't possibly be here for her. He must be a new donor. It was just a coincidence. That was all. Still, she found her heart hoping that maybe, just maybe, she was wrong.

****

Trevor's eyes swept the room, looking around to see if anyone else was as enthralled by the hot speaker's magnanimous gestures and thinly veiled venomous words as Rose seemed to be. He was vaguely curious to know what the sweetheart party diva could have possibly done to rate such ire, but he found himself more interested in Rose.

The way she stood there reminded him of a Greek statue, full rich curves practically inviting a man to touch and explore them. Some women's bodies were naturally designed to be sexually alluring to a man, and Rose was one of those women.

Those generous curves bent together into a luscious indentation at her waist before blossoming into a full backside. Everything about her sparked desire in him. He found himself mentally comparing her to last month's ex-girlfriend.

The thought brought on a fresh, agonizing pain. That woman's fuller figure was paired with devilish fun, a come hither voice, soft plush shoulders, and minx-like bedroom antics that held him spellbound for so long he hadn't thought it possible to consider another woman.

That was before he'd discovered that he wasn't her one-and-only. He was the one she came to when her heart was wounded and her vanity needed soothing after some perceived slight from her preferred lover. That lover, Brandon, was standing next to Rose.

He felt a knot forming in his stomach. Was Rose with Brandon? Where was Sky?

As the speech ended, he casually sauntered over to Rose with a careless, laid-back shuffle, trying to pretend he didn't care and that it didn't matter to him. He forced his posture to relax, his arms dangling at his side and swaying back and forth like a hammock in the breeze. He tried to mentally prepare himself for this encounter.

Brandon disappeared into the shrinking crowd. A gentleman with a large gut hanging over his belt stood casually chatting with Rose. He wore a blue shirt, khakis, and dockers. It was a bit conservative for his liking, but the man was considerably older.

Trevor held his breath, waiting his turn to speak to her. Before he got his opportunity, she darted into the darkened hallway. Trevor decided to follow after her, hoping to get her alone.

****

"Rose! I need your help." Haillie's voice called to her from the hallway. Rose slipped out the door as soon as Michael's back was turned to her. Haillie was standing in the supply closet.

She gestured to Rose and shut the door behind
her.

"What do you need?" Rose wanted to get back
to the party. She wanted to talk to Trevor and
find out what he was doing there, but her sister's
career was on the line. If she needed help, Rose
could delay what she wanted until after she
secured her sister's future.

"I need the keys to Michael's office." Haillie
hissed.

Rose grimaced. "What on earth for? You know
what will happen if I get caught, right? We're
both going to get fired."

Haillie gave Rose her best puppy dog eyes.
"Please. I can't serve these people on paper
plates with plastic cutlery. You know what will
happen if I do. Michael's got a set of dishes that
will be perfect right in his office. We can put
them all back when we're done."

Rose sighed, closed her eyes, and fished out the
set of office keys from her pocket. She held
them out without looking at Haillie. "You know

I'm no good at lying. I can't see you taking these."

She heard the jingle of the keys and felt the tug on her fingers and let go. She waited until she heard footsteps disappearing down the hallway to turn off the lights and head out the door.

"I thought you would never come out here." A strangely familiar voice spoke from the darkened, shadowed outline of a man. She strained her eyes, trying to see who it was, and fought back her irrational fears of rape and murder as the man stepped closer to her.

"Who are you?" She noted the absent weight of her purse at her side and, therefore, the absence of the pepper spray she kept on a keychain. She cursed herself twice over.

Taking a half step back toward the pounding bass and safety of the numbers gathered in the impromptu party she queried her predator again, this time adding "What do you want?"

The voice creepily answered "You."

Rose felt her breath catch in her throat. Her worst nightmares were coming true. She wondered if she would have time to scream and then wondered if anyone would hear her over the blare of the music if she did.

Rose decided that honesty was the best policy. "Me? I'm pretty sure you don't. I mean, I'm at least 50 pounds overweight and I talk too much and there are a lot of girls around that are a whole lot prettier than I am."

The unexpected laughter that came from the figure in front of her caught her by surprise. She was pretty sure she recognized it from her lunch this afternoon. "Trevor? Is that you?"

"Yes, it's me." His voice confirmed.

She reached over to flick on the light from the supply closet. "You scared me half to death. What on earth are you doing out here?'

She could clearly see his broad shoulders, the chiseled pecs rising and falling underneath his tailored cotton dress shirt. Her mouth went suddenly, inexplicably dry as a vision of her hands running across those pecs came to mind.

He reached out and put a hand to brace himself against one wall while his other hand gently cupped her chin in his warm fingers, lifting her face up. She noticed his biceps straining against the threads of the fitted shirt and suddenly forgot to breathe.

His eyes lingered on her lips and she wondered if he was going to kiss her. Part of her wanted him to. Part of her was terrified that if he did, she wouldn't want him to stop with just that kiss.

His question took her by surprise. "I saw you standing with Brandon earlier. Are you aware he has a girlfriend?"

Confusion interrupted the stirrings of desire. She licked her lips, struggling to moisten them enough to answer him. "Brandon? Donor Brandon? No, I really don't keep up with the personal lives of our benefactors. That's Virginia's job. Why?"

Trevor's eyes studied her face like a hawk might study its prey, as if looking for any hint that she was lying to him. A slow smile stretched across his lips as his face drew closer to hers. "Because I don't like to share."

A question rose to the surface of her mind but was quickly submerged beneath the hot waves of desire that washed over her as his lips claimed hers for the very first time. The siren call of his Greek god body enveloped her and left no room for the rest of the world as she fingered the fabric on the sleeve of the arm that now encircled her in a passionate embrace.

Chapter 20.

"Where did you come up with these?" Lisa looked at Haillie with sudden suspicion as she fingered the oddly familiar porcelain plates.

Haillie gave her a sly grin. "Let's just say I borrowed them."

Lisa could smell trouble, but decided not to dig deeper. The less she knew, the less involved she would be when trouble hit the fan.

Just when Lisa thought things couldn't get worse, Haillie delivered another bomb. "We're going to have to change the portions for dinner. It's no longer just the board members we've got to impress. Michael and Virginia took the liberty of inviting our top donors along with some journalists and celebrity bloggers."

Her mouth dropped open. Trouble now smelled a whole lot like one giant, sewage covered rat. "You're kidding me? What was he thinking? He's going to sabotage our biggest fundraiser of the year? Our clients depend on the money we raise from this!"

White hot rage surged through Lisa at the thought of the collateral damage this petty attempt at destroying Haillie was going to cause. She'd just staked her career on the success of Elegant Events and Michael's antics were threatening that success. This was personal. "Leave it to me."

"I trust you. I'll leave it in your capable hands. " Haillie gave her a conspiratorial smile and headed out the door on her way back to the party room.

****

Brandon's eyes lingered on the doorway, watching for Haillie's return. He wondered where she was and what she was doing. A twinge of guilt came over him. He should be home, with Sky, not here with Haillie.
He told himself he was just being polite. It was polite to excuse yourself to the host or hostess of a party before leaving. That was basic manners, and no Avery would ever be so rude as to leave without following proper etiquette.

Never mind that it gave him an opportunity to speak to her and to hear her voice again. He sighed and scratched his forehead. Who was he kidding?

Sky was safe. She was predictable. She was stable. She was a good woman with an honorable career, an everyday hero who saved the lives of infants with her skills, knowledge, and expertise.

He admired her. He respected her. But there was no passion between them. As long as he was with Sky, he could keep his heart carefully tucked away in its safety deposit box knowing she would never touch it.

Never again would he have to worry about getting hurt as he had with Virginia. Never again would he need to concern himself about being rejected or abandoned. Sky was reliable, dependable, and always there for him.

Haillie was anything but predictable. Her presence was a wrecking ball in his carefully constructed, if deadly dull, life. He knew that he should stay as far away from her as he could possibly get.

Whenever she was around, his heart began reminding him of what it felt like before he'd buried it behind the impenetrable walls of steel. He yearned to feel that sense of close connection he'd once shared with Virginia before Michael she returned to Micheal.

He wondered what it was that Haillie possessed that Sky did not. What was the difference between the two women? If he could just understand that, maybe he could purge himself of the urge he felt to bask in the warmth of Haillie's many charms.

****

Haillie stepped back into the room and surveyed the guests with a practiced eye. People were clustered in small groups, chatting while drinking from flutes of champagne and sparkling punch, but the life was missing from the party. This was the kind of boring, lifeless event that donors expected, but it was not the kind of event that attracted new donors and set record-breaking numbers for attendance.

That kind of event required more, and more was exactly what Haillie intended to give them. She stepped over to the DJ booth where Liam was standing and gave them both a conspiratorial wink. "Ready to get this party started for real?"

The three bent their heads together as Haillie relayed her instructions. Her eyes searched for a familiar face, someone she could rely upon to follow her lead and help break the ice. Brandon's blonde head standing in the corner was just the ticket.

She walked over to him and tapped him on the shoulder. "Care to dance?"

His eyebrows rose but he let her lead him onto the dance floor. "You're assuming I can dance."

She winked. "I know my wealthy socialites. Learning to dance is part of learning the necessary social graces to fit in with the crowd."

He chuckled. "Yes, but some of us are better at it than others."

Brandon led her into the open center of the room and the first beats of a spirited tango began to play. He took slow, steady steps toward her, and she placed her right hand in his left as they faced one another.

They began the spirited dance, each one matching the footsteps of the other in time to the beat. She let him take the lead, following him through twists and turns as they moved across the floor. She ignored the oohs and ahhs she heard coming from the edges, allowing her world to collapse down until there was nothing but Brandon and the music remaining.

Her fears for the future of Elegant Events, her concerns about the decision of the board, her worries about the impact that Michael and Victoria's scheming would have on her future all melted away as she focused on those gorgeous blue eyes and the strength of the arms that held her.

He led her in a particularly spirited series of spins followed by a dip so deep her hair nearly brushed the floor and brought her up. She was tempted to capture those smirking lips with her own but resisted the temptation and released her hand instead to turn away from him, allowing him to chase her for a few steps before he reclaimed her hand and led her into another turn.

They finished the dance with a flourish as the music ended. She looked over at Brandon and gave him a well deserved seductive smile. "See? I was right. You can dance."

****

Fun. That was the thing that was missing from his relationship with Sky. Pure, unadulterated fun. There wasn't a spontaneous bone in Sky's body. Everything she did was planned, calculated, and regimented.

She would never have invited him to dance, never taken the risk of a tango, never let anyone see her publicly enjoying herself. The woman kept a bowling alley hidden in the basement of her four story home the way some people kept sex dungeons. It was as if she were afraid someone might think she'd ever had a frivolous thought.

His eyes left Haillie's for just a moment when he spotted a familiar face staring at him from the doorway. He sucked in his breath. "Sky."

He breathed the name like it was a death sentence. Haillie looked over at the woman standing in the direction where Brandon's eyes were focused.

"Sky?" she repeated, a clear question in her voice.
"Sky." He affirmed. He realized that name needed a little explanation to help make sense of it. "My girlfriend."

Haillie tensed as she looked over at Brandon. "Your girlfriend?"

He took slow steps toward Sky, preparing himself mentally for the confrontation. Sky did not like surprises. Her eyes never left his face. He expected her to be angry. But there was something else in her eyes, an emotion he didn't recognize.

"We need to talk." Was all she said to him.

He glanced over at Haillie. The hurt in her eyes was clear and he wished a thousand times over he could undo it. "I'm sorry. I never meant…"

She held her hands up, as if to ward him off. "You don't owe me an explanation. I've got a party to tend to and you...well, you've got your hands full."

Brandon wanted to stop her. The thought of not seeing her again was like the thought of the sun never rising again. He knew in that moment he could not continue his relationship with Sky. He didn't know if he could win Haillie back, but he wasn't ready to live the rest of his life without really living it.

He turned and followed Sky out into the dim hallway toward the elevator. "You're right. We do need to talk."

Sky sat on a bench beside the elevator and looked at her hands. Her voice was low as she spoke. "I don't think I've seen you so passionate, so alive, and so happy in the entire time I've been with you, Brandon. I kept telling myself that you just needed time to get over Virginia and then you would love me, but it never happened. You're dutiful. You're attentive. But I don't want to be somebody's duty."

She looked up at him. Tears ran down her cheeks. "I want something more than you can give me. Don't think I haven't heard what you tell people about why you're with me when I'm not around, when people ask you why you settle for a plain Jane like me instead of someone like Haillie. I don't want to be your safe choice. I don't want to be the woman you keep around because you're afraid to get hurt."

Brandon felt suddenly ashamed of himself. He sat down beside her. "You deserve better. I wish I could give that to you, but I can't. I'm just sorry it took me so long to see it."

She leaned her head against his shoulder for just a moment. "I forgive you. It's not just your fault. I should have had the courage to end this earlier, when I found a man that wanted me for me. But I messed up, and I lost him. I don't know if I can get him back, but I know I've got to try."

She sighed heavily and stood up. "I've got to get home and get some sleep. I've got a 9 month old baby on the operating table first thing tomorrow morning." She chuckled and shook her head. "Sometimes I think I'm the one in need of a heart transplant."

He watched as she stepped into the elevator. He didn't move to stop her. He wasn't even bothered by the revelation about her finding someone else. There was no jealousy, only a small hope that she would find the happiness he'd been unable to bring her.

He turned back toward the lights and the music of the party. He hoped it wasn't too late to fix things with Haillie.

****

Haillie struggled against the tears that threatened to burst from her ducts. She had no right to be hurt. Brandon had never made any promises to her. He'd never once asked her to do more than join him for lunch.

So why did she feel just the same as the day she'd found out that Michael was cheating on her? Why did she feel as if he'd betrayed her trust? Their lunch that was intimate, true, but there had been no kisses, no hand holding, nothing beyond what might be expected of two business people getting to know one another.

The chemistry she felt might well be one sided. Maybe she'd imagined it. She thought of James and a blush came to her cheeks. Brandon wasn't the only one with someone they were seeing. Even if she wasn't serious about that relationship, it still existed.

Her heart told her that Brandon owed her an apology, but her head was telling her that was nonsense. They'd encountered one another all of three times: that unfortunate morning jog, the lunch date, and tonight's gala sneak peek. It was beyond silly to think of him as a lover. She barely knew him.

She stepped into the lady's wash room to give herself a moment to pull herself together. The drama with Brandon aside, she had a party to run. The details mattered. The votes would be coming soon, and she needed this contract more than she needed a relationship.

****

Brandon searched the dancing, laughing people in the gathering for a sign of Haillie but didn't see her anywhere. He suddenly felt tired. Incredibly tired, as if the laughter and the joy on the faces around him was draining him of his energy.

He sought out Virginia to make his excuses. He was ready to go home. He found her standing outside of Michael's office.

She was on the phone. Her back was turned to him. "This plan was a disaster! No, I don't know how she did it. Everything we did to try and discredit her, and the witch turned it around. She's going to come out smelling like roses. The bloggers are loving her, the donors are having the time of their lives, and we'll be the ones in breach of contract if we fire her now."

She paused to listen to the voice on the other end of the line before continuing. "There isn't anything left. I can't afford to lose him, but I can't get rid of her."

He couldn't believe what he was hearing. He'd never seen this side of Virginia before. "Get married or else? Do you think he'll go for it?"

His eyes widened. What on earth was she planning now? "Nan, that's genius! Thanks. I'll get to work on it now. I'll let you know how it turns out."

He realized that she'd been trying to ruin Haillie, to run her out of the company and discredit her. This Virginia was a far cry from the woman he'd loved long ago. He wanted nothing more to do with her. She'd become a petty, trifling witch who didn't care who she hurt as long as she got what she wanted.

Virginia's face fell as she whirled around to head toward the party and spotted him. "Brandon! I -"

He held up a hand. "I think I've heard all I needed to hear from you."

She winced as if he'd slapped her. "You don't understand."

He locked eyes with her, hands on his hips. "Let me tell you what you need to understand. If you try breaking your contract with Haillie again, I will make sure that every blogger in that room gets to hear what I just heard. They're going to know that you set her up. They're going to know that you were undermining her. They're also going to know that she pulled through spectacularly in spite of you. I'll personally make sure that your donors dry up faster than water in the Sahara. Is. That. Clear?"

Virginia's face was drained of color. She nodded mutely. She reached out a hand toward him but he shrugged it off. "Good luck to you. I hope he says yes. You deserve a lifetime of that."

He turned on his heel, feeling grateful for the first time that she'd broken things off with him for Michael, of all people. He needed to find Haillie. She deserved to know the truth.

****

Virginia stared at Brandon's retreating figure. Tears fell like a waterfall from her cheeks.

Breaking off the relationship with Brandon hadn't been her idea. It was her parents' idea. They'd lost every penny of their inheritance. Her trust fund was the only money the family had left, and stock market fluctuations meant there wasn't much of that left.

Her engagement to Michael was a desperate attempt to save her family, and herself, from being left destitute and penniless. Brandon's family had money, but not enough money to save her family's fortunes.

Hiring Haillie was an act of desperation, an attempt to finally cement her relationship with Michael by reminding him of all the reasons why he was better off with her. She hadn't anticipated reigniting the sparks that drew them together in the first place.

Everything in her life was falling apart. She was losing everything, and Haillie was at the center of it all. She could not understand it. She couldn't understand why she was losing everything to her. Even Brandon seemed taken by her.

She straightened herself up and pulled herself together. It was time to play the last card left in her deck: the marriage card.

Chapter 21

"This has got to be the best sneak peek event I've ever attended! If this is the sneak peek, I can only imagine what the real thing is going to be like. I'll be telling everyone about it." The blogger was shaking Michael's hand with a vigor that set his teeth on edge. He was fairly certain the man was going to shake the hand right off his body.

"We're honored you could make it and so glad you enjoyed it." Micheal could feel his blood pressure rising beyond the recommended parameters his doctor set. He struggled to keep his voice under control.

He wanted to scream in frustration. He'd tried to destroy Haillie and she was going to come out smelling like roses. There was no way the board was going to agree to get rid of her, not after this.

Trevor wrote a $50,000 check to the charity on his way out the door. "I'll have to admit I was reluctant to attend tonight's get together. These things are usually not worth my time." His eyes flicked to Rose for a moment and then back to Michael. "You've got something special in this place, and I can't wait to see where it goes from here."

Brandon was the last of the extra guests to leave. Despite the smile that was on the younger man's face, there was an edge to his voice that Michael didn't understand, but what he did understand was the threat Brandon seemed to be making. "You've gone to a lot of trouble to put this little event together. I wish our events were half as good as this one. If you're not careful, I might just snatch the event planner who helped you with it right out from underneath your nose."

Michael forced a chuckle. "No need to steal her. If you'd like her number, I'll be happy to share it with you. After all, Everyday People is in business to help everyday people make it in business."

When the last donor and guest journalist had left the room, the board gathered around the table. Michael stood in front of them. "As you all know, the contract with Haillie Prescott and Elegant Events was dependent upon demonstration of capability. Tonight's sneak peek was that demonstration. All who are in favor of retaining Haillie's services say 'Aye'."

Haillie stood off to the side. Her face held no expression. She said not one word in her defense. She seemed content to let her work do the talking for her, and her work tonight had been exceptional.

As the Chair of the Board, he didn't get a vote unless there was a tie breaker needed. Lisa and Rose both glared at him as they cast their vote. Kevin stood side-by-side with Lisa to cast his vote. The vote was unanimous in its "Aye."

To Micahel's surprise, even his darling fiancee, Virginia, voiced her Aye vote. He made a mental note to question her about that. This, after all, had been her big idea, not his.

Michael was furious. He was furious with Virginia, who'd put him in this situation to begin with, and he was even more furious with Haillie for refusing to give him an excuse to fire her the way he'd hoped she would.

He understood that Lisa's vote was her usual display of defiance against his control. He'd come to expect that from her. He'd have gotten rid of her years ago, but having her as an employee of Everyday People allowed him to write off the payments he made to Liam as a tax deductible expense and these days he needed all the tax deductions he could get.

Rose's vote was also easily understood. She would vote for her sister no matter what happened. Rose's greatest strength was her loyalty to those she loved. It was also her greatest weakness. While there were days he wondered why he kept Rose around, he knew the truth: Rose was a pawn that allowed him to manipulate and control Haillie from a distance. As long as he controlled Rose's paycheck, he controlled Haillie. But that control did come at a price.

Kevin's vote for Haillie, though, made him grit his teeth in frustrated anger. While he knew Kevin was sleeping with Lisa, Michael could have let that pass as long as the man had remained loyal to him. After all, it was Michael's training and his programs, run through Everyday People, that lifted Kevin from the streets and launched Kevin's first enterprise.

Of course, that help had come with an agreement. He held a silent partnership of Kevin's business until such time as Kevin paid back in full the investment Everyday People made in him. As silent partner, he could squeeze Kevin out at any time and send him back to the streets from which he came. That thought was the only thing that kept a smile on his face as the votes came in against him.

Let Kevin have Lisa and the responsibility of caring for Liam with it. It was Michael who'd turned that cold fish into his own personal gold mine, not Kevin. She would be worthless without him.

He could have Michael's sloppy seconds if he wanted them. Let that polo shirt wearing cement cretin keep building his little projects. It was still making money for Everyday People, and that money allowed Michael to draw a comfortable, tax-free salary until he could get access to Virginia's trust fund.

He stormed out of the board room without a single word and headed toward the garage. Virginia ran to catch up with him, but he was too angry to slow down. He mentally cursed the wretched wench for coming up with the idea to challenge Haillie with a full presentation.

He'd warned her, but Virginia hadn't listened. First, she'd insisted on hiring Haillie over his objections and now she'd pushed full ahead with her plan. The whole mess was in his lap and the board was losing respect for him.

He slammed the car door shut and waited for Virginia, his mind on Haillie. He needed to get her out of the office before she ruined everything he'd spent the last ten years working to build. Whenever she was around, things started slipping out of his control.

He sat there, tapping his fingers on the steering wheel, thinking. There was a chink in her armor. He just had to find it.

Virginia knocked on the glass of the passenger seat. His head snapped to attention as he looked at her. He briefly considered driving off without her, but he wasn't about to throw away years of work in a moment of passion. He unlocked the doors.

"Get in already." He snarled the words, in no mood for an argument.

She glanced over at him, clearly hurt. "Are you okay?"

His jaw tightened as he turned the key in the ignition. "I'm thinking. I know that's a novel idea to someone like you, but we grown ups like to do that from time to time."

She tensed. "Michael, I know you're upset with me for the vote, but I can explain…"

That was the straw that broke the camel's back. "I TOLD you not to do this, didn't I? I told you not to hire her, and you ignored me. I told you not to push her, and you ignored me. You can shut your tiny little mouth. I've heard everything out of you that I need to hear."

Her face scrunched up and Michael knew she was about to start crying. He didn't care. He was tired of her and tired of the waterworks. If not for her money, he'd have ended things a long time ago. But he couldn't afford to lose the money, so he reigned in his anger and mustered up an apology instead. "I'm sorry. I shouldn't have yelled at you. It's just..."

* * * *

Virgina blinked back the tears. She was used to his moods. She just wasn't prepared for this one. She'd never seen him this out-of-control with his anger. She felt like taking off her engagement ring and throwing it in his face. But she couldn't afford to lose him. She couldn't afford to lose his money.

His apology, she knew, was forced. He didn't mean it. He was boiling with anger at what he saw as her betrayal. A vote for Haillie, in his eyes, was a vote against him. She tried again.

"You don't understand. Brandon overheard me talking about the plan and he threatened to pull his donations and to spread what he heard everywhere. He was going to destroy Everyday People if I didn't vote for her. He's crazy about her." Virginia let it all out in a rush.

Everything, that was, except the part about forcing Michael to marry her. Michael pounded his fist on the steering wheel. "That wench is going to steal everything from me! First the votes, now the donors, what's next? The company??"

They pulled into the garage of the house and Virginia headed out the door, taking the lead up the stairs. Shoes lined up in a row in the mud room greeted them as they came in the door. She took off her shoes in a hurry, eager to flee the blast of anger that was heading toward the house.

She took the steps two at a time. She was tired of hearing about Haillie. She'd heard the rants too many times over the years. She was tired of the constant comparisons, and even more tired of paying for Haillie's sins.

The fun of being on Michael's arm and being able to freely spend his money ran out a long time ago. She'd listened for two years to his constant whining about Haillie when she was his wife. Her compensation for that was an Alfa Romero and then a condominium on the right side of town, all while her friends were slaving away in college waiting for their trust funds to become available. The whining made it easy for her to listen to his rants while they traveled the world in grand style as Micheal's mistress on her tour de whore. That was the year he left his wife, convinced she was his only possible ticket to a lifetime of happiness.

She imagined that life with Michael would continue to be one grand adventure. She'd thought that once Haillie was out of their lives, she wouldn't have to hear about her again. She'd thought wrong.

Michael expected her to be at home and by his side during his business meetings. He expected her to fill the place Haillie once had. The weight of his expectations was overwhelming to her.

He became obsessed with Haillie. Between constant comparisons to her and his hiring of her sister so he could spy on her and gloat about her inability to get over him, Virginia felt like she was living with two people instead of just one: Michael and the ghost of Haillie past. She wasn't Haillie and she had no desire to be Haillie.

She didn't want to be the next Mrs. Prescott and spend the rest of her life with a man who clearly was not over his ex. She thought that maybe if she brought Haillie on board, he would see how pathetic she was and finally let go of her for good. Instead, it just made everything worse.

She had done her part and supported him in a plan to rid himself of the agoraphobic harlot, as he put it. She remembered to lock up the office so Haillie couldn't get in to set up her presentation. Every possible detail to ensure her failure was set up around her, yet she still found a way around them and won. Haillie had risen to the challenge, no if and or buts. It was a fact that couldn't be changed, moving on was their only option. She just hoped he could see that.

She sighed as she stood on the second floor landing, watching him kick the garbage cans in a fit of anger. This was becoming a new normal for him. Ever since Haillie joined the non-profit, he would flare up in random emotional outbursts. These, and the recent bouts of flacid attempts at love making, left her convinced more than ever that he and Haillie were far from over.

Below her the epithets were streaming with the force and regularity of a waterfall. They were spraying back up into a mumbled mash of curses that were regurgitated, recycled and put back into more creative sentences with Haillie's name as a central part of those sentences.

What she wanted to watch of Michael's tantrum show was already done. He was nearing the conclusion. Minutes ticked away as he began throwing unbreakable things at the wall. The maid would have a task on her hand tomorrow morning.

She needed out. She wanted Brandon, but he had Sky. There was that hot guy in the parking garage, James something. Yes. That would do nicely. She decided she would have him before she married Michael. Maybe after, too, if he could be discreet.

She went to her private office to make a phone call to Nan. The walk to her sitting room was short. The noise from downstairs was dying down, and she drowned out the dying embers of his fiery fit by turning up the volume from the TV as she dialed Nan's number.

On the fifth ring Nan picked up, just as the beginning music of her favorite TV show's theme song began to play. Virginia was relieved. "Nan, you got home okay?"

Nan's voice cackled across the line. "Oh, dearie, Don't you worry about me. I always get home okay. I carry my bodyguard with me. Seven shots is all I need."

Virginia frowned. "Nan, you aren't supposed to have that anymore. You shot the Instacart guy and had to pay him a settlement."

Nan made a hmph sound into the phone. "I still say he looked suspicious. He was hanging around my door making noises."

Virginia sighed heavily. "He was dropping off your groceries, Nan." She muted her show and pushed the lever down on her comfy chair, elevating her feet to an optimal tv watching position.

Nan clucked her tongue disapprovingly. "He could have been quiet about it. Dropping off groceries and breaking into someone's house aren't comparable."

Virginia changed tactics. She knew she wasn't going to convince her Nan that the man wasn't trying to break in and rob the place. "Nan, the judge let you off with a warning."

She could practically see the scowl on her Nan's face. "The judge was on the take."

She felt exasperated. They'd had this disagreement numerous times. "He was in our favor, Nan."

Nan's voice was filled with skepticism. "It didn't feel like a favor to my bank account."

She tried again. "Nan, you shot a man through the door. You didn't even try to warn him"

Nan began a familiar rant. "Phewy, y'all kids ain't made like they were in my day. Just today some girl in an elevator was showing a full turkey breast of titties. I could see the man near her practically drooling over them, but he couldn't get up the nerve to ask her out. What do they teach these days? How to whine, sue, and sex. Sodom and gomorrah, I say."

Virginia rolled her eyes. "Nan, I need some advice. The party didn't turn out the way we planned. Michael's all stirred up now, and I doubt it's the right time to put pressure on him for the next part of the plan."

Nan snorted. "I bet you he's hollering right now, isn't he? The man reminds me of Ronald, my fourth husband."

Virginia grimaced. "Nan, isn't that the one you shot? I don't see how the two are related."

Nan's reply was quick this time. "Is he carrying on like a two year old?"

Embarrassed, she answered with a low, "Yes."

Nan cackled. "See? Just like Ronald. That man had a temper, but I put the fear of God in Him. And a couple of bullets, but who's counting? Sweetie, I'm getting you a Seecamp LSW .32. You shoot him once and he'll start acting like a man. Believe me, there are few things that get a man's attention as fast as a bullet in the bum"

Virginia didn't doubt her Nan was right, but she wasn't quite ready to start shooting Michael, no matter how tempting the thought may be. "Nan. I'm going to watch tv. Good night. Put your weapon in the nightstand drawer."

Nan humphed. "That's too far away." She paused for a moment. "If you want to fix this business with Michael, leverage Haillie's success in your favor. The woman is driving him mad. Tell him that you're not convinced that he really loves you."

Virginia shook her head and hung up. She had done her good niece duty. Anyone might say she was a terrible fiancée, but she had done that duty today, too. She was doing the best she could to take care of everyone else's needs, and getting none of her own met.

Her eyelids gently slid down as the chair massager got to work on her back. The sandman was calling. That was the one male call that she could take without disrupting her peace of mind. She had been a good girl today and she deserved some rest. She would give Nan's suggestion a try the next day.

* * * *

"What is wrong with me?" Michael stared at himself in the mirror. He was exhausted from dancing around the house like a buffoon. Now that he'd calmed down, even he could admit to how overly dramatic he was being. What was it about Haillie that got to him?

A semblance of an answer swirled around in his head. The words Haillie spoke to him on a day he'd come to visit her brownstone out of what he told himself was morbid curiosity during the years of self-imposed exile came to mind, along with a vision of that finger pointing to him, exposing flaws no one else's eyes had ever seen to the open air, laying him bare.

She'd hurled the words at him, one mean-spirited thought after the other, and each one true in its own right even though he'd denied them all that day and told her she was crazy. The words that struck him the hardest were about the baby she'd miscarried.

"You never even cared about what that did to me. You never cared about the way we lost our baby. All you cared about was your flipping money and how glad you were that you wouldn't have to be 'saddled' with another Liam."

Tears had sparkled in her eyes, but she'd not given him the satisfaction of seeing her cry.

"There's no amount of money in the world that will ever make you a man in my eyes. Men don't abandon their children like you did Liam. Lisa has to practically chase you down and force you to spend time with him. You treat him like garbage beneath your feet."

He'd tried to object. "I pay good money for that boy's education. I make sure he has everything he needs."

She'd hit home with the sneer in her next words. "Everything that money can buy except a father that wants him. You disgust me. You don't deserve Liam. You didn't deserve this baby. And you don't deserve me."

He'd said something forgettable in return, but those words stuck with him. She was right. He hadn't deserved Haillie. He'd always known that. He just couldn't understand why she'd never been able to see it.

He didn't deserve to be a father. Liam deserved better. The baby was better off without him, too. He was no good for anybody.

No matter how hard he worked, no matter how much he made, no matter how much he tried to do for others, at the end of the day, he couldn't escape the truth. He was just what his mother always told him he would be: a no good, no account, worthless man, just like his father before him.

A compulsory yearning for alcohol reared its head. The alcohol allowed him to forget his pain, at least for a little while. He was hauled toward the library by a power that was much greater and much stronger than his own will.

Mid-pour in the room that reflected his humble beginnings to his tidy life before Haillie and her words came to haunt him, he made an unwavering decision.

Down came the glass from his lips. He set it back on the counter. His thoughts focused on what he was about to do, he pinched Virginia's keys from the crystal bowl just outside the garage door. The purr of the engine coming to life echoed the distant humm in his loins that was both familiar and strange.

He threw the car in reverse and clicked the garage door opener, watching it clank open notch by notch. He floored the gas pedal, clearing the door by centimeters. The force of it made him feel alive as he sped down the driveway. It was time to bury this for good.

Chapter 22

Exhaustion was a mile marker Haillee passed six
hours ago. If she stopped to rest on the highway
of success now, it would be an inebriation out-
cold type of sleep. In three more exits, she
would be in the rural area of too tired to get a
wink of rest.

Her door swung open and she dropped her bags.
She craved to join her purse and Louis Vitton's
back on the foyer. Buckling knees did more than
agree, they gave out. Two hands swooped in to
sweep her back up on her feet.

Her eyes widened in shock. "What the..?"

She was greeted with a full view of his cowlick
and receding hairline.

"Hi." She didn't think as her eyes opened, she
interlocked her fingers around his neck and
bought her lips to meet his. She kissed him with
an aching need that begged to be fulfilled.

He returned the passionate lip lock. Her fingers
trailed from his neck to his shoulders down to

the top button of his shirt. She fumbled with his buttons.

He gently pulled the fingers away, kissing her finger tips with a tenderness that sent hot shivers down her body. "I'm enjoying this, but are you sure you want to do this? You were fainting from exhaustion just seconds ago."

She impatiently dug underneath his shirt to touch his bare skin. "Save me the energy of taking myself to bed and I'll muster up the momentum to make you a happy man."

James scooped her up in his arms. "Yes. Ma'am." He headed toward the stairs, then paused. "Where is your bedroom?"
She chuckled. "We've made love twice and you don't know where my bedroom is yet?"

He turned around and started heading to the front door. She looked up at him, bewildered by the behavior. "Where are you going?"
He grinned down at her. "I'm assuming your room is in the backseat of a Lincoln. Can you call the car service, cause I'm not sure I can keep my vitality up for a half an hour waiting for your room to get here?" He kissed her again.

She playfully slapped him on his pec. "Second door on the left at the top of the stairs." James bolted up the stairs.

* * *

Virgina's car glided into a parallel parking space. Micheal sat inside with the engine running while a war raged between his flight or fight responses. Six times he put the car into gear, ordering himself to leave, only to then park and repeat the process all over again until the transmission was making a weird noise. He shut off the engine and stepped out of the car.

He was vulnerable. He was fragile, and he was as sad as he had been angry for a decade. He was free from something that held him, yet he felt it was about to pull him under.

Panic rose as he climbed the stairs to her front door. He felt like a condemned man preparing to meet the executioner.

* * *

"What on earth led a man like you to become a parking lot attendant? Surely you are capable of greater things?" Haillie wrapped one leg around James and his perfect youthful physique. In between frantic kisses, she peppered him with questions.

James returned a kiss but deflected her question with one of his own. "Why did you let me assume you were Crystal instead of telling me you were Haillie?"

She giggled while drawing circles around his nipple. She kissed him above it. "Does it matter? You figured it out."

His finger lifted her chin and he looked into her eyes. "It matters. I want to know the real you, not the you that you pretend to be."

She smiled coyly and purred "I want to know you, too." Her head disappeared beneath the covers.

He groaned an oooh as he felt her mouth on the inside of his thigh, but gently removed her and pulled her from beneath the covers, waiting until she locked eyes with him. His voice was as firm and unrelenting as another portion of his anatomy. "I really do want to know you."

She pressed herself up against him and kissed his neck. "I've been in this house for ten years. I'm single. I'm into you. Is there anything else that matters?"

James slid further away from her grasp. Haillie's face scrunched up. She stiffened and her voice had an edge to it that was both defensive and angry. "What's wrong? You're a man. Don't you like sex?"

He reached for her arms, pulling her closer to him. "I am, and yes - I do very much like sex. I just like to know a little more about the woman I take to bed than the location of a few erogenous zones."

Her lips formed a pout, and James was tempted to give in. She was adorable when she pouted. "I'm too exhausted to start a get to know you conversation. Can we do it over coffee in the morning?"

He kissed her cheek. "Are you asking me to stay over?"

She gave him a suspicious look. "Sure, just as long as you don't ask any more questions and I can get some sleep?"

He sighed and kissed the top of her head. "Good night, then."

Haillie rolled over onto her side of the bed and cut out the lights. Her whisper caught up to him just as he was getting comfortable. "You'll have to do the walk of shame."

He shook his head. "For you? It's never shameful."

* * *

Haillie's eyes shut and sleep was blissfully descending upon her in the dark room until the silence was shattered by the vibration as James's phone rang.

Haillie felt annoyed. First, he'd interrupted a very promising liaison. Now, his phone was interrupting her sleep. She considered silencing it, but it might be something important. She raised her voice. "James! Your phone."

His eyes opened groggily and he looked over at her. "What?"

She pointed at the phone dancing on the nightstand. "It's vibrating."

James's eyes shot open. His arms searched around in the dark looking for the buzzing plastic rectangle.

"Hello." He mumbled into the phone receiver. "Who is this?"

"Your mom, dear." He turned to look at Haillie, discreetly covering the phone and got out of bed, heading toward the water closet.

Haillie, eyes barely opened, started to mouth a question. "Who's on the phone?" Then, she caught herself. She had no right to ask him about a life she wasn't part of and didn't desire to be caught up in at this time.

If she started asking about his phone calls, he would expect an answer in the morning to the questions he wanted her to answer. He didn't belong there. Having him in her bedroom was fine, but her heart couldn't afford to make room for him in her life. She wasn't ready.

He whispered from the bathroom door " I'll take the call in here."

He closed the door behind him, but not before she heard him say, "Ma, what?"

* * *

His mother sounded practically giddy with excitement. "Well, how did it go with Ms. Prescott?"

He thought of the look of jubilation he'd seen on Haillie's face when she'd left the parking garage. "The servers were a lifesaver. Thank you, mom. I'll find a way to pay you back for the overtime."

His mother demured. "No need, dear. We're just so happy to hear from you."

Her words made him feel guilty. "I'm sorry I had to reach out to you. Ms. Prescott was in an impossible situation."

She cooed. "I'm just happy we could help."

He grimaced. "Tell dad I know I owe him."

James could her talking to someone else. "Warren, he says he knows he owes you."

He heard his father's voice reply. "Forget it, he's my son. I just want him to visit the office."

James inwardly groaned. This was the life he desperately wanted to avoid. He didn't want to take over his father's business. "When dad? When do you need me to be there? What time?"

His father's voice was eager as if he'd just been promised an early Christmas. "Tomorrow."

James couldn't make it and keep his current job. "I have to work."

His father sounded offended. "You call a minimum wage job work? I'm offering you a real job."

He regretted getting his father's hopes up. "Dad, I'm sorry I called."

His mother's voice was filled with rebuke. "Don't push him away again."

His father's voice was stiff, unrelenting. "But you did call, and a deal is a deal. I expect you in the office bright and early tomorrow morning."

James was desperate. "What if I could pay you back for the overtime, or I could work at Eden's Hanging Garden?"

His father scoffed. "I didn't work for 40 years to build that place to see my only son work in the kitchens. You own the place, and you're going to give the employees the wrong idea."

He pleaded with his father even though he knew this was a battle he was not going to win. "Dad, I haven't asked anything of you for years now. I didn't ask you tonight for my sake. It was for one of our own."

His mother's voice was low but he could hear her pleading with his father in the background. "Take it easy. We want him to come home."

He'd always been able to count on his mother to win over his father when push came to shove. She was the only woman he'd ever loved, and it showed in the way they treated one another. "Fine, considering the circumstances. You'll have to go to a social event of our choosing as a respectable Everton. None of that parking lot attire. And I mean it."

James's heart fell. Attending a major social event as James Everton III was going to put an end to all the work he'd done to try and find a woman who would see past the parking lot attendant or the money to the man beneath it all. He wanted a love like his parents had - one that was genuine and would last a lifetime, but finding that kind of love was hard when all most women saw were the dollar signs.

As a parking lot attendant, it was true that fewer women noticed him or took the time to speak to him but those few that did were worth getting to know. They were usually pretty down-to-earth. Parking lot attendant James didn't have to worry about a woman googling him so she could arrange a "chance" meeting with him, or watching mothers, cougars, and desperate debutantes fawning over his money and status. He could be himself. He wasn't ready for Haillie to discover the truth about who he was. Not yet.

Not until he could be sure she loved him for who he was, not what he had in his bank account or the titles that he'd inherited.

He knew enough about her to understand why she wasn't ready to open up about her past. The tabloids had been filled with sightings of Michael and his mistress during the last two years of their short marriage. Then came the rumored miscarriage, followed with reports of an attempted suicide.

Now that he knew her better, he was pretty sure the last two hadn't happened how they were rumored to have taken place. Haillie was not malicious, just hurt. She was like a wounded animal that needed a safe place to shelter so she could heal, and he was determined to give that to her for as long as she needed it. He would provide whatever help the power behind his name could give to shield her from the devastating blows of Michael Prescott.

* * *

The doorbell rang. "James, can you get that?" The door to the bathroom didn't open. Broken undertones of a conversation were drifting through the door. She felt her heart sink. It was probably his twenty-six year old girlfriend who was waiting for him at home.

She could imagine him lying to her right now about where he was and why he would come home smelling like Haillie's perfume. That was how men were. At least, that was how the men she seemed to fall in love with were. Happily ever after just wasn't for her. She would settle for happy for now.

Propelling herself out of bed, she slipped on her slippers and snatched James's shirt from his side of her bed before she jogged down the stairs.

* * *

Michael began finalizing his options as he waited at the bottom of her stairs. He remembered how fresh faced and beautiful she'd looked in that white gown while she walked down the aisle toward him. He'd been captivated by the stroll of her walk, the shimmer in her eyes when she laughed, and the flashing glints of love when he caught her stealing glances out of the corners of her eyes at him.

He'd felt like the man who had lassoed a star and brought it to earth. He knew it didn't belong there with him. He knew it would eventually miss the sky and yearn to return to it, but the light of it dazzled him too much and he found himself yearning to claim it.

The longer the star was with him, though, the more its light began to fade and dim. The very thing he'd loved most about it he was killing by capturing it. That was how things had been with Haillie.

He should have had the courage to set her free when he saw what his love was doing to her, but he couldn't make himself let go. So he'd latched onto Virginia. He'd let the affair be as public as their marriage had been, hoping she would do what he didn't have the courage to do and leave. Her loyalty and her faithfulness in the face of his infidelity infuriated him beyond reason. He'd wanted to shake her until her teeth rattled, but even if he'd done that much, she'd have stayed.

He divorced her, hoping she'd finally get it through that thick skull of hers, but she didn't fight back like he'd hoped she would. The light in her just died out completely and the radiant light that once shone in his darkness collapsed in on itself into a black hole of misery that threatened to suck in everything around it.
He should walk away. He knew he should walk away. He turned and started down the steps, but he couldn't make himself leave. Before he knew it, he'd rung the doorbell. His heart fluttered as he remembered the love he felt for her, the many beautiful smiles they'd shared during intimate

moments that time could not erase, and the way her eyes never left him when he looked particularly dapper. Even now the thought of that look was enough to send an electric pulse of desire through him.

No one could hold a candle to Haillie in her full glory, a glory he'd thought was long dead. Tonight, he'd been reminded of what it had been like to have her by his side, and a nagging guilt came with that memory. He felt a compulsion to shed that guilt.

He was devastated and worn out from all the anger he'd carried over the words he hadn't found the courage to say. There were still so many blanks to be filled, and tonight was as good a night as any to finish what he'd started back then.

He rang the bell again. The trembling had gone and now he was ready to stand up to her.

She opened the door wearing nothing but a man's shirt that brushed the top of her knees. She couldn't have looked sexier if she'd have been dressed in lingerie. He nearly forgot what he intended to say. "What the..,."

He took his eyes off her, allowing himself to regain composure. "Hi. I'm sure you weren't expecting me to be on the other side of this door."

Her arms crossed and her voice was tight. "No, I wasn't. What will it take for you to leave my doorstep?"

He looked her in the eyes from the bottom step. "For you to listen to me."

He could tell by the way her jaw was set and her mouth was turned down that she was angry. "I listened to you for the two years we dated, the four years we were married, and for the last ten years of the hell I've spent inside this brownstone. I've listened to you for the last two weeks as you have done everything you could to destroy me, to sabotage my work, and to break me down." She shook her head. "I am done listening. It's your turn."

He held up his hands, palms open to her. "I didn't come here to fight."

She snorted. "You never do. Yet somehow we always end up fighting, and you always end up blaming me for starting it. Why can't you just leave me alone?"

He winced at the truth of that statement. "I came to apologize."

She crossed her arms over her chest and leaned up against the door jam. "Bull. . ."

He went into the apology he had practiced on the drive over. "I wasn't happy you lost the baby."

Haillie's face lost all color. Her eyes stared at him. The only indication that his words had reached her was the lone tear that dripped down her cheek and off her chin.

* * *

Haillie felt cold slowly engulf her heart, freezing her in place. She was an ice sculpture, frozen, and too cold to be defrosted by mere words. She stood on the edge of an emptiness so deep that it had taken her the better part of a decade to find her way out of it.

She didn't remember doing it, but she must have stepped aside because Michael followed after her and closed the door behind him. The thud wasn't heard. The warmth of his arms as he wrapped her in a hug she would once have died to feel again was unable to reach her this time. He whimpered, "I'm sorry," as he laid his head on top of hers. She felt the raindrops of his sorrow in her hair. "I made a mistake. I did want him. It wouldn't have been a repeat of Liam like I said.

A spark of anger ignited within her, melting the ice and releasing her frostbitten heart. The painful needles of feeling being restored were reminders of every night she'd spent alone in her misery, her loneliness, and her pain. The only thought screaming through her mind was "You're too late."

Michael lifted his head. His voice was filled with pleading. She could see he was sincere, but it didn't reach her. She was beyond him.

"Haillie, say something! I didn't mean any of it. I know I hurt you when I said I didn't want another Liam and a life-sucking woman at the teat. I would do anything, anything at all, to take that back."

He closed his blood shot, tear filled eyes and his lips found hers. He thrust his tongue into her mouth. She expected to feel something, but she didn't. She was shocked by the realization. She felt nothing for him.

She stood still. Her eyes remained out of focus. She just stared at him as if she didn't see him. He proceeded to try and unbutton the top button of her shirt while begging, "Haillie, please say something. Anything."

The rooms in the mental prison where she'd lived for the last decade were collapsing, burning, exploding, and being rebuilt at the same time. She gagged on all the dead baby jokes he'd made in the aftermath of her miscarriage, as if her pain and the death of their child meant nothing to him. Michael kissed the exposed flesh showing under the shirt.

A part of her mind showed her a vision of what was going to happen. It was the same thing that always happened when Michael came to visit her. She would end up, on her back, looking at herself in the mirror as he laid her down on the table in the foyer. He would pull her hair and groan with pleasure while she would lie there as dead to what was happening as the hopes of the little person the nurse had placed in her arms on that horrible day.

Her little girl would have been twelve. She often wondered what the child would have looked like. The yearly anniversary of that event were especially dark days, days that she often spent comforted solely by numerous glasses of whiskey that dulled a pain that never truly went away. She'd faced all of that alone, without Michael, just as she had the miscarriage.
A tsunami of emotions once held back by those carefully constructed walls flooded over her, threatening to drown her in a well of feelings she didn't welcome and hadn't wanted. They had been shut up and ignored for too long. They would no longer be denied.

She felt another button come undone. From long habit, her hands went up intending to undo the buttons so this could be over and done with. She would tell herself he was sorry this time and he came to apologize with each button that popped out of its folds, but the end result was always the same. He would get what he wanted from her and leave her empty and alone.

She pushed his hands away and slapped him in the face. "NO! Not this time."

Rage gave her strength she didn't know she had. She shoved him hard. "You don't have a right to apologize. That was MY baby."

She took a step forward, pushing him closer to the door. "You don't get it! You just don't. You...killed...ME!"

He held his hand out to her. "Haillie. Sweetie." The term of endearment enraged her further. She shook her head vigorously. "No. Not a hand. Not a finger. No more. I don't need your apologies. You can drown with your demons alone."

His anger flared, "I didn't kill you. You did that. I've been good to you. I..."

She slapped him, hard. "You've been good to me? You bastard! Take your words and stick them where the sun doesn't shine. They're as empty as you are. I won't.... I won't accept it."

He sneered in her face. "You accept my money and my job, but when it's your turn to accept an apology you're an ice cold b…"

Every word he spoke added fuel to a fire that she could no longer control. "I was never a female dog with you. I was in the boardroom because I had to be but you didn't like it. You didn't like my company, you didn't like the competition. I walked away for you. You took it all. ALL."

She screamed it from the bottom of her gut "All! You had to have everything and you want to talk about being GOOD to me?"

She tore the syllables from her soul. She bent at the waist and screamed at him again, as if to blow him and his impression of her life away. "You can't have me, but you are going to deal with me."

She stood up and locked eyes with him. An F4 tornado of emotion was building up in her gut. "You never did know me. You thought I was like Elena, your first wife. You thought I was going to use my purse strings to keep your dick and your dignity on a leash. You thought I was like Lisa, who you blamed for making you live up to the responsibility of being a father. You thought I would be as malleable as she is when it comes to you. But I'm not either of them. I never was."

She took slow deliberate steps toward him, her irises focused on him "I didn't need you. I had a tech company on the cusp, but I sold it to you along with a non-compete clause because I wasn't interested in controlling you. I wanted to support you in your dreams, and I became your event planning wife."

She lunged at him "You made me leave my bedrest so I could be your arm candy night after night. You didn't care about me. You didn't care about what I was going through. All you cared about was your friends and your time and your money. To hell with you and all of it. You don't get to apologize."

* * *

James heard the raised voices coming from downstairs and decided to check on Haillie. It was an odd time of night for visitors.

He made it to the last step in time to see Michael lower his shoulder and body check Haillie. Her petite frame didn't stand a chance against the larger man's bulk. Her body went soaring.

James made it across the room in time for her to land on him. It knocked the wind out of him, but he was otherwise unharmed. She hardly even noticed his efforts. Before he could stop her, she'd scrambled to her feet and was taunting

Michael. "You think that's good enough? I am going to beat you like a punching bag."

She grabbed up a baseball bat from under the sofa and charged across the room. James was a second too late to stop her. She hissed a threat to Michael. "I'll make you regret having ever come here."

James got to his feet and grabbed her shoulders, trying to hold her back. "Let me go or I swear I will beat you, too."

Micheal started to laugh. He laughed harder as she struggled against James's grip. Between fits of laughter he pointed to James "Now you're sleeping your way to the top? Looks like I came to say sorry to a strumpet."

James glared at Michael and prayed Haillie wouldn't catch onto his meaning. This was not how he wanted Haillie to find out about him.

* * *

Haillie was still swinging but Michael's laughter was taking the fire out of it. The bat dropped to her feet. "I'm proud to be with him. I don't care that he's a parking lot attendant. He's more of a man than you'll ever be."

She reached for James's hand and interlocked her fingers with his. "Let yourself out, baby killer. We're going back to bed."

Michael wasn't even looking at her. His stare was dead set on James. "We both know what you are. Are they going to be happy when they realize you're with her? Look out, Rapunzel, they'll be locking you back up in that ivory tower by the morning. Enjoy your evening."

Haillie knew that tone. It was his "victory" gloat. Somewhere in her screaming, she'd made a mistake. She reviewed the conversation line by line. It wasn't her. It took approximately nineteen seconds to connect the dots and realize his reference to Rapunzel had nothing to do with her.

She whirled around to face James. Memories of the group he'd been part of when she'd walked into the Around the Corner Cafe came to mind. The cafe was not a hang out for parking lot attendants. It was a hang out where up-and-coming executives and bored trust fund babies discussed philosophy and politics of the average man's plight. James had fit right in with them. She kept her tone soft, but she could not disguise the edge in it. "Do you have something you want to tell me?"

She could see the guilt written on his face. His adam's apple bobbed as he swallowed hard. "No."

She didn't turn around. "Michael. Tell me."

She didn't have to see Michael's face to hear the glee in it. "The boy you're so happily allowing into your bed is one James Edward Everton the Third, the sole heir of the family you sold your business to for pennies on the dollar."

The look of anguish on James's face told her it was true. He'd lied to her. He was just one more man lying to her. She was done with that.

She unlaced her fingers, unbuttoned the shirt, and handed it to him. "Take it and get out. If you come back, I swear I'll shoot first and ask questions later."

He pleaded with her. "Please," he begged. "Let me explain."

Haillie didn't want to hear it. "Get! Out!"

James held up his hands. "I haven't…"

She pointed toward the door and picked up the bat. "Out. Now!"

James's shoulders slumped. He opened the door barefoot and shirtless and left.

Micheal shut the door behind him with the words, "Goodbye to the trash of the good class."

Haillie sat on the couch and curled up. Micheal went to the alcohol cabinet in the kitchen off the formal living room.

He came back with scotch and nudged her as he offered her the cup. His voice was contrite. "I really am sorry. It was my fault. It was all my fault." He admitted.

She shoved the drink away. "This isn't an invitation for you to stay. I want you out. I have work in a few hours. I need rest."

Micheal took off his jacket to cover her. The door opened before the jacket landed on Haillie's nude body. Every ounce of her hot chocolate brown skin was exposed to the chill of the evening air as the door swung open to reveal Virginia. She took one look at the two of them and their drinks.

She took the ring off her finger and threw it at him. Micheal put the jacket back on and dashed out the door. Haillie sat up in the empty house, picked up both drinks and downed them.

In the distance, she heard her cell phone ringing on the table. She recognized the ring tone as belonging to Elegant Events. She considered ignoring it for a brief moment. The emotional exchange with Michael and the revelations about James left her feeling drained and hollow. Elegant Events was the only lover she had energy left to serve. There were employees depending on her. She picked up the phone. "Hello?"

The voice was smooth as fine whiskey. She knew it right away. "Hi. I didn't think you'd be up. I planned out my three sentence voice message. Want to hear it?"

She chuckled as she coiled up on the couch. "What were you going to say?" Curiosity, more than a desire to entertain a prospective new love interest, motivated her. She wasn't sure she had room in her heart for more disappointment.

He spoke slowly, as if he were feeling his way across a high wire and were afraid he might fall at any moment, "I wanted to say I've been enchanted with you since I first saw you locked outside your house. It was the cutest birthday suit I've seen in a long time. Was it designer?"

She burst out laughing at the unexpected cheesiness of the pick up line. She wanted to stop herself, but she could feel her mind already working to draw up blueprints for the first floor of a new storage area for the messy feelings that weren't going to fit in the life of a successful event planner. She planned to build this one on the same smoking heap Michael and James had just burned down to ashes. She didn't have the energy to clear space for a new place.

"Why, yes. It's a Haillie's limited edition. Super expensive. Very exclusive."

His next words were a bald faced lie if she'd ever heard one, but she accepted them graciously. "I thought only the wealthy could afford suits without blemishes."

She smiled. "You missed the special stitching on the vintage edges, did you?"

His voice was a soft caress that sent warm shivers to the most intimate of spaces. "Can I talk to you over coffee or breakfast tomorrow?"

Her heart yelled, "NO!" It needed time to mend. Other regions of her body had their own response, "Get back in that saddle and ride till the cows come home."

She paused as her heart and her body began their argument. "I don't think you're in a position to offer me a coffee date."

His voice sounded curious. "Oh? Why's that?"

She repeated the bits of gossip about him that she'd heard at the party. "You have a girlfriend, and I'm not interested in a threesome."

He chuckled. "Had. I had a girlfriend. We both agreed that we weren't right for each other. I have no interest in a threesome, either."

A slow smile stretched across Haillie's face. "In that case, coffee. Only coffee." She hung up with the building project already beginning in her hippocampus.

Epilogue

Micheal was lagging behind in this foot race. Micheal yelled in desperation, "Virginia. Please, stop." He thought of the close friendship between the Everton's and Virginia's family. He'd struggled for years to get close to their level of society. With their financial backing, his non-profit could stop struggling.

Virginia found an extra burst of energy and she used it to beat him to his car. She took a moment before she slunked down into the driver's seat.

He spoke the words he knew she wanted to hear without effort. "There is no one else for me. I don't love Haillie. What you saw isn't what it looked like."

Once he made Virginia his wife, he would get access to the money left in trust for her. He needed that money. It was his best hope for saving Everyday People.

Tears sparkled on her lashes as she looked up at him. Her face was splotchy and red. "How do I know you're going to feel that way tomorrow? How can I be sure you don't still love Haillie?"

He went down on one knee and grasped her hand. "Because in just one week from today, you'll be Mrs. Michael Prescott."

She squealed, her face lighting up with glee. She threw her arms around his neck. He swallowed. Everything depended on this. "You'll accept me as a husband?"

She kissed him slowly. "Of course. "You make us legal and this" she swept a hand down the length of her, "is yours. All yours."

He sighed in relief and tried to catch his breath. Elena's words "You'll never make it without me" floated to the surface of his mind. He'd been 22 years old, and he'd believed her even though he hadn't wanted to. After all, she was more than twice his age. She'd never hesitated to remind him of his humble origins, or her role in helping him climb the social ladders needed to get the funding for his business ventures.

This move would prove her wrong. He was finally going to make it to the top. He wanted to do double middle fingers to the sky to let her know he was making it withoutt her, the way he always said he would. He reached up a hand and caressed the side of Virginia's face. "Let me go get your ring."

Virginia's face twisted. "No! You're not going back into that lotus lair. You'll buy me a brand new one. Let her keep that cheap piece of junk. I want 7 carats and a perfect cut princess diamond surrounded by sapphires."

Micheal grunted. He could already feel the dent in his wallet. Virginia exited the driver's side of his mercedes and reclaimed her Phantom. He got in the car on the driver's side of his automobile. He watched as she hopped out of her car and ran back to his.

She tapped on the window. He rolled it down "Yes, dear?"

She looked him in the eyes. Her jaw was set. "I want that tramp to plan my wedding."

Michael was suddenly confused. "Which tramp? Lady & Tramp events?"

She rolled her eyes. "No, I want Elegant Events to do it, and not one of her lackees. I want Haillie herself to plan my wedding. Make it happen." Her perfect white teeth gleamed in the moonlight like a piranha waiting for a large beast to step into its waters.

He could just imagine Haillie's face when he delivered this news. "Yes, dear." He thought, "Guess who's beating who, wench."

Virginia held his gaze. "I want it at Eden's Hanging Garden."

Micheal cleared that misunderstanding up quickly. "Darling, you know I would get you anything, but I'm having my Gala at Eden's Hanging Garden. Why don't we have the wedding at the premiere spot in the city?"

She gasped and put her hands over her mouth. "Skylight Beauties? Do you really think we can get a spot so soon? My friends booked that place a year or more in advance!"

He grinned in satisfaction. Haillie might be able to pull a small party off in a matter of hours, but there was no way she was going to be able to pull off an entire wedding at the most exclusive venue in town in just one week.

Elegant Events would be the laughing stock of the town. "Make your calls and get it in the society pages you want. Tell your friends. If Haillie can't handle something as simple as a booking at Skylight Beauties, nobody would blame us if we decided she wasn't up to the task of handling something as complex as a Gala."

He was smiling like the Cheshire cat as Virginia pulled away from the curb. He was going to body check all the progress Haillie thought she could make without him. If he couldn't have her love, he would destroy everything she loved until there was nothing left for her.

That night, he grieved the loss of his child for the first time with a bottle of whiskey for his only companion even as he mentally prepared himself for life with a child bride whose spending habits could suck his wallet dry within an hour.

Haillie wasn't coming back to him. She wasn't going to let him console himself in her arms and play the role of the dutiful mistress. She had James Everton in her bed now. He hoped she enjoyed herself for as long as it lasted.

He was going to destroy everything that brought her happiness and comfort until suicide seemed the only option left to her. He'd done it to Elena, and she was older, smarter, and pure moneyed evil. Destroying Haillie should be a piece of cake.

Made in the USA
Middletown, DE
02 October 2023

40010729R00269